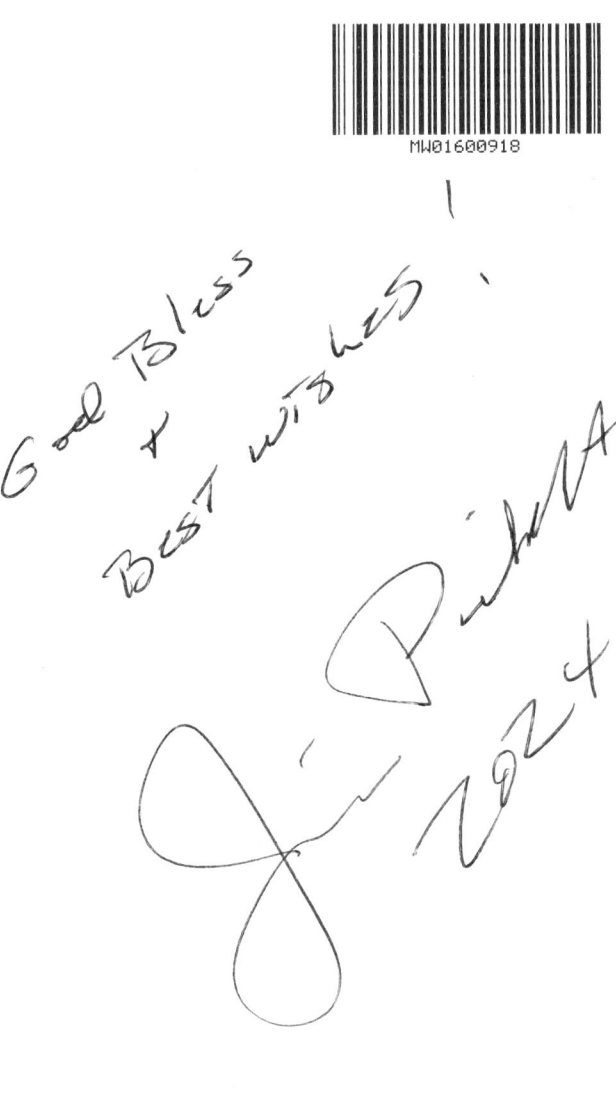

God Bless
+
Best wishes

The Taming of Kekionga
1812 - 1813

Dedication

This book is dedicated to my family, friends, military veterans who have served, those who are serving now and to the Native Americans who were here first.

The Taming of Kekionga
1812 - 1813

Jim Pickett

First Edition – 2023

First Editor Copyright – 2023
by Jim Pickett

ISBN: 979-8-9865327-3-8

OAK CREEK *media*
Bluffton, Indiana

Other Books Written By Jim Pickett

The Bones of Kekionga

The March to Kekionga

The Siege at Kekionga: Tecumseh's Uprising

Foreword and Introduction

What's in a title you may ask? The author takes the approach that it ought to tell something about what is in the book. The previous Kekionga historical narrative stories, *The Bones of Kekionga*, *The March to Kekionga* and *The Siege at Kekionga: Tecumseh's Uprising* centered basically around an Indian village at the headwaters of the Maumee River. Not just any ordinary village but a village that drew far more commerce at the time than Detroit for example. The village was strategically near a portage that carried trade goods and allowed travel from Lake Erie to the Gulf of Mexico and places in between. It also was a magnet for violence as Indian tribes and foreign countries fought to possess the land. President George Washington knew it as the Miami Villages for there were many communities along the rivers besides the larger Kekionga.

In the story you are about to read, *The Taming of Kekionga: 1812-1813*, Kekionga will now symbolize the Indian movement to stop the westward momentum of the United States. Although there will be some scenes that happen near this village, the September of 1812, seven-day siege is over and retributions against the offending Indians are being directed by General William Henry Harrison. More warriors and this time United Kingdom forces are on the way to destroy a fort that has been built at the headwaters of the Maumee River.

In this narrative, the War of 1812, also known as the Second War for Independence, is erupting across the Old Northwest Territory. Not to disregard the war theatre east of the Appalachians, upper New York, the east coast and down south, but for this story, a continuation of *The Siege of Kekionga: Tecumseh's Uprising*, the focus is on how it expands hundreds of miles away from Kekionga. From Kentucky, Indiana, Ohio, Pennsylvania, Michigan, Lake Erie and into Canada; the United States, Great Britain and the Native Americans draw battle lines, fight the horrendous weather conditions, fatal diseases and illnesses that for more than a year defines an expanding country, a wanna be Empire and a people who just want to be.

The author thanks those who thought enough of 'The Siege' and the Kekionga series to insist on a follow up story, here it is. Through the eyes and voices of the characters that the author has added and those of the people who were actually there, hang on. It will jump around just like the previous Kekionga stories in order to stay in chronological order and to give both and sometimes, in this case, three perspectives or viewpoints. Rest assured it will all come together in the end. Dozens of sources were used to be accurate and educational.

Want to know more about this time period and events? Check the back of the book in the accreditations and further reading section. Also, a section that lists the fictional and non-fictional names of the different people in the book has been added.

Now, prepare yourself to go back in time, first to 1920, and then to September of 1812.

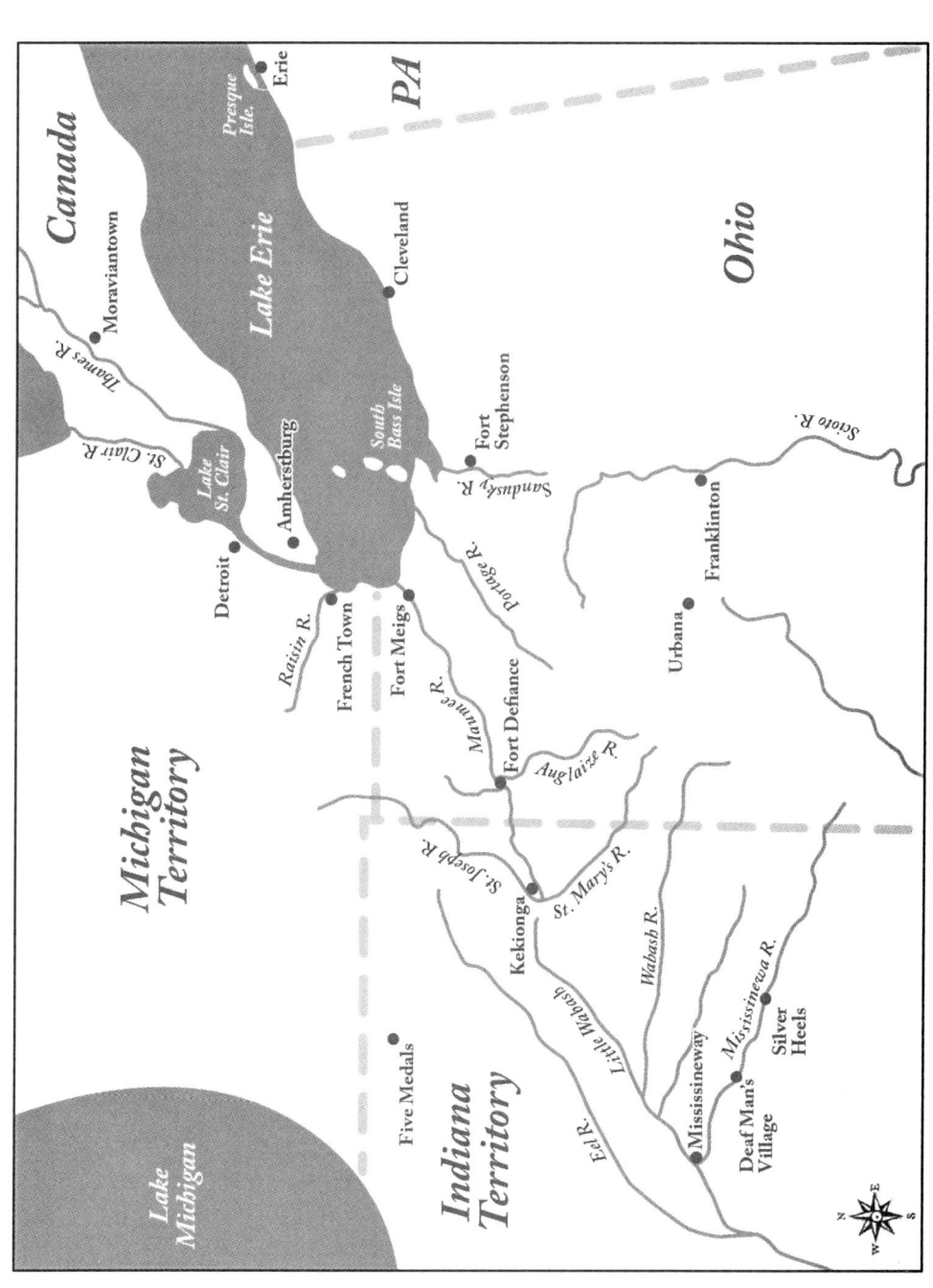

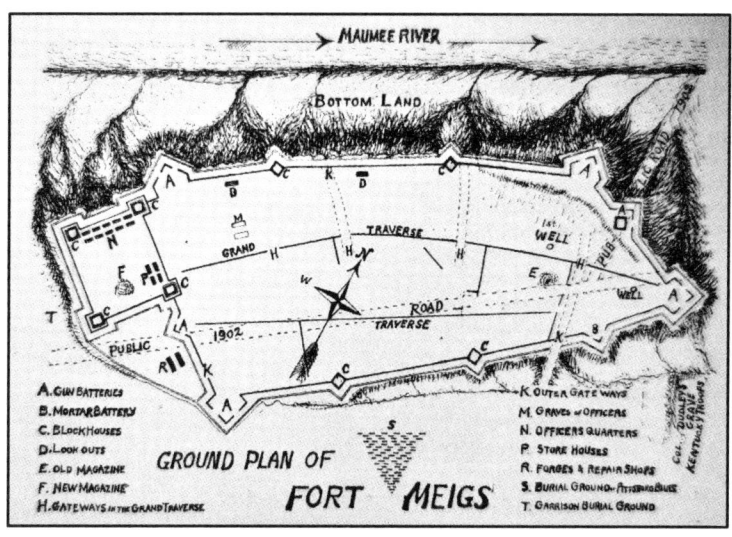

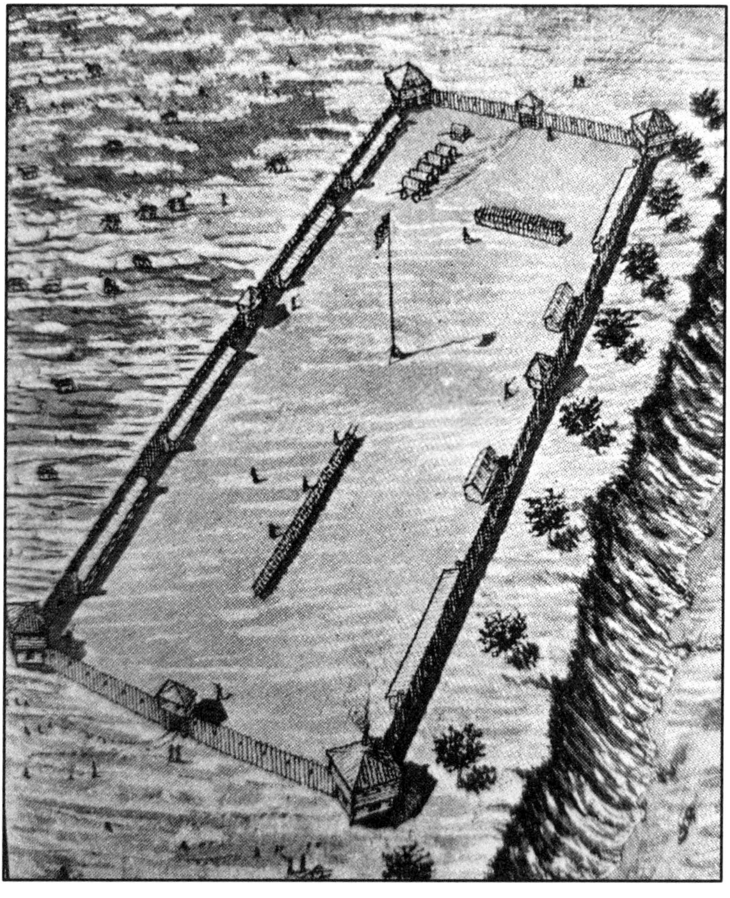

MAUMEE RIVER

BOTTOM LAND

GROUND PLAN OF
FORT MEIGS

A. GUN BATTERIES
B. MORTAR BATTERY
C. BLOCK HOUSES
D. LOOK OUTS
E. OLD MAGAZINE
F. NEW MAGAZINE
H. GATEWAYS IN THE GRAND TRAVERSE

K. OUTER GATE WAYS
M. GRAVES of OFFICERS
N. OFFICERS QUARTERS
P. STORE HOUSES
R. FORGES & REPAIR SHOPS
S. BURIAL GROUND of PITTSBURG BLUES
T. GARRISON BURIAL GROUND

Fort Winchester

Tecumseh

Oliver Hazard Perry

William Henry Harrison

Chapter 1

October 1920 — Aboite Township, Allen County, Indiana

"Did you see that, Nyle?"

"Did I see what, Stan? Some old bones and skulls again? Ha!"

"There was some movement down that hallway," explains a bemused Stan as he and his brother install a new phone line in an old home west of the city that they work and live in.

"Dad burn, brother, I thought we were past all that ghost stuff," laments Nyle.

"Where's my pliers?" inquires Stan. "I know I brought them in with me when we first got here."

"Maybe Ostrander took them. Ha!" answers Nyle.

"I guess I'll have to go out and get another pair from the truck. Plus, my lunch box is missing," adds Stan.

"Probably forgetfulness. You know we are almost 30 years old now!" jokes Nyle. "Bring my lunch box in too, will you, Stan? It's almost chow time."

While Nyle looks around at the older interior structure, the lady who lives in the home with her husband carries a lunch pail and pair of pliers in her hand down the long hall toward Nyle.

"I don't know why, but I found these behind my washing machine in the laundry room. I might as well ask: Do these belong to you?" inquires the lady, holding them out.

"Yes, my brother is missing those items."

"Indian guest playing tricks again," informs the lady. "This old house was built in 1839 and has had a lot of history around it. The portage passed right by here with natives carrying trade goods. Also, many French, British and American armies over the years back in the day traveled through here. Why, rumor is that La Balme's Massacre took place near here instead of up north in Whitley County."

"Ma'am, I don't know anything about what you're talking about. My brother Stan is the one who knows and enjoys history. Most of his knowledge came from a guy named Bob Gavin."

"Oh, I know Bob!" apprises the lady. "My husband and I met him at the History Round Table meeting at the library downtown many years ago. We'll see him again next month. I'll tell him I saw you guys. By the way, is it going to be long distance calling into Fort Wayne?"

"'Fraid so, ma'am," says Nyle. "See that crank on the side of the phone box? Ya just turn that real fast a few times, and you'll get the phone operator. Just tell her who you want to talk to. After Stan and I get this set up, we'll show you how."

"It'll be nice to call someone. It gets a little lonely out here, and with the mysterious things that go on, I can't thank you enough."

"Our pleasure, ma'am. It's our job."

After the lady leaves behind the pliers and lunch box and swiftly moves back down the hallway, Nyle walks around the room studying pictures hanging on the interior wall of the federal-style brick building. He stares out a bay window and doesn't notice Stan walking up from behind.

Stan places his hand on his brother's shoulder and at the same time yells, "BOO!"

"Ahhh! Dad burn you, you son of a gun! Don't you ever do that again. Geez! You trying to give me a heart attack?"

"Relax, Nyle. It's just me. Who did you expect?"

"Well, I don't know. By the way, the lady found your pliers and lunch pail behind the washing machine in the laundry room. You weren't in there, were you?"

"Say what? No, I wasn't in there. I don't even know where that room is. She's not playin' a joke, is she, Nyle?"

"No, I don't think so. She doesn't seem the type to do that, but she knows Bob Gavin and a lot about the history around here. Says things come up missing in this old house and end up in a spot she knows she wouldn't have left them."

"This reminds me of our friends Ann and Jim that lived up by Churubusco, down a long lane that led to the Blue River. They would go for a trip into town and leave a light on, but when they came back, the light would be off. At first they thought they had an electrical issue. Other times, they would leave no lights on and come back with a light on or flickering as they approached the house."

"Oh, now I remember that. Yeah, I think someone was playing a trick on them," reasons Nyle.

In walks the lady, and with a loud voice, she says, "You boys need anything, just let me know!"

Both Nyle and Stan jump, startled.

"Yyyyou bet, ma'am," answers Nyle.

"You were tellin' Nyle about some history around this old place and that you know our friend Bob Gavin. What else can you recount?" asks Stan.

"Yeah, well, ol' Bob was tellin' us that Indians carried goods and canoes along the old portage trail that connected the St. Marys River to the Little Wabash River right out front of the house here to the put-in place on the Aboite River," she answers. "Later, stagecoach and canal boat travelers would stay in this very house to rest and have a meal."

"No kiddin'?" expresses Stan and Nyle together.

"Another thing, boys, the canal boat would travel across the Aboite Creek by what they called an aqueduct, a water bridge over a body of water."

"That's all very interesting," says Stan, "but about that spirit you say might be playing tricks. Our friend living along the Blue River near 'Busco says she has had a little Indian boy appear and brush up alongside of her as she would wash the supper dishes while staring out the window at the river. Then she'd catch a glimpse of him dashing away. You ever experience that, ma'am?" asks Stan.

"Now mister, if that ever happened to me, do you think I would ever admit to it? People would think I was crazy."

"Sorry ma'am, but Nyle and I have had our share of experiences the last few years that we can't explain, and I was just wondering."

The lady wipes her hands on her apron and shakes her head slowly and replies, "Some things are best left unexplained. You boys seem to have a good sense of history. When you have a moment, just allow yourselves to go back in time, listen and visualize what it was like long ago."

"Yes ma'am, we will," replies Stan.

Chapter 2

September 13–14, 1812
Michigan Territory/Indiana Territory

"Listen, Tecumseh, I've taken enough of your abuse. There is only so much I can do. I answer to the Crown, King George III of England, and I know you want your land back and so does Great Britain! If we work together, we can make this happen!" pleads Colonel Henry Proctor.

Waiting for the interpreter to finish, Tecumseh then speaks. "Your so-called Crown did not deliver the food we needed at the Auglaize villages and let us down at the Battle of Fort Recovery. Your people also promised help at the Battle of Fallen Timbers but closed the gates of Fort Miami just as my warriors approached!"

"There was not enough space in that fort to hold an additional thousand people," interjects Proctor. "I apologize for all that, but I am only a Colonel. Major General Brock is the one to talk to, but I will help you when I can. If you want to pass some blame, look at your brother, Tenskwatawa, the so-called Prophet, standing over there. Did he not go against your wishes at the battle on the Tippecanoe?"

Tecumseh pulls his knife out of its sheath and walks toward Proctor, flashing menacing eyes and infuriated by the accusation. Four British Redcoat guards step in with raised bayoneted muskets ready to thrust to protect their commandant. The Indian interpreter grabs Tecumseh's shoulder just as Proctor raises his right-hand palm to relieve the tension.

Tecumseh wisely backs off, knowing his aggression would cost him his life. Stepping away, he answers, "Yes, that was not wise, and my brother and I have discussed that. But do not forget, I have lost a father and two other brothers to the Long Knives and am running out of patience. We want revenge, and we demand the land that in our belief system belongs to every creature on this earth.

"These Americans destroy land and crops wherever they go. They even go half-starved to obtain what they want. Why do they not know, or even you great commander, or the father across the sea realize the Great Spirit has created everything, including you and me?"

After allowing the interpreter to finish, Proctor redirects. "I understand the sacrifice you and your people have made, and I give you my word I will do what I can for you. Look at the victory over the Americans here at Fort Detroit."

"What victory are you referring to? This cowardly American General Hull surrendering to us without firing shot? Ha! Or, how about a group of Americans at Fort Mackinac that surrendered not even knowing a war between your two countries had even been declared?"

Proctor, flummoxed by Tecumseh's wisdom and knowledge of events in North America, attempts to explain.

"To make things clear, my country is still involved in a war with France."

Understanding some English, Tecumseh reengages his thoughts. "England and France are always at war. Is that all your two countries know about? War and world domination? At least the Americans appear to have set their limits on the Mississippi River."

Starting to pick up on the Algonquin language a bit, Proctor doesn't wait for the interpreter. "Don't be naive, Chief! Power is contagious, and land is power. Did not the Miami and the Iroquois fight one another for decades over this territory? Good thing you had the insight to unite a confederation."

The interpreter finishes as an annoyed Tecumseh begins to respond, "Enough history. What are you doing to help stop the American intrusion? Fort Dearborn has been removed without your help. What about this Fort Harrison and the one at Kekionga that I refuse to call by name?"

Proctor answers, "I have sent Major Adam Muir and two hundred British infantry, four pieces of artillery, along with our Indian agent Matthew Elliott leading a thousand warriors up the Omee River toward the Miami villages of Kekionga."

As the translator finishes, Tecumseh finally smiles slightly.

One hundred sixty miles south and west of Detroit, farmer and scout E.J. Carlisle and son Wayne Pastor lead two teams of draft horses to a forty-man work detail led by Lieutenant Phillip Ostrander of Fort Wayne. The cutting of trees a mile west and south of the fort is part of repairing the outpost and outbuildings burned during a seven-day siege by the Miami and Potawatomi hostiles. The underbrush clearing ordered by General William H. Harrison for the area surrounding the garrison is hoped to prevent future Indian sneak attacks.

"Ya know, watching these trees come down reminds me of Running Deer spying on us Americans from the top of a tall oak," says EJ. "We were building Anthony Wayne's first Fort Wayne up on the hill by the cemetery. Man, did Running Deer come scrambling down once we started cutting that 'big boy.' Wonder where my friend got to during the siege?"

"To be honest, Dad, I saw him and Red Hawk hightailing across the St. Marys away from the fort when Harrison arrived. I had them both in my musket sights but didn't pull the trigger. I think Running Deer switched back to the Indian movement."

"I appreciate you not shootin' 'em, Son, but I find that hard to believe after all the reconnoitering he and I did together. Dad burn, he even went to Fort Dearborn with William Wells to help him out."

"You notice he and the thirty Miami he went up there with survived that massacre, don't ya?" offers Wayne Pastor. "I think he switched, just as Wells did when he joined Wayne to oppose the Indians."

"Yeah, but he gave me his word after I untied him the day you were born. An Indian's word is usually binding."

"I understand, Dad, but it's an agonizing decision. I went back and forth myself with Red Hawk down along the Wabash and Mississinewa rivers. I made some Indian friends that I will help if I get the chance.

Not all the Indians want war. There are many that just wanna live in peace and adjust to the American way of life."

"W.P., you've picked up on a few things around these parts of the country, and I appreciate that," compliments his father.

"I obtained a lot of that on our trip together down the Maumee to Lake Erie. Plus, you and mom have taught me everything I know, and I value that. Someday, I want to go back there."

"Where's that, Son?"

"Lake Erie. That lake is so big. Something is drawing me there. I just want to be a part of that."

"Maybe you will someday, W.P., maybe you will, but right now, we gotta haul some logs and help end this war."

As the two Carlisles walk toward Lieutenant Ostrander to receive their orders, a tree falls nearby, scattering dust, branches and leaves near the disgruntled officer.

"Dad burn you, Smitty, you trying to kill me? Be careful where you're droppin' 'em!"

"Sorry, Lieutenant, ha! You almost ended up like General Wayne down at Fort Adams."

"I don't see the humor in that, Smith. Wayne's still limping around from that episode!"

Private John Smith raises his authoritative voice and responds, "May I remind you, Lieutenant, the Gen'ral died of the gout, or something like that, back in 1796 and is buried on Presque Island in Lake Erie."

"You seem to be awfully well-informed for someone who is just a private," digs Ostrander.

"Like I been tellin' everyone for years, I should be a Gen'ral by now, since I been 'round 'em so much."

"You ain't pro'bly 'cause you stinks so bad!" yells E.J., cupping his hands to be heard over the axes chopping trunks.

"Why, dad burn you, E.J.! If Wayne Pastor weren't standing there with you, I'd come over and whip on you so fast."

"Ha! My wife, Charlotte, wouldn't take too kindly to that!" responds E.J.

"All right, enough of this nonsense," orders Ostrander. "Get those logs hooked up, you two, and drag them over to the fort!" Besides, Major Croghan might court-martial me if we don't get a move on."

"Yes sir, Lieutenant," obeys Wayne Pastor.

Ostrander continues to complain to no one in particular, "That young major ought to be answering to me, not vice versa, dad burnit."

"Yeah, what happened there?" asks E.J. while connecting a log to his team of horses.

"Oh, I think Croghan is related some way to George Rogers Clark, and Harrison thought he performed real well at the Tippecanoe battle last year.

"Did I not perform admirably here at Fort Wayne last week?" continues Ostrander. "I think I did. Go ask Indian agent Stickney and Lieutenant Curtis. Why, that drunken Captain Rhea wanted to surrender."

"You think Harrison's gonna hang 'im, Lieutenant?" asks Wayne Pastor.

Ignoring the question, Ostrander is distracted.

"Now what do we have here riding up? Dad-burned guards! What are you doing out there, twiddling your thumbs?"

Several soldiers grab their muskets as two Indians from the Miami nation ride in from the south. Breaking out of the forest the natives have wild game strapped over their horses.

Pulling his sword out of its scabbard, Ostrander walks toward the perplexed Indians and grabs their horse reins while asking his troops, "Who knows Algonquin around here?"

"I can help ya, Lieutenant," says Wayne Pastor, hustling over to the anxious natives.

"Much obliged, W.P., but be careful, it may be a trick," says Ostrander.

W.P. rattles off a question in Algonquin as the nervous Miami warriors answer and question back animatedly.

Wayne Pastor turns slightly, not taking his eyes off the Indians completely, and speaks to Ostrander. "They are wondering what happened.

"Hey Dad, come over here and give me a hand at this."

The Miami continue to speak their language, informing the Americans that they come in peace and are returning from Kentucky and a hunting trip.

At the same time, twenty-five miles west and south of Fort Wayne, the Indian village and trading post called the Forks of the Wabash receives the first of Harrison's two divisions led by General John Payne. Surprised, panic-stricken Indians yell in Algonquin, "Get to the canoes! Head for the Wabash! Paddle fast, the Long Knives are here!"

"Remember, General Payne, no one is to fire a shot unless the warriors turn and aim at them!" reminds William Henry Harrison. "Let the Indians go."

"Yes sir!"

"Colonel Allen? No firing unless a warrior aims at them."

"Yes sir! This place is practically deserted, anyways," responds the Kentucky politician and lawyer-turned-soldier. "Captain Garrard, pull your troops back, let 'em go!" orders Allen.

Several American troops raise their Kentucky long rifle, taking aim for a dubious shot, while four American drummers pound out the signal for the troops to return from their pursuit.

"Dag nabbit! If we had gotten here earlier, we could have wiped out the whole village, including the traitor Frenchmen marrying among these heathens," complains one militiaman who has traveled hundreds of miles seeking revenge.

"Now what good would that have done?" answers Colonel William Lewis.

No shots are fired out of respect for the popular General Harrison and his orders.

Harrison rides up, observing an assortment of more than one hundred Frenchmen, Miami, Potawatomi, Wea and Eel River Indians paddling down the Wabash. Others can be seen scattering into the forest.

"All right, you know what to do, General Payne."

Following Harrison's preplanned orders, he barks, "Colonel Lewis, gather up the housing and burn it. Captain Garrard, gather the crops and burn 'em. Colonel Allen, have your riflemen cover the perimeter. Shoot to kill if they come back on us."

"Yes sir, General."

Twelve miles north and east of Kekionga, Colonel Sam Wells of Kentucky leads a similar search-and-destroy mission along the St. Joseph River. Ordered by Harrison in retaliation for the seven-day attack on Forts Wayne, Harrison and Dearborn, Sam Wells heads first for the mouth of Cedar Creek, destroying all signs of Indian habitation. Two miles before reaching the Potawatomi village, he receives news from scout Ensign James Liggett.

"They're gone, Colonel. No sign of Chief Metea or his people lingering around."

"Very well, Liggett, the 17th will move in and destroy it then travel toward the Eel River and the trail to Fort Dearborn. See what you and your scouts can find up that way. Take what rations you need for two days, and we will meet you at that crossing."

"You bet, Sam," obeys Liggett, saluting.

Back at Fort Wayne, Ostrander is about to call it a day when a disturbance halts the action along the forest line.

A barefoot, long-haired, disheveled man, leading an old broken-down grey mare and his companion wolf, walk out of the trees.

"Not again, guards! What have you let in?"

"This is Mr. Chapman, Lieutenant. Remember?" reinforms E.J., "I was tellin' you about him awhile back."

"Yeah, but I don't recall the wolf."

"Oh, he's basically harmless!" shouts Chapman.

"What do you mean 'basically'?" inquires Ostrander.

"I healed his front right leg when he was a pup, and he's been following me ever since. Don't bother me, and he won't bother you unless you bother him. Ha!"

"What you doin' here, Johnny? It can be dangerous with the Indian uprisin' and all," asks E.J.

"Oh, the Indians don't trouble me. I'm just sayin' goodbye for a while. Headin' back to southern Ohio to see my half-brother Nathan and then back east for some seeds.

"Also, want to inform you folks, the wooly worms are warning of an early, harsh winter season coming."

"Oh, yeah, the nature guy who plants apple trees," mocks Ostrander. "You got insects talking to you now? Ha!"

"All of God's nature talks to all of us. One just has to be willing to listen, Officer. You guys take care. Remember, God loves you."

Chapter 3

September 15–19, 1812

Fort Dearborn Trail, 11 miles north and west of Kekionga

Colonel Sam Wells, brother of deceased Indian agent William Wells, leads his Kentucky 17th mounted infantry up to the dismounted scout Ensign Liggett.

"Thought maybe you'd want to pause here, Colonel," says Liggett. "A lot of markings on the trees and musket balls embedded. Looks like there was a battle. In fact, we took the liberty to bury a few skulls and bones."

"Yep. October 1790, Hardin's Defeat. General Harmar told me about it one time when I was visiting Fort Washington. Good job, Ensign. Gives me the willies here, let's move on," says Wells as he leans forward on his saddle horn, spits tobacco juice and waves his 800-man militia forward.

As Wells and his officer contingent of Liggett, Major George Davenport and Colonel Richard Johnson lead the detachment from Harrison's army north on the Fort Dearborn Trail, the consensus is to have Liggett and his scouts ride ahead. They are to find Potawatomi war Chief Five Medals' village on the Elkhart River and report back.

Leading the rest of his force, Wells reluctantly intends to pay a visit to a rumored cannibalistic Seek Indian village. This side visit would be a continuation of the search-and-destroy mission Harrison had ordered within a fifty-mile radius of Fort Wayne.

Twelve miles south of Wells' mission, Colonel James Simrall guides his 300 Kentucky militia dragoons, who are trained to fight either on horseback or on foot, in full gallop toward Chief Little Turtle's former Miami village along the Eel River.

"I don't like taking indirect orders from Harrison through a young kid like this Commander Croghan at Fort Wayne, but I like the action,

Major," says Simrall, heading his detachment into an unknown outcome.

"Yes sir, I understand," replies the subordinate.

"Let's swoop in before they know what's hit 'em," Simrall adds as he strategizes along the narrow Indian trail dashing by the vacated Chief Coesee's Indian village.

"Yes sir."

"We will take care of this place on the way back. Perhaps the warriors will have returned and we can eliminate a few before we report to Fort Wayne again," smirks Simrall.

Later that day at Fort Wayne, Harrison, freshly returned from his mission to the Forks of the Wabash, orders Croghan to throw a noose over the front gate.

"Let's get this inquiry concerning the conduct of Captain Rhea last week over with," orders the general. "I want him, the garrison and the entire army to understand the seriousness of this type of offense."

With the door to Rhea's office open so the noose could be seen, the former commander is brought before three officers presiding over the hearing.

As Rhea, Ostrander, Lieutenant Daniel Curtis and Indian agent Benjamin Stickney finish their testimony, Harrison stands up to speak. "I don't need to hear any more. We have things to do. I will speak for the Military Board of Inquiry that we can take that noose down.

"Stand up, Captain Rhea," orders Harrison. "Your conduct, Captain James Rhea, during the siege of Fort Wayne is egregious, traitorous and unacceptable." Harrison stares over at Rhea's wife, Polly, and young children seated next to her.

"Nevertheless, it is my opinion and decision to allow Captain Rhea, since his service prior to Fort Wayne has been admirable, to resign from the army and move on with his life supporting his young family. You have until December 31, 1812, Captain Rhea. This inquiry is over."

Viewing the proceedings, E.J. pulls his war veteran Uncle Isaac aside. "Between you and me, Ike, 'Mad' Anthony Wayne would have hung 'im."

"I'm certain of that, E.J.," concurs Ike.

Sixty miles northwest of Kekionga, Colonel Wells, having already found the Seek village deserted, enters Five Medals Village and greets Liggett. "What do you have, Ensign, besides another empty village?"

"Looks like about twenty acres of corn."

Wells looks back at George Davenport. "Destroy it, Major Davenport."

"Yes sir!" says Davenport, riding off and giving commands to his officers.

Liggett adds, "But we also have something unusual, and a couple of my scouts are complaining of illness after they first encountered this sorcerer-type woman, sir."

"Show me where she's at, Ensign."

As Wells gets off his horse, he hands the reins to a private and walks into a sacred Indian shrine. He views a deceased Indian woman sitting up facing east with owl and hawk claws, bills and bones in front of her.

"Indian spirit ritual, Ensign," opines Wells.

"We also have some evidence of British influence, Colonel," says Liggett, holding up a newspaper printed in Cincinnati and a box of confiscated American information about General Hull's surrender of 2,500 men at Fort Detroit. "From the looks, all of this was acquired from Amherstburg and London, Canada, Sam."

"Hmm, looks like we have a spy traveling about," says Wells. "Ok, Colonel Johnson. Destroy and burn the village."

"Yes sir."

"Liggett, take a company of Johnson's men, search and destroy anything in the area. Keep in mind we are heading back to Fort Wayne in two hours, though."

"Yes sir."

As Colonel Simrall's dragoons follow him into the deceased Little Turtle's old village, screams are heard from Miami women and children as they scramble away from the Americans. The natives rapidly climb the banks of the Eel River and run into the forest to avoid the saber-swinging horsemen.

"Don't harm them unless they turn on you!" tardily commands Simrall and his subordinate officers.

BAM! Bam! BAM!

Dragoons raise their rifles and fire as soon as they see a warrior raise a weapon. One old warrior is chopped down while raising a spear to defend his wife.

Black Loon, son of Little Turtle and father of Chief Coesse, runs upstream along the south bank from his favorite fishing hole. He stops to raise his British Brown Bessie musket to halt the slaughter.

BAM! Bam! finish the dragoons, who shoot Black Loon, the last of the defending warriors.

"Burn it all, chop down the crops, gather it and burn it!" yells Simrall. "Let the survivors go!"

Out of emotion, the colonel yells to the fleeing Indians, "Don't ever attack Fort Wayne or any other American fortress again!"

"What about this log building over here, Colonel?" inquires an officer.

"The order is to leave Chief Little Turtle's home alone. Go inside and confirm that, and leave it stand if it is. Destroy everything else! As soon as we are done here, we are moving south along the Eel and destroying anything we find!"

"Yes sir."

Eighty miles northeast of Kekionga along the Maumee River, British Major Adam Muir leads his 200 regulars and 1,000 warriors following Colonel Matthew Elliott's command toward Fort Wayne.

"Chief Winamac and Five Medals will be thrilled to see us," states the longtime British Indian agent, Elliott.

"I agree, but I wish we could move a little faster. These cannons are a burden," comments Muir.

"I know, but we need them. Those old walls I saw last spring won't be able to withstand the barrage that will allow the massacre of every single American inside."

The next day, back at Fort Wayne next to Kekionga, Sam Wells's troops return with the story of an eerie conquest.

"I think we've had a spell cast on us, fellas," relays a militiaman assisting a sick Kentuckian to the infirmary.

"Yeah, we had one of our boys die on us earlier today," comments another.

"I saw that dead Indian woman. She was an evil one, with claws and beaks of every animal and bird around placed in a basket," describes his friend.

Harrison greets Wells after Cornelius Washburn, Harrison's new bodyguard, allows everyone of importance into the general's office.

"We went as far as the Elkhart River area and destroyed every—"

"Yes, I heard the whole story from Washburn, Sam," interrupts Harrison. "We had something similar with a dead chief inside a small cabin at the Wabash forks, didn't we, Neil?"

"Yep, Indians are strange. I saw a lot of that in southern Ohio," says Washburn, clipping off a response.

"Get your men camped out around the fort on the west side, Sam. We have more troops coming in any day now," orders Harrison. "The move toward Fort Detroit is next. Hope your boys have winter clothing. It gets cold up here early."

"The boys didn't think about winter when we left Kentucky last spring, General. Thought it was going to be a quick fight and victory, and then head back home."

"Don't think so, Sam. I heard the same thing from Colonel Allen. So I put in a requisition order for winter clothing a few weeks ago. I also heard that the women folks of Kentucky are taking great pride in making them. How fast they'll get here will depend on the delivery by the independent contractors."

"Dad burn, General. I don't suppose we can wait a spell till that comes in?"

Hindering Wells and Harrison's conversation, Washburn raises his voice to stop valued scout Peter Navarre from barging in.

"Hold it right there, Navarre! What's your business?" yells Washburn.

"Hold it down out there, Neil!" says Harrison.

"Yes sir."

Whispering, Navarre answers, "I just want to give General Harrison a heads-up. Brigadier General James Winchester is marching this way with orders from Governor Meigs to take over the Army of the Northwest and send our men back to Piqua. Winchester says his seniority places him ahead of Harrison, and he won the argument. Oh, he's a crankety old war hawk."

"Don't be pulling my leg, Navarre. That won't go over well with the troops."

"Keep this secret, Neil. Inside information says it will only be temporary, and Harrison will be made Major General in charge of the whole operation."

Along the lower Maumee River above the rapids, Muir and Elliott's command hold up, waiting for British packhorse trains bringing supplies to catch up, when Miami Indian and former American scout Running Deer turns himself over to Elliott's lead warriors.

Stating he has news for the British and Indian commanders, Running Deer is roughly grabbed by the Miami braves, who recognize the longtime Kekionga warrior.

The unnaturally strong and athletic Running Deer shrugs off the physicalness and walks untouched between his escorts toward the delayed coalition force.

At the same time, forty miles south of Kekionga, Running Deer's son, Red Hawk, paddles his mother, Morning Bird, down the Wabash River toward the assumed safety of the Miami Indian village called Mississineway.

Red Hawk continues paddling as Morning Bird calls a greeting and waves to a warrior on top of the seventy-five-foot-high natural limestone wonder called "Hanging Rock."

"Why do you not greet the friendly brave on top of the lookout, Red Hawk?"

"It brings back a sorry episode in my young life, Mother," chats Red Hawk in Algonquin. "When Wayne Pastor and I attempted to join The Prophet and Tecumseh at Prophetstown near the Tippecanoe River, we had an altercation."

"Tell me, my son. Perhaps it will heal you."

Red Hawk begins, "My first love that I had met with my father during a trip to these parts was a beautiful Miami Indian maiden named Wy-nu-sa."

After Red Hawk finishes the story, Morning Bird, through tears, offers her sympathy. "It must be hard, my son. I'm just thankful you and Wayne Pastor are ok. Maybe this return will ease your pain."

Back at Fort Wayne, trusted French trader, trapper and scout Commandant Antoine Bondie holds a meeting to make assignments.

"E.J., I know Charlotte will not like this, but we need you with General Winchester using your experience and eyes to lead his force along the Maumee northeast toward Fort Defiance and eventually Detroit."

"No way, Antoine," says Charlotte, while hugging her husband, E.J.

"It'll be ok, Charlotte. Uncle Isaac will be here to take care of you and the kids in our new cabin."

"Dad burn, E.J. I was planning on going with you," decries Uncle Ike.

"We need some levelheadedness around here, Ike," says Bondie. "In fact, I wouldn't be surprised if there weren't reprisals from the

Indians for all the damage Harrison ordered. It is a dangerous situation. In my opinion, we should have never attacked these villages around here. It may have stirred up the friendly ones."

"It'll be alright, Charlotte," says E.J. "I know how to take care of myself, and Ike will be around to help you."

"Let's face it, E.J., you have been darn lucky," warns Charlotte.

"Can't disagree with that, Charlotte. Too many close calls," says E.J.

"Wayne Pastor—or should I call you W.P.?" asks Bondie.

"Doesn't matter," says Wayne Pastor. "What's the assignment?"

"You have been asked to go with Harrison back to Fort St. Marys. There is a special assignment brewing, and they need you to help lead it."

"I hope it leads to Lake Erie. I'd like to see that again."

"I just want to see you back here again, alive, Wayne Pastor," requests his mother.

"Captain Johnny Logan, Bright Horn and Captain Johnny, you'll be with Winchester also," directs Bondie. "According to Private John Smith and other scouts, a sizable British and Indian unit is heading this way."

"Also, Ensign Liggett from Sam Wells' company will be out there with you. As you can tell, it's a huge campaign, and as we say in French, 'Je vous souhaite bonne chance,' I wish you good luck."

Chapter 4

September 19–24, 1812 — Northwest Territory/Ohio

On a clear blue-sky morning, William Henry Harrison climbs the steps to the south gate overlook atop the entryway to Fort Wayne. Officers standing on the platform salute and then raise their arms toward the audience to quiet the murmur of the anticipating troops.

Harrison walks along the catwalk, straightening his black wool Bicorne hat and unfolding the speech that he has partially memorized. He positions himself above the entrance and takes a gander at a combined 2,500 American uniformed regulars on the left in shako hats and mostly Kentucky militia centered and to the right wearing a variety of sweat-stained and slouched round hats.

The regulars in sharp, blue uniforms holding shining, bayoneted 1795 Springfield smooth-bore muskets contrast with the colorful, long hunting shirts of the Kentucky militiamen, leaning on their long rifles and staring up through unkempt, lengthy hair.

A tear forms as Harrison clears his throat and then, almost shouting so he can be heard, begins, "Good morning, gentlemen and you ladies that grace us with your presence! As I gaze at you sitting and standing before me on the hill that reaches up to the 1794 original Fort Wayne and a cemetery that holds some of our brave pioneers, and I see around me the damage of the 1800 fortress that some of you here so capably defended, it pains me to realize how much sacrifice has already been made.

"By now, most of you have heard that General James Winchester has been called up from his retirement in Tennessee to lead our forces against Great Britain and a confederation of hostile Native Americans.

"'If anything could soften the regret which I have at parting with troops that have so entirely won my confidence and affection, it is the circumstance of committing them to the charge of one of the heroes of our glorious Revolution, a man distinguished as much for the services he has rendered his country as for the possession of every qualification which constitutes a gentleman!

"The glorious nation of the United States of America of which every one of you characterizes will be triumphant no matter who leads you in resisting a force representing our motherland of the United Kingdom. Great Britain and the coalition of Indian nations united by the Shawnee chief of war Tecumseh cannot stop the God-fearing country that we inherited.

"We conquered the British previously with our forefathers, and we shall do the same with the current generation. As the distinguished Kentuckian Henry Clay has stated, 'It is not now a question for freemen and patriots to discuss. It exists; and it is by open and manly war only that we can get through it with honor and advantage to the country. Our wrongs have been great; our cause is just; and if we are decided and firm, success is inevitable!'"

Applause, whistles, and cheers, more for Henry Clay than for Harrison, swell and then subside as the general waits strategically for just the right moment to finish his speech.

"Let me reassure you that, God willing, I shall expedite all of you again in some capacity in the imminent future! God bless and keep you all!"

With that, Harrison folds his speech, salutes the troops, turns and salutes General Winchester standing at the end of the overlook, and walks off to even more thunderous cheers, whistles and applause resounding up and down the converging three rivers behind him.

Three days later, General James Winchester follows the sounds of a ten-man fife and drum corps across the Maumee River at Harmar's Ford in order to follow Anthony Wayne's trail to Fort Defiance, where the Auglaize River enters the main stream. With scouts fully miles ahead and a detachment of fatigues protected by riflemen widening Wayne's overgrown trail, one advance guard is still detained. A sobbing Charlotte and her three children clinging to E.J. strive to prevent him from leaving.

Uncle Ike pulls on Charlotte, attempting to release E.J. so he can climb aboard Thunder his chestnut brown Appaloosa.

"Look, Charlotte, Reverend Wallace has already prayed over you, E.J. and the kids. It's all in God's hands, and we will see what happens," says Uncle Isaac.

"Yeah, I know, for some reason I just wish Mr. Chapman was here," responds Charlotte.

E.J., with tears in his eyes, turns in his saddle, waving at his family as he rides away along the south bank of the Maumee toward the ford that leads to the vacant Indian village called Kekionga.

E.J., by chance, sidles up to Colonel John Allen of Kentucky while crossing the shallow, rock-laden river bottom.

"Pretty tough, isn't it?" speaks Allen, noticing the tears after he had observed E.J. saying goodbye to his family.

"Yep," responds E.J., wiping his face embarrassingly.

"I had the same thing back in Kentucky leaving my wife. She's going to light a candle every night till I get back to Shelbyville. I had a successful law practice and even ran for governor, but that dad-burned Charles Scott somehow beat me by one vote."

E.J. shakes his head slightly and smiles.

"So when Henry Clay came home from Washington and inspired us all, I was the first to sign up. I tell you this not to brag but to inform you we all are leaving something behind for this noble cause."

"Thanks, Colonel, I needed that. I'll have to say goodbye for now and head up to General Winchester to let him know I'm proceeding out ahead. I hope to see you again."

"I'm sure you will, and good luck. E.J. is it?"

"Yes sir."

Allen nods, returning a salute to Carlisle.

Proceeding along the Cincinnati Trail also known as Wayne's Trace, William Henry Harrison leads his smaller contingent to the fifty-five-mile mark and eyes lead scout Peter Navarre riding up to him from the south.

Navarre speaks first. "We are a day's ride from St. Marys, and this spot, as you can see, General, has two converging streams and some high ground to camp on. What you say we call it a day and spend the night here?"

"I like it, Mr. Navarre," answers Harrison. "What do you think, Colonel Wells?"

"Yes sir. I'm ready to call it a day, as well, General. Looks like it's been used before. The redoubt breastworks are already assembled.

"Wayne Pastor, you and Davenport set up the camp. Get the horses watered downstream. Officers, see that the marquis tent is at the top of the rise.

"Ya know, Mr. Washburn, this is the most relaxed I have been in several weeks," says Harrison.

"Don't put your guard down, General," warns Washburn. "Those redskins are watching. Several villages are in the area."

"Navarre, keep your scouts out there," says Harrison, "but I want you to join us tonight after supper for some games of whist."

"Yes sir, be glad to join ya."

"Colonel Simrall, rotate your three hundred dragoons around the camp as pickets tonight," orders Harrison, "and then I want to talk to you during supper at my campfire."

"Yes sir."

As the encampment settles in, Harrison walks up to his marquis tent entrance and notices the guard is nervous.

"What's the matter, soldier?" asks Harrison, returning the salute. "What you got in your mouth? You have a tooth ache?"

"No sir, just a musket ball, sir. Relieves the tension, sir."

"Private, the camp is completely surrounded by troops."

"Yes sir, I understand. I'm kind of new to this, but I overheard, and it is rumored heads of men killed were being cut off by the Indians. Then they are being displayed on poles."

"Private, things like that have been going on for some time by both sides. If you're dead, you're dead. It doesn't matter. It's called intimidation. Work as a unit with your outfit, and do the best you can, understand?"

"Yes sir."

"And don't ruin that musket ball, you might need it. Ha!" utters Harrison, chortling as he walks away.

Sitting around the campfire in front of the commander's tent, Harrison looks at Colonel Simrall.

"Colonel, I don't want you to be a Wetzel."

"What's that, General?" asks Simrall.

"I heard what you and some of your men did at Little Turtle's village and along the Eel River. Lewis Wetzel, in some guys' eyes, was a real hero while he was alive. Others consider him a cold-blooded murderer.

"He never saw an Indian he liked. Probably because he witnessed his parents' death at the hands of some warriors when he was a kid. I can't imagine what that was like, but it's no excuse. We gotta stop this revenge motive.

"I'd like to negotiate with the Indians some more and obtain land out here and, if possible, live among them. You understand?"

"I think so, sir."

"War is war, Simrall. But don't be a Wetzel."

"I'll try, sir."

Ten minutes later, Harrison's tent is lit up with oil lamps, laughter and good-natured fun. A half-soused Neil Washburn slams down a deck of playing cards on a pine-plank table supported by empty whiskey barrels as Harrison pours himself a mug full of hooch while yelling, "How in the world, Washburn, are you supposed to protect me from those Injuns when you can't tell an ace of spades from a hole in the ground?"

A fiddler back in the corner plays lively music as Sam Wells, Wayne Pastor, Simrall and the good-natured Private John Smith pull up a camp stool or barrel to sit on.

"We got too many for whist. Let's play that new game from New Orleans I just learned called poker," suggests Harrison.

"Hey, everybody get your mug full. We gotta lighten up before we get back to the war at Fort St. Marys tomorrow," yells Harrison.

"I don't know poker, General," says W.P.

"Oh, we'll teach ya," says a winking Washburn, slapping Wayne Pastor on the back.

"Five-card stud," yells Harrison over the fiddler music while dealing.

"Have some more to drink, boys. Shoot, we may be up dancing before the night is over. Ha!"

Guards on the perimeter of camp hear the laughter but become anxious as the horses stomp around lightly, appearing uneasy while they graze, drink water from the stream and occasionally look up quickly. Over 300 troops are spread around Harrison's marquis tent, attending their campfires with five or six to each one, sipping on their allotted whiskey or hard cider.

Two other officers, already feeling a little tipsy, have joined Harrison's card game, and voices get louder.

"I told you, two pair does not beat three of a kind!" explains Harrison to the newcomers.

"How can three little deuces beat two kings of England?" complains an officer.

"Well, no one expected us to win the Rev war either, did they?" jokes the young W.P., exposing some historical knowledge as well as easing the tension.

"They just do!" yells John Smith. "Either learn the game or get the heck out of here!"

"I don't think that's as funny as you think since you are sitting over there with most of my money, you sissy little redneck!" yells the first officer, bumping the table and knocking some cards and coins onto the floor.

"Oh no, I've seen this before," says John Smith, sitting next to W.P.

"Settle down, boys," says Harrison. "It's just a friendly game."

"It's not a friendly game when you got two cheaters sitting across from me, General!" says one of the officers, staring at Smith.

"Who you calling a cheat?" asks Smitty.

"I'll give you two guesses, and the first one don't count."

Smith grabs the pine table and flips it at the offending guest.

The officer stands, turns and grabs the whiskey barrel behind him, tossing it at Smith. The spigot flies off and whiskey sprays, blinding Washburn for a second just as he takes a swing at who he thinks is a guest officer and strikes Harrison in the jaw by mistake.

Sam Wells stands up just in time to deflect an empty barrel flying at Harrison.

Harrison snatches the fiddle bow from the fiddler and starts whipping on the officers until it breaks, flies off and accidentally hits Simrall.

Stung by the fiddle bow, Simrall seizes the string instrument from the musician by the fingerboard and smashes it over both insolent officers' heads.

Washburn and Smith grab the back of the collar of the two officers, direct them toward the marquis entrance and kick them in the rear end, propelling the two through the tent flaps and into three gathering curious soldiers, finally finding a landing spot in the fire pit ten feet away.

"WHOO, WHOOOO!" holler the officers, reacting to the hot coals.

Staggering, Smitty and Washburn turn to extend hands in congratulations but, because of their inebriation, miss each other and bang skulls instead.

"Dad burn, you guys are nuts!" says Harrison, shaking his head.

Chapter 5

September 25–27, 1812 — Indiana Territory / Ohio

Approaching the Indian village on the Wabash River at the mouth of the Mississinewa River, Red Hawk and his mother, Morning Bird, wave to hailing Miami, Potawatomi and Delaware women along the bank.

"This will be a good place for you to stay, Mother, while I help our people's cause against the evil whites."

"I was wondering why you have been so quiet, Red Hawk. The Tecumseh influence along this waterway still exists, does it not?" speaks Morning Bird.

"This is everyone's land, and I will fight for it against Harrison. As I have been telling you, he has swindled much of this land from Little Turtle and other lesser chiefs that have no authority to make these treaties. Harrison liquors up these chiefs, and they sign anything to get more alcohol.

"One thing Little Turtle was right about," continues Red Hawk, "is that 'liquor is to be feared more than the gun or tomahawk.' That is the end of that. I stand with Tecumseh and the English."

"I fear, my son, the gun and the long knife will be your demise."

"At least, my mother, I will go to the spirit world knowing I did all I could to please the great Kitchi Manitou."

As Red Hawk sculls to the shore of the Indian village of Mississineway, memories of a conflict with warriors accusing him of murder flood back. Then a friendly, familiar voice breaks those thoughts and penetrates the other greetings.

"Look who we have welcoming us," says Red Hawk, "one of your long-ago friends from Kekionga!"

"Is it Maconaquah?" asks Morning Bird excitedly.

"Let me help you out," says the delighted old friend.

"My son, Red Hawk, was telling me several months ago that he and Wayne Pastor were thankful for your intervening in a misunderstanding they had with warriors here."

"Not sure who Wayne Pastor is. I remember White Snake being here with your son, Red Hawk."

"Yes, that's him," says Morning Bird, "the boy who wanted to become a Miami that lived among you for a few months."

"I knew there was something about him that did not make sense. Nice boy, though," voices Maconaquah.

As the middle-aged woman shows Morning Bird and the leery Red Hawk around the Indian village, they hear the Algonquin chatter about the two strangers from Kekionga and who they are.

As they stroll, they meet some of Maconaquah's friends tending fires that have black kettles hanging over them. Smelling the cooking stew made from the steady diet that the gardens along the river produce, they overhear how some of the villagers relaxing in front of their birch bark-covered wigwams and longhouses want nothing but peace with the whites.

Others, with a more antagonistic attitude advocate using the villages along the Mississinewa as a staging area to attack new American settlers entering the territory.

"War is all we hear about in this village. I am glad it is more peaceful upriver at my village," says Maconaquah.

"Personally, I for one am sick of the fighting and bloodshed," adds Morning Bird. "It seems it is all I have seen my entire life."

"Even my husband, Shepocanah, if you remember, Morning Bird, was injured at the Battle of Fallen Timbers and lost his hearing."

"I remember. That was nice of you to nurse him back to health and then for him to take you as his wife."

"We moved from Kekionga, as you know, down the Wabash and live nine miles up the Mississinewa in a hamlet named for my husband called Deaf Man's Village.

"Shepocanah and I have had four children. Two boys have died from disease, but our two girls are young and spirited.

"Red Hawk, here, is my surviving son. Running Deer and I had a daughter, but she too died of disease our village shaman could not cure."

"Morning Bird, Deaf Man's Village appears to be safe from the violence the Americans bring and welcomes you and all races, and the trade is vigorous."

"In order for that to continue, Maconaquah, Tecumseh's movement will have to continue," says Red Hawk finally contributing to the conversation. "With the British assistance, the Americans can be stopped."

"Well, you and your thoughts may be in luck any day now, Red Hawk," replies the former Frances Slocum. "Your hero is rumored to be arriving soon to meet with anti-American warriors and chiefs at the "moon rock."

"You can probably find warriors with your same sentiments and follow them to the rock when it is time."

Seventy-five miles north, along the Maumee River near the rapids, Running Deer is escorted to the delayed British and Indian joint venture campsite of Major Adam Muir and British Indian agent Matthew Elliott.

Waiting for boats and supplies to arrive that will propel them to victory at Fort Wayne, the two view the proud Miami warrior approaching with several escorts guarding him.

"We found this brave, or spy, traveling this way along the river. We remember him as a scout for the Americans at Fort Wayne," says a Miami warrior.

"That is true," pleads Running Deer, "I was scouting for the Long Knives but am true to my heritage and live for the existence of my people."

"How do we know you are not a spy?" argues the Wyandot Chief Roundhead from the Detroit area.

"Yes, you have been a spy with your white-man friend named Carlisle. Your son and his son are friends. I know I have seen them," informs another subchief.

"If that is true, you cannot have it both ways," says Muir, leaning forward on his stump stool, through an interpreter.

Forty miles south and west of Muir's campsite, an advance American guard and spy, Ensign James Liggett, eats a late dinner around a campfire with four soldiers he is assigned to lead in an exploratory venture ahead of General Winchester's force.

After already sending one of his men back to Winchester to warn him of many signs of Indian activity, Liggett settles in for a night's rest when, out of the darkness, startling circumstances occur.

"Levez la main," speaks a Frenchman, bursting from the forest accompanied by eight red-and-black-painted warriors, who surround the five seated Americans.

Not sure what the Frenchman has said, Liggett attempts the foreign language, "Mon francais n'est pas bon." Then in English he repeats, "Not sure what you want, since I do not speak good French.

"Easy boys," says Liggett to his subordinates in English, trying to ease the tension, "at least the white man is French."

"Stand up," speaks the Frenchman in broken English, waving his arms upward.

"What is this all about?" asks Liggett in English.

"Come with us to the British camp for interrogation. Wear your weapons until we get there. But keep your hands away from the trigger. You will not be harmed," says the Indian leader.

While the Americans follow the Frenchman northeast along the north bank of the Maumee, the warriors chatter to each other in Algonquin, trusting the Kentuckians do not understand them.

Sidling alongside the Americans, the Indians slowly remove their tomahawks, and the lead warrior screams, "AHYAAA!"

Unexpectedly, the Americans each receive a blow to the head, killing them instantly with the exception of Liggett, who upon hearing the initial screech moved enough to sustain a glancing chop to the shoulder. He sprints away toward a cluster of nearby oak trees, holding his arm and seeking protection, when he undergoes three fatal musket ball shots to his chest just as he looks back.

"AHYAAAAW!" scream the warriors scalping the Americans and waving them overhead.

Back at the British-Indian camp, Brown Bess muskets are pointed at Running Deer as he is tied up.

Attempting to be more convincing, Running Deer speaks in Algonquin, "I fought with Little Turtle at the victory in the Battle of Kekionga. I was there at the victory over General St. Clair at what is now Fort Recovery, and I fought against the one who never slept at Fallen Timbers. I have scars to prove it."

"You liar! Everyone has scars, this is an unforgiving land, we cannot take a chance," says Matthew Elliott.

"I'm telling you the truth. General Harrison has removed the siege at Fort Wayne, and the Americans are coming this way."

"You are nothing more, nothing less than a William Wells," says Muir.

"Yes, a two-faced spy who doesn't know who he is," says Elliott, signaling his warriors to take Running Deer into a temporary wigwam as a prisoner.

Meanwhile at Fort St. Marys, the Presbyterian Reverend Matthew Wallace, Harrison's army chaplain, speaks to the general just as a messenger is about to hand Harrison a large envelope.

"I see you are missing a couple tombac buttons from your sleeve, General."

"Not only that, Reverend, we have some horses missing from last night. Probably lost the buttons while I was saddling my horse this morning," answers Harrison.

"What about last night?"

"The horses or the card game that got a little carried away, Reverend?" asks Harrison.

"The Bible mentions the word drunk 81 times," says the chaplain.

"I think I can do a better job controlling that," says the general. "I hope you can forgive me."

"It is not me you need forgiveness from, General."

"Point well taken, and now you'll have to excuse me, Reverend."

"Of course, General."

Turning to the messenger, Harrison receives and opens the envelope in front of Colonel Wells and begins to read the orders from the war department of President James Madison.

Reading parts aloud, he informs Wells that Harrison is now the Major General of the Army of the Northwest and has been propelled ahead of Winchester in rank.

"Well, I'll be! Navarre was right," reacts Harrison.

"Yes sir. Congratulations, sir. Couldn't be a better choice. So what is next, General?" asks Wells anxiously.

"As I read and digest this, Colonel Wells, we have about thirty-five hundred militia troops heading this way from Virginia and Pennsylvania to join us in a three-prong attack on Fort Detroit. Seems General Hull's militia has been paroled by the British, and the regulars along with Hull are imprisoned in Quebec, Canada.

"Ok, I think I have a grasp on what to do, but it's going to be complex," begins Harrison. "I'm heading to Piqua and Franklinton to get some troops trained up and moving this way. You will lead a force up the Auglaize River toward Fort Defiance. Use the river for supply movement if it is deep enough. Build some interior forts to protect our supply line.

"I will catch up with you, but we will need a larger fort at Defiance. I will supervise that after I give Winchester his bad news. I do not look forward to that, Sam."

"I bet not, sir."

"Artillery, according to the orders in my hand, is heading this way with the Virginians and Pennsylvanians. It doesn't say who their leader is or when they will get here."

A day after Liggett's recon mission is discovered and wiped out by the Frenchman and Indians, Captain Ballard with a fifty-man 17th Kentucky Infantry recon of his own come across the mutilated and dismembered American bodies. Two have to be cut down from cottonwoods. Immediately, Ballard's detachment goes into a defensive mode by stacking logs and branches into protective cover while shallow graves are dug for the former comrades.

"The Indians are still out there. I have noticed a few watching us. Not sure how many, though," says Ballard to Lieutenant Harrison Munday.

"I think if they outnumbered us, they would be attacking by now," says Munday.

"Maybe so. But let's do this. Lead twenty-five men and act like you are leaving, but circle around behind them, attack and force them this way," orders Ballard. "Got it?"

"Yes sir, let's do it," says Munday. "When you hear the war whoops, that will be us, and you'll know it's on."

"Ok, we just about have these guys buried," informs Ballard. "We're gonna stay low and quiet here, hoping the Indians think we all left."

Word of the plan is passed down the line, and Munday takes his twenty-five with him, noisily, as if leaving, they back track the original route.

Ten minutes go by and all is silent, when one of Ballard's subordinates whispers.

"Pssst, Captain. I see 'em comin'."

Ballard whispers back while cocking his musket, "Stay down. The rest of his command follows suit with a series of musket cocking taking place in anticipation.

The noise alerts the keenly sensory warriors, and they stop thirty feet away from Ballard's position, looking intently and sensing danger, but it's too late.

"Ahhhhyaa! Ahhhayyaa!"

BAM! Bam! BAM! is the sound of Munday's detachment charging from behind with muskets blasting.

"Now men!" commands Ballard as his force rises slightly and fires, knocking down surprised and terrified approaching warriors with buck and ball.

Bam! Bam! BAM!

"Cease fire, men. We don't want to hit Munday and friends."

"But some are getting away, sir!" cries a subordinate.

"Stay here! This could be the lead of a larger force coming this way. Go get your souvenirs from these redskins if you wish, but we gotta head back to General Winchester."

Three of Harrison Munday's men are seen running after the fleeing warriors.

"Munday, pull your guys back! No chase! Get your boys back here!" calls Ballard.

"Dang! I like our aggressiveness, but that is not smart," says Ballard to two of his ranks.

Chapter 6

October 1–5, 1812 — Indiana Territory / Ohio

Just outside the walls of Fort Wayne, carpentry activities pierce the solitude as outbuildings are being rebuilt after having been destroyed by the seven-day siege the previous month.

"Hey, Lieutenant Ostrander," says Uncle Isaac, climbing down a wooden ladder, "I can't thank you and your fatigue enough for helping me work on E.J. and Charlotte's cabin and barn for them."

"Well, this time the family is a little closer to the fort," says Ostrander.

"Yes, Lieutenant," says Charlotte, "I can keep better track of the boys and little Hannah May with all the underbrush cleared away, also."

"You're welcome, ma'am. Just keep your musket nearby. I'm a little uneasy since the main army has moved toward Fort Defiance."

In the distance, a five-man special force of riders is seen approaching on Wayne Trace toward the fort's south main gate.

"Those couriers don't look familiar, Lieutenant," says Ike. "At least it's not that ornery old Private Smith, is it? Ha!"

"Naw, we couldn't be that lucky. It's special scout and messenger Peter Navarre leading the way.

"He once was held captive by the British. Released and told to go home," says Ostrander. "He'll be hung if he is caught helping Americans again."

"Hung or burned. That's pretty much the way it is with all scouts and messengers helping the enemy," says the veteran Uncle Isaac. "That's why we worry about E.J."

"E.J.'s pretty good, Ike. He knows his way around better than most. Excuse me, Ike. I better go check on what the news is," says Ostrander.

Along the Wabash River forty-five miles south, Shawnee Chief Tecumseh and seventy-five escort warriors gallop into Miami Chief

Charley's region and locate the sacred "moon rock," a rare Indiana geological formation.

A ceremony of worship around the fifteen-foot-long-by-twelve-foot-wide, six-foot-high granite slab that resembles the lunar surface has begun.

Out of respect, Tecumseh holds his horse and warriors away from the ceremony. He walks toward the gathering and falls to his knees next to a surprised and honored Red Hawk. Although tired from their long ride from Canada, the other warriors join him.

Chants that worship the Great Spirit, the moon and all things on earth that are alive and inanimate are uttered.

Chiefs Shepocanah, Majenica, White Loon, Charley, Silver Heels and Captain Squirrel finally rise to their feet and are pleased to see Tecumseh has arrived with his braves. Slowly and spirit-honoring, Tecumseh and his warriors rise to their feet and greet the chiefs.

Ordered to form a circle, all of the colorfully clothed Indians sit back down cross-legged as Tecumseh enters the ring.

"My Miami, Delaware and Potawatomi friends, my Shawnee brothers and I are honored to meet with you today at this distinguished spot. Let me question you. Are you ready to give up this rock to the whites?" asks the Algonquin speaking Tecumseh, dressed in his winter garb slowly pacing the hallowed grounds.

"Do you know what they will do with this rock?" asks Tecumseh rhetorically as he removes his outer robe and hands it to a warrior to keep for him. "They will bust it up just like they want to bust up the Great Spirit's coalition of tribes.

"Never forget where we have come from and who placed us here and where we all go when the life we have on this grand plane comes to an end!"

Grunts and guttural sounds of approval abound.

"I see the deaf-man chief here. Where is Godfroy and Pechewa, the wildcat? I trust you will pass this next information onto them, for my warriors and I cannot stay long.

"The British support us, and we must support them, for together we can prevent these Americans from ever settling in the Great Spirit's land we call home.

"Some of you want to give in to the whites and adjust to their way of life and live among them," addresses Tecumseh, shaking his head. "Such foolishness. The Americans will claim this land and more and will not stop at anything until it is theirs.

"You like whiskey? Of course, some of you do. They will use it to have you sign anything!

"Be wary of an attack from a place called Fort Harrison to your west! Be wary from my former homeland of Ohio, to the east!

"The whites' numbers are increasing. If we as an alliance can keep Mississineway and the Mississinewa River a sanctuary and staging area for raids against the settler incursion, success will be ours. Train your warriors well. Raise your families strong. Grow your crops abundantly! Fight, if necessary, as one fist, because separately, just as a single stick, we will break!"

With that, the chiefs rise in unison and cheer their leader, assuring him of their allegiance.

"AHHHYAAA! AHYAAA!"

As quickly as he had arrived, Tecumseh and his warriors are gone in a cloud of dust visiting other villages in the Indiana Territory and then back toward Canada.

At the British-Indian camp along the Maumee River, after the interrogation of Running Deer and listening to more witnesses testify against him, a verdict is announced by Elliott, "Burn him!"

"I agree, do away with him, or he will turn against us again," claims Chief Roundhead.

While being escorted away to a temporary wigwam by a sympathetic warrior he is asked, "Do you wish to prepare yourself for your death?"

"Yeesss," answers the dejected Running Deer, wearing leggings and wrapped in a large blanket robe to ward off the cool autumn wind.

While Running Deer strips himself of his clothes and uses a scalping knife to remove his body hair, a plant root mixture is placed next to him to paint his torso, arms and legs.

One hundred feet from the Maumee River, a nine-inch-diameter pole of a slow burning oak is sunk deeply into the ground pointing vertically. While branches, wood brush and old dried logs are placed a few feet away in a position to be pushed around the victim, Running Deer chants a death hymn as he applies a black bear grease concoction also provided for him to his body.

"Is this necessary, Elliott? Are we barbarians?" asks Muir. Just hang him and get it over with."

"It must be tortuous or it will continue to happen, Major Muir," says Elliott.

A quarter mile away, cautiously and slowly making his way down the Maumee River horseless is deerskin-clad E.J. Carlisle. Unsure of what is ahead, E.J. stays low behind a hollow log when he hears five warriors approaching from behind. To stay hidden the frontiersman crawls inside the log and lies quietly as the braves trot by ten feet away.

E.J.'s senses pick up a hint of smoke that indicates a camp is nearby. Dragging his Springfield Model 1795 musket by his side, he exits the log and crawls to a clearing that looks down on a camp. He spots a ten-foot-high post 150 yards in the distance surrounded by Indians, flammable wood and brush even closer to the post.

E.J. observes a familiar, black-painted Indian, naked but for a breechcloth, being led with his hands tied behind his back to the pole. A small group of warriors pound drums and ceremonial dancing begins to take place by others clockwise around the pole.

"That's my friend Running Deer," says E.J. softly to himself. "This can't be happening."

E.J. looks at his Springfield and thinks, "I'll have to get closer."

Beginning to crawl forward, he feels a hand grab his foot.

"Oh crap."

"Shhh, quiet. You're gonna need this," says the stranger just as E.J. looks back and sees a not-quite-so-familiar grimy face and hand offering a seventy-inch-long Kentucky long rifle to him.

"Can you shoot him from here?" asks the stranger.

"I think so," says E.J. "Who are you, mister?"

"Kenton, Simon Kenton. You want me to take him? I'm gettin' old, but I can still barrel 'im from here."

"Thanks, Mr. Kenton," whispers E.J. "I trained with Anthony Wayne. I think I can hit 'im."

"Be ready to run, young man. Cause they'll be madder than a hornet in a wasp's nest that you ruined their fun."

Placing the gun butt against his right shoulder and extending the barrel over the top of a dead, fallen ash tree log, E.J. looks through the sight down the barrel at a warrior with a torch, prepared to light the brush pile around Running Deer.

E.J. licks his finger to check the wind and thinks to himself, "Do I take out the warrior or Running Deer?"

With the two almost lined up directly, E.J. briefly deliberates, "Maybe I can get them both. At least Running Deer won't suffer."

Seeing his opportunity, E.J. cocks the hammer with his right thumb, looks through the sight and squeezes the trigger ever so slowly.

BAM!!

Waiting for a reaction, Kenton giggles and says, "You got 'im, boy!"

E.J. watches the Indian with the torch fall, shot fatally through the heart, and Running Deer's hands go free at the same time.

Warriors seated rise stunned, looking around to see where the shot came from, while Running Deer, recognizing his chance to get away, breaks through the circle of braves and, with his God-given speed, takes advantage of his head start, pulling away from his nearest pursuer south along the river path.

A cool breeze disperses the telltale long rifle smoke, allowing the two pioneer scouts to head away from the river into the deep forest undetected. The dead warrior's torch falls and ignites branches intended for Running Deer's death. The resultant fire spreads smoke and soot, blinding some warriors temporarily. Simultaneously and miraculously, shipments carrying needed supplies arrive on the river, with hollers of greetings adding to the chaos.

Seventy-five miles upstream at Fort Wayne, disgruntlement takes place again. "That does it!" complains Lieutenant Phillip Ostrander, a siege-resistant hero at Fort Wayne, who exits the fort's front gate and heads toward Uncle Isaac finishing the barn roof. "I've just about had it with this military life."

"What happened, Lieutenant?" asks a blue-dressed and aproned Charlotte tending the fort garden nearby.

"Yeah, what's happening, Commander is it?" asks Ike.

"No, it is not Commander. I've been bypassed again. Some guy named Captain Moore from the 19th Infantry is taking over. Don't know much about him, but he rode in with Navarre."

"Gee, you'd think fort veteran Lieutenant Curtis would have even been given a chance," says Uncle Ike.

"Oh, I'm better than Curtis, dad burnit," says Ostrander egotistically.

"They are sending this kid Croghan to Fort Defiance. Can you believe it! From Fort Wayne to Fort Defiance and closer to the war. This kid has connections somewhere."

"Maybe he's just good at what he does, Lieutenant," says Charlotte, taking hold of Hannah May's hand and leading her into the cabin, away from the cursing and complaining.

"Have you seen the boys, Uncle Isaac?" asks Charlotte.

"They were playing over along Shawnee Creek last time I saw them," says Ike.

"I think it's that dad-gum Indian agent Benjamin Stickney's doing," offers Ostrander. "He saw me have a few drinks with Commander

Rhea during the siege," mumbles Ostrander as he strides over to help Ike finish the roof.

Forty-eight miles away and a few days before Croghan switches to Fort Defiance as commander, those occupying the dilapidated trading post nervously view the 1,200-man British and Indian force pulling Fort Wayne-bound artillery pieces up the south Maumee River trail toward the mouth of the Auglaize River.

Struggling to handle the forested road, Major Muir and Matthew Elliott call for a halt. Warrior scouts are seen crossing the 100-yard-wide Maumee toward them from north to south at a ford.

"The Americans are coming with a large army down the north bank of the Maumee heading right for us," announces a warrior spy. "Fort Wayne, as we have picked up on, was relieved by Harrison several days ago."

"This would be a good place to take a stand, Major Muir," suggests one of his officers.

"Yes, Commander Muir, we have the artillery and ammunition to meet them head-on. They are on the other side of the river. Let's strategize a way to defeat them," mentions another officer, carefully monitoring Muir's puzzling demeanor.

"Our mission was to knock the walls of Fort Wayne down. That mission has obviously had to be scuttled. The fort is no longer surrounded by warriors. We must turn around," orders Muir.

The Indians who can understand a little English look at each other astonishingly and in Algonquin begin to chatter.

"This cannot happen," decries Roundhead, "we can defeat them!"

The British interpreters tell Muir and Elliott of the disbelief.

"You're not telling me anything I can't understand," yells Elliott at the interpreters.

"Reconsider, Major Muir. The Indians are ready to fight for our cause and the crown," pleads Elliott.

"To fight the Americans here is not our orders from Colonel Proctor, Mr. Elliott. The orders are to knock down the walls of Fort

Wayne. Since that cannot be done, by chance of an American army in our way, we shall turn around immediately and expedite our way back to Detroit.

"To move faster, we shall roll the artillery into the river so the Americans cannot use them and we may retreat more rapidly. Do I make myself clear, Mr. Elliott?"

"These cannons, stop Americans," offers another war chief in his broken English.

"These cannons are not made for forest warfare. They were made for open-field warfare, Chief!" informs Muir.

"Royal Regiment, do your duty and roll them into the river!"

With that, the Royal Regiment of Artillery follow the command and give a hefty five-man shove, propelling one at a time the four pieces into the Maumee River north and downstream from the Auglaize River.

Chapter 7

October–November 1812 — Indiana Territory / Ohio

Fifty-nine miles south and west of Kekionga at Mississineway and the older one across the Mississinewa called Osage, life is fairly normal. Most of the residents feel safe from the American armies. Tecumseh has visited to reassure his leadership. A hunting trip involving a large percentage of the warriors at Mississineway is being planned. The braves will head to the Kentucky hunting grounds to bring back protein that the venison provides to balance their mostly vegetarian diet.

"Red Hawk and I will visit you the next full moon, Maconaquah," says Morning Bird as she and her son wave. Maconaquah's husband, Shepocanah, and two young daughters paddle against the strong Mississinewa current back to their home called Deaf Man's Village nine miles away. Chief Silver Heels strokes alongside Shepocanah with his entourage in three supply-filled birch bark canoes heading toward his village, which is one of four clustered and seemingly protected from the outside world.

"You are not going on hunting trip, Red Hawk?" asks Morning Bird.

"Mother, let's get you established here first before I go traveling about. Tecumseh needs me, but I am uneasy about the Americans pursuing our people up or down the Wabash to these villages.

"Now, with so many of my brothers leaving, I am a little more concerned," says Red Hawk pulling his robe closer around him to resist the chill as they walk to their new and unfinished willow sapling-framed wigwam.

Southwest from Fort Defiance five miles, American General James Winchester has been camped in the same spot for three days.

E.J. Carlisle and Simon Kenton, fresh from saving Running Deer, report that the British and Indian coalition led by Muir has turned back.

"Good reporting, boys," says Winchester.

"Oh, I like hearing that you think I'm still a boy, General," says the fifty-seven-year-old Kenton.

"Well, my sixty-year-old body tells me I'm older than you, but we are still going at it, aren't we?"

"Yep," says Kenton, "and I've got to head to Piqua, organize the militia and lead the Ohioans toward DEEtroit and DEEfeat those dad-burned Brits."

"Thanks for your help, Mr. Kenton, and the use of the long rifle," says E.J. "What a shot, huh?"

"One for the ages, kid."

"You'll have to tell me about that, E.J.," requests Colonel John Allen of Kentucky, sidling up to his new friend from Fort Wayne.

"He can tell you about it after we get General Tupper organized and sent downriver to spy what's ahead," orders Winchester, again delaying his army's advancement.

Twenty-eight miles directly south of Fort Defiance, General Harrison leads 3,000 American troops north through the Great Black Swamp following the Auglaize River and orders the completion of Fort Jennings.

"I can't imagine anyone wanting to attack this garrison in this location, Colonel Wells, but those rascally Indians are everywhere, and they know this land better than we do."

"Yes sir, General. By the way, here is Reverend Wallace, as you requested," says Wells.

Ignoring the army chaplain for a moment to finish his thoughts, Harrison continues, "This fort, Colonel Wells, will go along with Forts Barbee, Amanda and Findlay under construction as well.

"Reverend Wallace, with Winter coming soon, I would like to request a prayer to expedite the war strategy I am concerned about. Things are moving too slow to satisfy my plans."

Wallace begins by stating, "Keep in mind, General, any request to God will happen if it is his will."

"Yes, Reverend," responds Harrison.

The army pastor immediately pulls his Bible out but recites from memory Matthew 6:34: "Therefore do not worry about tomorrow, General, for tomorrow will worry about itself. Each day has enough trouble of its own.

"General, I have been around enough Indian warfare to know that what you are doing may be slow and methodical, but your planning and actions comfort me, and I feel the Lord is with you."

"Amen, Reverend," says Harrison, staring at him. "Thank you. But answer me this. Who is truly our enemy? The Indians or is it the British?"

"Romans 16:20, General, 'The God of Peace will soon crush Satan under your feet. The grace of our Lord Jesus be with you.'"

"Amen again, Reverend."

Looking back down at a crude map, Harrison places a lead block-printer's weight with 4th inscribed on it to hold it down against a cool breeze.

"Look up here, Colonel Wells," says Harrison, pointing his right index finger at the map of Ohio. "Where the Little Auglaize River flows and meets the Auglaize. Let's place a fort there, also."

"Yes sir."

"Scouts say the depth of the water increases, and supplies will be more easily floated," says Harrison. Engineers are in northern Ohio, as well, Colonel, trying to figure out where to cross the Black Swamp for the new militia from Pennsylvania and Virginia."

Three days later, Winchester finally brings his left wing along the north side of the Maumee River to a ford that crosses to the south leading to a trail up the bank to Fort Defiance that has had eighteen years to deteriorate.

"Never been here before, but I like the location overlooking the Maumee and the Auglaize, Colonel Allen," comments General Winchester.

"You may not want to bring everyone across, General, until we see what we have up there," says Allen, surveying from a distance. "Doesn't look very big, sir."

"Report is that it has been abandoned from military use for some time going back to the Indian wars," says Winchester. "They have turned it more into a trading post."

Riding up closer, the officers notice pointed abatis logs and fascines laying estray, covered by growing weeds. Broken limbs from a few trees left thriving are scattered about for shade and the drawbridge that leads across a twelve-foot-wide trench, now full of rainwater, appears to have a safety issue.

"Keep half the units on the north side with the cattle and hog herds, finish bringing the artillery, Allen, and those with us across," orders Winchester.

"Play a little louder, musicians! Let 'em know we are here!"

"Get more pickets and spies out, Allen. Let's don't invite a surprise attack."

"Yes sir."

"Hope supplies are coming in soon, Colonel," says Winchester. "You look a little uncomfortable with your summer linen and worn shoes."

"I am, sir and I hope so too."

Two days later across the Auglaize River ford south of Defiance arrives William Henry Harrison with his troops, swelling the left wing of his planned attack of Detroit to 4,000.

Shouts of, "Here comes Harrison!" from the excited Winchester force is heard as the new Major General rides in with Sam Wells and clustered aide-de-camps toward the sorry Fort Defiance.

Winchester walks out the open gate of the 1794 fort across a creaky drawbridge toward Harrison, thinking he is still in charge.

"Welcome, Harrison."

"Good morning, General Winchester, but from the looks, you have had better," says Harrison, pulling out an envelope that contains the news that the old veteran has been relieved, and Harrison is taking over.

Two minutes after reading the contents, Winchester comments, "I see it's signed 'President James Madison.'"

"Yes," says Harrison, "it's official. But I want you to stay on as commander of my left wing."

"Yes sir," says the elderly general, reluctantly saluting.

"We need a new fort," says Harrison. "It needs to be at least ten times bigger than Wayne's old one."

"Get engineer William Atherton on its design, Winchester. Place it along the west bank of the Auglaize south of Fort Defiance. I want four huge blockhouses. It has to be able to hold supplies and stop the British as well as the Indians. Get it started now!" orders Harrison.

Back at Fort Wayne, a revenge factor plays out.

"Get in the fort, Charlotte!" yells resident Antoine Bondie, scampering around the outside of Fort Wayne, waving his arms.

"Get your kids inside, Charlotte. The natives are surrounding us again!"

"Oh, shoot! Come on, boys! Where's Hannah May?"

"I saw her at the Shawnee Creek catching crawdads a half hour ago, Ma!" yells Bennie, the oldest son.

"Hannah May! Hannah May! You get home right now!" shouts Charlotte as she heads toward the narrow three-foot-wide stream 400 yards away. Seven mounted Miami and Potawatomi riding down and up the creek bank toward the cabin halt her progress.

"Stop, Ma. It's too late!" shouts her youngest boy, Teddy. "Head for the fort!"

"Yeah, Ma! Into the fort! Hannah's probably hiding, anyway!" offers the oldest. "She's good at that!"

"I can't allow those redskins to have my baby!" screams Charlotte, running into the new two-story log cabin.

Charlotte reappears with a loaded 1795 Springfield musket pointing at now 500 red-and-black-painted warriors surrounding the newly repaired Fort Wayne.

"Oh my God!" murmurs Charlotte, seeing the futility and dropping to her knees crying as her boys, Uncle Isaac and Bondie help her up to her feet and practically drag her into the fort.

"I don't know how much more of this I can take!" sobs Charlotte. "I want E.J.!"

The Indians' advancement stops, not because of Charlotte's rifle but because twenty-five American infantrymen wearing leather shako plumed headwear stare over the twelve-foot-high picket walls, pointing their Springfield rifles. More firepower points out the embrasures of the southwest blockhouse as a five-and-a-half-inch howitzer is maneuvered to fire out the west portal.

Commander Moore walks out the south main gate to supervise the local residents still entering. On the other side of the stockade, two horseback saddled messengers exit the river gate down the bank, hopefully unnoticed, along the Maumee River toward Fort Defiance carrying the news of a second siege.

"Ahhhyaaa!" yells a tomahawk-swinging Potawatomi Chief Five Medals, steaming at what had happened to his village on the Elkhart River and those within fifty miles of the fort.

Raising his tomahawk again, he screams, "AHHHYAAA!!"

Echoing his sentiments, 500 warriors shriek, "AHHHYAAA!!"

At sunset, fifty campfires are viewed around Fort Wayne by blockhouse sentries enclosing the palisade.

"We have enough food stored up for a while, Mr. Stickney," says Captain Moore. "Do you think we can negotiate?"

"Didn't work before, Captain, but it's different this time," says the Indian agent.

"How's that, Mr. Stickney?"

"There is a real good chance they have the little Carlisle girl. A hostage like that is a deal maker or breaker."

"You don't think they'll …" hesitates Moore, "in front of her family and us?"

"Let's pray they don't, Captain," says Stickney.

A hundred and ten miles southwest of Kekionga, trouble stirs. Like a wild grassfire, William Henry Harrison has more problems in the Indiana Territory, where a year ago he thought was under control.

Prophetstown and the Tippecanoe area now see General Samuel Hopkins of Kentucky leading 1,250 militia from Illinois, Indiana and Kentucky up a tributary of the Wabash River called Wildcat Creek.

"I don't know why I have to justify this venture to you, Colonel Russell," says Hopkins.

"Seems like a waste," says Russell, "having this huge army following behind us on a search-and-destroy mission.

"No Indian chief in his right mind, especially one rumored to be Tecumseh's brother Kumakskau, is going to take us on, and for sure we are not going to sneak up on anyone."

"I get what you mean," says Hopkins, "but everyone's wary after one of our detachments lost a militia brother yesterday."

"I understand, General, but it may be the price we have to pay for the Pigeon Roost and Fort Dearborn massacres, and the fact American graves from last year's Battle of Tippecanoe were dug up and desecrated. I can't tell ya how mad people back home are. They want revenge," says Russell, combing the horizon ahead looking for any sign of trouble.

"My blood's curdling as you speak, Colonel. I agree we will have to send out more detachments to search and destroy the villages in a timely manner.

"Bring up Colonels Miller and Wilcox, Colonel Russell, and give them sixty men to scour this unknown creek to the east."

"Yes sir, General," says Russell. "I think sixty men have a good chance of returning with results as opposed to one scout."

A half mile away, a hundred Shawnee and Winnebago warriors, led by Kumakskau, stay hidden as Tecumseh's younger brother recalls advice he was taught: "The Americans will chase you if given a good reason."

Observing the defeatable American detachment forming and then following the bank of Wildcat Creek toward him, orders to his warriors break the silence.

"Bring the dead American, and we will post him on the other side of the bend in the stream behind us," commands Kumakskau.

"I want White Cloud to stand with the dead one. White Cloud is the only one I cannot defeat in our wrestling matches. Ha!" says Tecumseh's little brother. "He is brave and has a swift pony."

"The body will not stand on its own," says White Cloud.

"Remove the American head and place on pole," says Kumakskau.

"Listen, White Cloud, when the Americans see you with the pole, they will chase you. Lead them into the deep ravine ahead. There will be no escape for them."

"Yes, Kumakskau. Good plan," compliments the surrounding warrior advisers in Algonquin.

"Let's get hidden up ahead," says the chief, waving his hundred warriors to follow him.

Colonel Wilcox and Miller lead the Indiana Rangers easterly along the conducible terrain on horseback, spurring occasionally to prod the saddle-bred horses over a hill.

Suddenly, Wilcox lifts his arm and calls a halt.

"What's that up ahead, Colonel Miller?"

"That's Private Wade next to that warrior, Colonel," says Captain Beckes, standing in his stirrups from directly behind Wilcox. "I'd recognize him anywhere. He's my best friend!"

"AYYYAAA! Ya-haaa!" taunts White Cloud, waving Wade's scalp.

"Let's go! Let's get him!" orders Wilcox, pulling his arm forward to signal his rangers.

"Be careful now, Colonel," warns Miller following slightly behind him.

"Let's go, it's just one of them," responds Wilcox, tired of the cautious behavior of the Hopkins expedition. "We're here to search and destroy!"

Riding full bore leading his sixty men, the detachment hesitates only at the pole to examine the head of Wade.

"Yeah, that's him. Those dirty dogs! We'll bury him later. Let's make this redskin pay!" yells Wilcox.

The Americans follow White Cloud's trail along the creek up and down some small hills that lead them blindly into a steep hundred-foot-high gorge that Wildcat Creek flows through. Hidden warriors blend in with nature and wait in ambush.

Galloping blindly into the ambush, a surprised American force hears the result of their lack of caution.

Bam! Bam! BAM, B-bam! Ignite the Native American British flintlock muskets that knock down several Indiana Rangers into the creek bed or along the bank. The hidden warriors pounce on the Americans and finish them off with tomahawks and scalping knives.

Waving the hair or beheaded enemy, the warriors crow, "AyaHYYA."

Shocked by the Indians storming in on horseback, Miller and Wilcox bellow their orders, "Up the ravine, men!"

Fifteen Americans are killed while the remaining force dig in with their spurs to drive their horses up the ravine and out of danger. Before they can get over the summit, three more rangers are pulled from their slow-moving, ascending horses and have their lives ended.

Chapter 8

November–December 1812 — Indiana Territory / Ohio

Standing in the middle of his newly constructed fort next to Anthony Wayne's old one, Harrison, who is directing interior construction, turns his attention to two riders bursting through the carelessly open west gate of Fort Winchester.

With three acres around him, guards still had little time to warn either bodyguard Cornelius Washburn or Harrison of the riders. Sliding off their sweaty, panting horses, the messengers from Fort Wayne quickly salute Harrison as Harrison cavalrymen trying to catch up ride in behind them.

"The fort has been surrounded, sir!" informs the breathless emissaries at the same time.

"Take it easy, boys. What fort?" asks Harrison, pointing at the least nervous one.

"Fort Wayne, sir. They need help again."

Harrison looks down, takes his bicorne hat off, smooths back his hair, turns to Washburn and pronounces, "This time, Corny, we will have to make sure it won't happen again."

"Yep. The Indians have had a chance to calm down, General," says Cornelius.

Harrison calls over an aide-de-camp and releases his orders. "Bring me Colonel Allen Trimble and his 2nd Ohio Regiment."

"Yes sir."

"Inform them to prepare horseback to return to Fort Wayne to relieve them of another siege. Our spies have been warning us of a possible Chief Five Medals reprisal. Drive the natives back to the Elkhart and into the Michigan Territory if they have to."

"Yes sir."

Three days later, Harrison heads to Franklinton in Ohio to help train the new militia pouring in from Kentucky, Ohio and Virginia.

General Winchester, who has been appeased by the naming of the new fort after him, sends Kentucky militia northeasterly toward the Maumee rapids, but because of an early winter storm, Colonel John Allen has to halt just six miles northeast of Fort Winchester.

"This snow is getting too deep and piling up fast, Colonel," says militiaman Eli Darnell. "It's blowing sideways, and the trail's nearly impossible to detect."

"Where's Wells at?" asks Allen blinded by the snow. "I can't see him up ahead."

"Wait, there he is in front, Colonel," answers Darnell. "They are dismounting."

With the Maumee River to their right flowing steadily at a five-miles-per-hour pace, the plummeting temperatures still form ice along the edges of the riverbank.

"Allen, is that you?" calls Sam Wells, walking back through the sudden three-foot snow depth.

"Yeah, it's me. What do you want to do?"

"It's late afternoon. Let's dig in and set up camp. Get some fires going and move out in the morning."

"Dad burn. What did that old coot send us out into?" asks Allen.

"He doesn't care. He's just following orders to advance. Chances are he is sitting in that cozy fort named after him next to a fireplace. Told me he couldn't wait any longer for supplies," explains Wells.

"Darnell, get some boys setting up tents and lean-tos for shelter, and start cutting some wood. The cattle and hogs gotta be penned in, also!" yells Allen.

"Yes, sir!"

Hundreds of Kentuckians of the 17th riflemen and 1st and 5th Kentucky regiments without winter attire make do in their summer clothing. Having left Piqua, Ohio, last August in a hurry to rescue Fort Wayne, northern Ohio winter weather has no mercy.

Meanwhile, Colonel Allen Trimble and his 500 Ohio volunteers follow orders and arrive at Kekionga to suppress an Indian encirclement of Fort Wayne. Warriors offer little resistance as the Americans cross Harmar's Ford at a gallop north to south.

Mounting their Indian ponies, the native Americans head northwesterly, connecting with the Fort Dearborn Trail.

"Yeah! Hooray! Yeehaa!" cheer the hat tossing in the air, grateful fort occupants, who had to hold out just half the time of the previous siege.

"Mom, help is here!" says Teddy, attempting to comfort Charlotte.

"Well, Teddy. If they can find Hannah May and place her on my lap, we will then have something to be truly happy about. Until then, I don't care whether I'm safe or not."

"Aw Ma, they'll find her real soon. Hannah is pro'bly hidin' along that old creek bed inside a log. Don't ya think, Bennie?"

"Yeah, there's hundreds of places she could be hidin'. She ain't gonna let no Injun capture her."

"Where have you been learnin' that kind of grammar, young man? There ain't no such word as ain't!" corrects the overtaxed Charlotte.

"Come on, Charlotte," interrupts Uncle Isaac. "Let's go see what's left of our homes."

"I'm sorry, Ike," says Charlotte. "I keep forgetting you have a home also."

"Didn't even have to fire a shot, Colonel," informs Fort Commander Hugh Moore, stepping out of the garrison through some falling snow flurries for the first time in four days.

"That's good, Commander, you saved ammunition," responds Trimble. "I think the immediate area is safe, but we are going to form up and drive the redskins as far as we can."

An aide to Trimble overhears and speaks up. "That's a nice idea, sir, but out of the five hundred men we have, only about half share your sentiments."

"What's that, Corporal?"

"Most would rather stay here and protect the fort than go off in the direction you want to go. Too many horror stories, sir."

At Franklinton, in central Ohio, those looking for a mission get one.

"Finally, we get to move out of this camp and get some action," says Wayne Pastor Carlisle, the native of Kekionga.

"Kid, you are too anxious for me. Do you know what we are heading into?" says trader, interpreter and hired guide William Connor of the Indiana Territory.

"What?" asks W.P. "You, me and four other scouts leading this search-and-destroy detachment?"

"In a few days, young man, we will either be stirring up a hornets nest, dead or both," says Connor.

"Yeah, you're probably right, Mr. Connor. I lived among those people as an Indian for a while with an Indian family led by Shepocanah and Maconaquah."

"You know them?" asks Connor.

"Yes sir, I do," says W.P. "Shepocanah was a little rough, but the lady treated me well. Pro'bly because I was from her one-time home of Kekionga."

"I have been trading in that area for quite some time," says Connor. "I hope we can get a peaceful solution before these dragoons cut loose, if you know what I mean."

Three days later after leaving Ohio, the secret mission commanded by Lieutenant Colonel John B. Campbell of the Kentucky 19th Infantry enters the Indiana Territory and the headwaters of both the Wabash and the desired Mississinewa River. Snow blowing sideways at twenty-five miles an hour forces the 600 Americans to pull down their hats and draw closer their brown, blue and grey wool coats.

Squinting through the blizzard conditions, Campbell and dragoon leader Simrall of the Little Turtle's village debacle spot W.P. approaching.

"It's ok, Colonel, it's Carlisle. He's a good kid. I was once in a poker game with him. He's pretty lucky, which is a good thing," opines a grinning Simrall.

"Colonel Campbell, Colonel Simrall," greets W.P. "We will be following a stream for a while, but it will grow into a fast-moving Mississinewa River until it empties into the Wabash. Be prepared to give up our surprise unless you want to pick up the pace fairly soon. Injuns have a way of keeping an eye on things."

"Let's camp here, Simrall, and get our mission done tomorrow fresh in the morning and get back to Ohio," orders Campbell.

"Sounds good to me," says Simrall. "Let's build some fires and warm up."

"You may not want to build them too large, Colonel," says Wayne Pastor. "The natives will pick up on that, too."

"Of course, W.P., thanks," says Simrall. "It's gonna be a long, cold night."

"I want you, Connor and the four other scouts advancing ahead tonight. I want a full report in the morning on how many villages we may encounter before we reach Mississineway and its twin, Osage, across the river. Got it?"

"You bet, sir. See you in the morning," salutes the obedient Carlisle while kneeing his thoroughbred stallion to break through the drifting snow.

Back ninety miles north and six miles from Fort Winchester at American Camp No. 3, the cold and snow is not the only enemy. Riding in are scouts Captain Johnny Logan, Bright Horn and Captain John, all three Shawnee seemingly helping the United States's cause.

"Hold it right there!" calls out a guard, pointing his rifle at Johnny Logan.

"We have been chased for the last two miles," explains Logan in his Algonquin and broken English.

"What do you mean chased?" intervenes veteran military scout Captain Ballard. "Nobody could be out in these conditions."

"What do we have here, Captain?" asks Colonel Wells, pulling up his wool coat and drawing his sword.

"These three are obviously Indians but just rode on in," says Ballard.

"We hhhave scouting nnews," says a suddenly nervous Logan. "The Miami are near and keeping an eye on you all the wway to the rapids."

"Tell us something we don't know already. I think they are spies," says Ballard.

"We are not spies. Do you not remember me helping evacuate Fort Wayne before the siege, and then later during the blockade, bringing news to Fort Wayne that Harrison was on the way?"

"I don't know anything about the Fort Wayne siege," says Ballard. "I do know that my friend Ensign Liggett was killed spying, and I had to bury him. How come you three are still alive?"

"Take it easy, Captain Ballard," intervenes Wells. "You know we have Indians working with us."

"Very few that I'm aware of," says Ballard.
"Captain Johnny Logan here is also known as Spemica Lawba. Bright Horn? Well, I have seen him at Indian agent John Johnston's home at Piqua and heard their names mentioned."

"I don't trust any Indian, Colonel," snarls Ballard.

"Give 'em a chance," says Colonel John Allen, popping in to hear the fuss. "We are stuck in this storm, and we need all the help we can get. Offer them some food and send them out again. It's not like our situation is totally unknown."

"I don't like it, Colonel. They may ride all the way to Colonel Proctor and have all the British in North America on top of us."

"We do not like British. We help Americans. I was adopted by Americans," says Logan. "How do you think I got my name?"

"All right, all right. We are too far from Fort Winchester to discuss it with the general. Go ahead, Captain Johnny Logan. Go bring us some news," orders Wells.

Forty miles away, having winter conditions of their own, the elderly, graying Uncle Isaac and attractive, brown-haired Charlotte

Carlisle start a fire in E.J. and Charlotte's cabin as they clean up after the second Fort Wayne siege. Disheartened that Hannah May was nowhere to be found, the two take solace.

The cabin door opens allowing a cold draft, removing heat from the cabin and stirring Charlotte to yell without looking, "Close that door, you youngins!"

"Glad you still think I'm a youngin!" grins E.J., carrying Teddy in his arms with Bennie hugging and walking next to him.

Charlotte turns to the door to see a man closing the entry. "Oh my God, E.J., you're back!" voices a surprised Charlotte with excitement.

"Whooee!" yells Uncle Ike with relief.

"Some storm, huh?" reacts E.J. out of embarrassment. "Didn't know I'd get this kinda greeting."

"Oh E.J., we've been stuck in that fort surrounded by Indians, and Hannah May, we think, has been taken by those savages!" expresses Charlotte. "Wayne Pastor is over in Ohio, last we heard, and these boys are helpful, but they don't know how to talk."

"Aww Ma," says Bennie and Teddy together.

"Dad burn, now Charlotte. All this in just the few weeks I've been gone? Geez, Uncle Ike, what's been going on?"

Uncle Isaac catches E.J. up on the news in more detail. Charlotte can't stop hugging and kissing her husband, while the boys hang onto their dad and fill in when Ike has to catch his breath.

"I'll tell ya what right now," says E.J., "as soon as we get settled around here, I'm gonna get on the trail of Hannah May and get her back, Lord willing."

"I want my baby back," interrupts Charlotte.

"I know you do, honey. So do I. Chances are the Indians won't harm her. Probably adopting her out. Just gotta find where she's at, and I think I know who can help.

"The Pastor and John Chapman said we need to talk to God all the time, not just when we need something, but let me give it a try. Father God in heaven, we thank you for everything we have and all that you have provided for us. Forgive us our sins. Come into our hearts and help us, Holy Spirit, in our needs. Amen."

"Thanks, E.J. You're not bad at that praying stuff," says Uncle Ike.

"Yeah, well, thanks. But I'm still not sure, according to John Chapman, how God knows every hair on our head."

Chapter 9

Late November–December 1812 — Indiana Territory / Ohio

Relaxed as if just wanting to conduct some trade business, the well-known William Connor enters a longhouse near Deaf Man's Village. Walking in on a heated conversation on Indian strategy and leadership, the Colonel Campbell guide Connor listens intently.

"Look, we have met with Harrison earlier this fall and have told him we want peace," says Shepocanah.

"That was before our great victory on Wildcat Creek," says young war hawk Miami Chief Majenica. "Harrison does not want peace. Why did he send that army up the Wabash to Pechewa's Creek if he wanted peace?

"I disagree with this deaf man, Shepocanah. He has served his purpose. He is too old to lead us. Look at him, he cannot hear us," says the colorfully robed Majenica.

As hand signing takes place for the confused Shepocanah to understand, a Delaware chief speaks up, defending him.

"He has much more exper—"

"He knows nothing anymore," interrupts Majenica in Algonquin, speaking too fast for the signers and Shepocanah to fully understand. "He would rather trade and live peacefully with his strange wife. I am much more in tune with what is going on. I am stronger and wiser than this pastured bull!"

Connor, comprehending enough to see a fight is imminent, watches closely as Shepocanah rises out of his crossed-legged position to grab for the young chief, surprisingly quicker than most thought he could, putting Majenica on his back. Then the reverse happens and the two are rolling around just missing the fire in the center of the council house.

Majenica, a full six feet tall and forty years younger, gets the advantage on the deaf man and pulls a nine-inch hunting knife out of its leather sheath.

"Break it up!" roars Chief Francis Godfroy, a larger and stronger man, grabbing Majenica's hair to pull him away and stepping on the younger warrior's wrist until the knife is released.

With the assistance of Chiefs Little Thunder, Sakima and Delaware Silver Heels, each combatant's supporters are subdued, and calm is restored.

Not far from Connor's longhouse encounter at the Indian powwow, Wayne Pastor recognizes the lay of the land and creeps toward Maconaquah's cabin.

Seeing her throw some water out the door, he whistles to get her attention.

"Over here, Maconaquah," whispers W.P. loud enough over the blowing wind to draw her to his location.

"Who is it?"

"It's White Snake."

Wearing an Indian robe-type clothing that he had brought along on the mission to get by, he informs her, "The Americans are near. I just want you to know if fighting breaks out, be careful."

"Hey, your Algonquin is getting better. But I wouldn't be too confident if you get caught," says Maconaquah, smiling through a glimpse of moonlight. "For your information, White Snake, Red Hawk and his mother are staying in this village, but not sure where they ended up tonight."

"Oh, that's just great. Now I have three of you to worry about."

Back on the Maumee at Winchester's Camp No. 3, conditions worsen, with rain drenching the tents. Dry, warm clothing, food, and supplies of salt and flour not arriving and Indians being a constant threat is wearing on the forty-acre camp full of hundreds of mostly Kentuckian militia and infantry.

Three American camp leaders meet to discuss the situation. "We're going to have to build more shelters and picket walls,"

Commands Colonel Sam Wells. "Get these guys out of the water. Warm them up!"

"We have some sick ones, Colonel," says Allen. "Fever, chills, coughing up blood, you name it."

"Sounds like typhoid fever, diphtheria. Dad burn, it's relentless," says Wells. "Can we go back to Fort Winchester, Captain Ballard?"

"Not an option at this point, sir. Most would freeze to death. The trail is nearly impassable with waste-high and higher snowdrifts! Best to stay by the fires, in my opinion, and hope the weather breaks and supplies get here soon."

Dropping in on the meeting as another night of falling temperatures brings more misery is Private Eli Darnell, one of the hearty ones.

"We had to bury our first two victims of this fiasco, sir. Good men, too. I knew 'em both. They couldn't stop shakin'. They've stopped shaking now."

Twenty miles down the Maumee on the south side, American scouts—Shawnee Captain Johnny Logan, Bright Horn and Captain John—ride in the dark on a mission to prove their worth. Their horses plod on in a parallel path to the river where it is passable. They realize it is dangerous, but the snow is too deep to go anywhere else, and if stopped, they will rely on their bilingual ability to get by.

"Hold it right there," orders a British voice.

"Minwakijigan," says an Indian, almost simultaneously, in Algonquin.

From behind a bush covered with snow, a Brit sympathizer and four warrior scouts mosey their horses cautiously to encircle Johnny Logan's trio.

"Your names?" orders Matthew Elliott Jr., the youngest son of the British Indian agent with the same name.

"We are scouting for the English," disinforms Logan in Algonquin.

"I don't believe him, Mr. Elliott," says Elliott's co-leader, Chief Winamac, who had helped lead the siege on Fort Wayne in September. "Pull your coat from your face."

Doing what he is ordered, the sporadic moonlight reflects on Johnny Logan's features.

"Ha, I thought I recognized that voice. He's an American scout named Spemica Lawba, and I would assume his friend Bright Horn is next to him," says Winamac. "I don't know the third one."

"Let's take them to my father and Major Muir," says Elliott, Jr.

Unknowingly following Captain Logan's tracks a half mile back from Winamac and young Elliott, E.J. is lost in thoughts about Hannah May. Springing out of the shadows of a clump of trees leaps an athletic warrior onto E.J.'s horse, knocking the scout into the snow. The momentum rolls the pair toward the freezing cold river, stopping just short of a steep bank by three young tree saplings.

As the two grapple, E.J. obtains some leverage, gains advantage, breaks away and stands up, separating from his attacker and letting him get into an offensive position.

Thinking he recognizes the exposed aggressor's profile, E.J., before he can say anything, is smacked in the face by the attacker's thrown snow clump, which blinds E.J. for a second. The skilled warrior tackles E.J. again and draws a knife to finish him off.

Pulling E.J.'s robe away to expose his head for a scalp cut, the Indian stops short when he hears a familiar voice.

"Running Deer! Stop! It's me, E.J.!"

"E.J.?" thinks Running Deer, snapping out of his warrior- like trance.

Moonlight briefly exposes both faces.

Releasing his grip, standing up slowly and catching his breath, Running Deer reaches down to help his friend up.

"You are lucky I didn't just go ahead and shoot you when I could," speaks Running Deer. "But I didn't want to give away my location."

"Actually, we are both lucky," explains E.J. as he rises to his feet, and both embrace each other in friendship. "I was the one who shot the brave that was ready to torch the branches around you."

"That was you?"

"Actually with the aid of the good Lord and friend Simon Kenton's long rifle, you got away."

"I remember hearing a crack," says Running Deer, "and seeing the torch warrior's strange look, and then my hands were free. Broke the wrist binding in two."

"Some shot, huh?" asks E.J. "May I ask what you are doing out here?"

"To be honest I think I am a man without a nation. I thought you were a British allied warrior following me," answers Running Deer.

After the two explain their situations further, E.J. fills Running Deer in about Hannah May.

"I once remember an American girl being brought to Kekionga many years ago. They named her Little Bear or Maconaquah, I think," says Running Deer. My wife, Morning Bird, became friends with her. Sometimes things turn out ok. Hannah May could be anywhere, you know."

"That's what I told Charlotte," says E.J.

"She's probably going to be adopted," says Running Deer. "I will be keeping my eyes and ears open for any rumor. Not all villages are against the Americans, you know, and something like this will not remain a secret."

"For now, will you stay with me, Running Deer?" requests E.J.

"Of course, you are my friend, E.J."

Twenty miles from the secret military objective of Mississineway, W.P. and William Connor meet a guide from Campbell's army.

"What are you doing out here?" asks Connor.

"Campbell is right behind me."

Glancing at his watch, W.P. states, "It's 4 a.m. Campbell was going to camp several miles back from here and wait for us."

"Changed his mind. Too cold. They camped, got a little rest and are preparing to attack at daybreak."

"That first village is but a half mile from here. Good chance we and the army could be spotted soon," says Wayne Pastor.

"I agree, W.P. Let's move back to Campbell's camp," says Connor.

At the advanced Campbell campsite, W.P. sees a friend on sentry duty named Nathaniel Vernon of the Pittsburgh Blues.

"W.P., we came up last night, and I can hardly stay awake. Started walking our horses, and now I can't feel my feet."

"Probably best staying on your horse, Nathaniel," says Wayne Pastor. "At least the snow has slowed."

"We're attacking at dawn. Gotta see 'em to shoot 'em," says Vernon.

"Where's Campbell, Nathan?" asks Wayne Pastor.

"Keep going straight ahead. He's talking to the cavalry commander."

Connor and Wayne Pastor ride up just in time to hear Campbell's last instructions.

"Look, Captain, we have orders that if we encounter Chiefs Richardville, Pecanne, Silver Heels, White Loon or any of Little Turtle's sons or brothers, we are not to harm them."

"But Colonel—"

"Oh, and also James Godfroy."

"Colonel, how are we supposed to know who they are or what they look like in the dark or otherwise? They all look similar. It's not like they have a name pinned on them or are in a uniform."

"Just figure it out, Captain, and deal with it!"

An hour later, the army moves up, and before daybreak, an early rising Indian that has spotted them is heard shouting a warning to the Indians in fourteen wigwams and a longhouse at the first village the Americans encounter.

Wayne Pastor, Connor and the five guides stay with Campbell, observing a strung-out half-mile-wide army of 600 approaching and enveloping the village. The captain of the cavalry gets anxious and takes his sector of the force and attacks.

Bam! BAM! BAM!

The warrior calling out the alarm is shot down. Then as the cavalry rides through, they shoot with their short rifle yagers and pistols anyone coming out of their lodge.

Ending before it gets seriously started, the captain yells an order to his cavalry, "Cease fire! Fire only if you are threatened!"

"It's nothing but women and children, sir!" shouts a sergeant. "The warriors have scattered into the forest."

As the rest of the army moves in, Campbell commands, "Round them up and move them into the longhouse, Major Davenport. Take their weapons and get a count of the dead and wounded."

"Yes sir, Colonel!"

"My God," exclaims W.P., "shot some of 'em down before they could give up."

"I don't like it either," says Connor, "but war is war."

"Yeah, but they may have been friendly to the U.S.," says Wayne Pastor, watching wigwams and corn being gathered, piled up and burned and dogs, cattle and horses being shot.

"You will pay for this! Tecumseh is here! He will come after you!" yell Indian women in Algonquin.

"Yeah, yeah, yeah," yells a sergeant, using his horse to force them to a temporary prison, "just get into the longhouse!"

Guides yell for Campbell. "Let's go, Commander, there are more villages downriver!"

As they ride northerly for another attack, Campbell says to Simrall, "Did you see the size of that dead negro back there?"

"Yes, I did, Colonel. Didn't have a chance. Probably a former slave that thought he was safe out here in this wilderness."

"Nobody is safe anywhere anymore!" says Campbell spurring his horse forward.

Two more villages are destroyed, with lodgings and crops burned, but the horses and some of the cattle are gathered, rounded up and prepared to be taken back to the first village that was attacked.

"We are camping at the original village for the night," says Campbell.

Arriving back at Chief Metocinyah's community, orders are commanded: "Form a square, build redoubts, organize your watches, get some grub and bed down!"

With all anxious to eat and settle down to relax, only the northwest bastion is effectively built.

Women yelling from the longhouse are heard, "Let us out! Let us go! Tecumseh will get you!"

"I'm tempted to set that on fire if they don't shut up soon," states a private nearby in between bites.

After a meal of nearly the last of the rations are consumed, a meeting takes place in Campbell's marquee tent among officers.

"That was not the brightest thing to do, Colonel," says Lieutenant Simrall, "ordering the burning of most of the crops that we could have kept to eat on the way back."

"I appreciate your honesty, Lieutenant, but feel free to speak up before mistakes are made. The boys got a little carried away before I thought about that," says Campbell. "What are the numbers? Did I hear eight Indian warriors? Forty or forty-two captives in that longhouse?

"Yes, Colonel," says Simrall. "Much of their livestock killed, fifty lodges piled and burned. We have about a hundred horses captured on a tie line out there in the center of the camp, being fed what we have left."

"In fact, we have a long five days ride home," informs a guide. "I think it's time to head back."

"I'd like to know, why did we not have much resistance after the first attack?" asks Simrall. "It's as if they knew we were coming."

"I don't know about that, but we did lose two men by accident. One was shot and killed by mistake by our own boys," informs Major Davenport.

"With a shortage of food and the destruction of three Indian villages, I think the message to the redskins is very clear. You're not safe anywhere," says Campbell.

"In fact, Harrison told me the long-range mission is to drive the Indians north to Canada. Let the British deal with 'em. Open this land up to new settlers."

"I agree, Colonel," says Simrall. "Hardly a man on this mission has not lost a family member to the Miami or Shawnee and others."

"That's it, spread the word. We're heading back to Fort Greeneville first thing in the morning. Inform the prisoners, allow them to make preparations. They'll make a good swap to get some loved ones returned from captivity."

Chapter 10

Late November–December 1812 — Ohio / Indiana Territory

Along the Maumee River treachery takes place.

"Dismount your horses, throw down your muskets and hand your weapons to us," instructs Matthew Elliott Jr.

"Pejig inini animosh," says Captain Johnny Logan.

"Ikwe waba ozawa," answers Bright Horn.

"What are you talking about?" asks Winamac. "You heard, Mr. Elliott! Dismount your horses and hand your weapons to us!"

"Nibi miskwa' midjin," responds Captain John, the third American scout.

"Water and eat?" a puzzled Winamac asks in English.

Chattering in predetermined code that would be used if they ever got caught, Captain Johnny Logan hands a loaded flintlock pistol to one of the Miami warrior scouts barrel-first and pulls the trigger.

BAM!

Having killed the warrior outright, Logan draws a hidden pistol before anyone can react and fires at Elliott striking him in the chest.

Shots by all involved go off in every direction, laming horses and humans alike.

"Ahya! Ohhh!"

Logan is hit as well as enemy Chief Winamac, while Bright Horn and Captain John fall into the snow on dying horses. Captain John and Bright Horn pull and fire their concealed weapons through their robes taking down another warrior leaving only one of the original five enemy unhurt.

Chief Winamac, writhing in pain, dies moments later after Captain John swiftly removes Winamac's flowing-black haired scalp.

Logan weakened by the shock of being shot and loss of blood, limps to Matthew Elliott Jr.'s horse and struggles to mount.

Before the group can ride back upstream and get away, the wounded Bright Horn has to snatch the reins of Winamac's horse and pull himself on. He gives a heeled rib-kick to his horse and follows his friends close behind.

With Captain Logan's group having no return gunfire available, the single surviving Miami now unpinned by his fallen horse stands and aims his heavier flintlock musket and shoots.

BAM!

"AHyya!" reacts Bright Horn.

Struck in the hip by the musket ball, he still manages to unsheathe his hunting knife on his moving horse and from 30 feet away deftly flips it right handed behind his back into the exposed chest of the enemy warrior.

"Ayyya!" anguishes the surprised brave staggering.

Clutching the horse's neck with two arms to stay on, Bright Horn knees his mount in the ribs again to catch up with the escaping Johnny Logan.

Captain John, having miraculously escaped injury, holds Winamac's scalp with a stick, riding alongside and bracing the wounded Johnny Logan.

Logan falls off his horse and Captain John stops to help Logan back on to escape any further confrontations that the heard gun shots could create.

Hearing the shots upstream, E.J. and Running Deer quicken their horses' gait cautiously toward two figures helping a third onto his ride.

Pointing his Springfield musket, E.J. calls out, "Who goes there?"

"E.J., is that you?" replies Bright Horn.

"Yes, what's going on?"

"We escaped the enemy, but Captain Johnny is hurt bad," answers Captain John for the injured Bright Horn, struggling to get back on his horse.

"Come on. Let's get these two to Camp No. 3," says E.J. "Watch for anyone trailing us, Running Deer."

"You bet, E.J.," says Running Deer, picking up on his American phrases.

"It may take us a while, but we'll get some help for you friends. On the gallop? You guys ok with that?"

"Kupi," says Captain John affirmatively in Algonquin.

"Dad burn, what are you doin' with that scalp, Captain John?" asks E.J.

At the American camp at Chief Metocinyah's village on the Mississinewa River, American invaders are partially asleep after several false alarms.

300 Miami, Potawatomi and Delaware warriors answer the call to stop any further advancement of the US troops toward Mississineway.

Under the leadership of Miami Chief Francis Godfroy, many braves have to ride or run two hours to Colonel Campbell's American encampment.

Creeping slowly toward the American camp and finally feeling like he is contributing to Tecumseh's cause is Red Hawk. Reaching a point where he can hear the enemy sentries talking, he listens.

"I'm getting five dollars a month and twelve for my horse I brought along," says Ivan Davis.

"Yeah, me too," speaks Nathaniel Vernon fighting back a yawn.

"Dad burn, Nathan, we have traveled well over a hundred miles, and except for that little action yesterday, we have nothin' to show for it. What a waste," complains Davis.

"Shhh," says Nathan. "You hear something?"

"I've been hearing something all night, Vernon, but I don't want to be accused of causing a false alarm again like I did at 4 a.m. The ridicule is relentless, and these guys are all awake now."

"Boy, I don't know. This could be more than a deer walking by," says Nathan Vernon.

Peering over the logs and protection of the northwest redoubt, Vernon briefly checks his watch that says 8 a.m. and hears steps running at him.

"Who goes there?" shouts Vernon.

"Potawatomi, dad burn you!" calls an Indian.

"AAAYYYYAAAA! AAYAAA!" sound dozens of war-whooping warriors attacking the temporary fortification.

Captain Bennoni Pierce of the Ohio volunteers, commanding the redoubt, runs up to defend and receives a musket ball to the head by an Indian.

The camp is alarmed as the warriors quickly overrun the redoubt and engage the Americans in fierce spear and tomahawk to sword and musket bayonet combat.

"Bring up the Pittsburgh Blues, Major Bell!" yells Colonel Campbell over the bursts of gun and pistol fire mixed in with death screams on both sides.

"AHHYAahhahh!" Sixty Pennsylvania bayoneted volunteers imitate the Indian cry as they pour into the melee, some swinging swords and engaging the warriors ferociously, not giving the Indians a chance to reload.

Wayne Pastor and the guides stay near Campbell, armed and ready to help when needed.

The blue color schemed Blues head for the heaviest Indian concentration, and the natives retreat, giving the Americans a chance to regroup and reload. Still, scattered shots from outside the American perimeter on the left and right wing pick off troops exposed in the early morning darkness by a fire blazing in the middle of the camp.

Private William Northcutt of the Bourbon County Blues extinguishes the fire and heads for the most heated clash.

Horses lined in the center of the camp are shot wholesale by the Indians to prevent Americans from hiding, having protection and getting away too fast. Exposed soldiers now have to lay down behind the dead and dying horses still kicking.

The southwest corner of the camp has Indians attacking and screaming from behind Campbell.

"Ayyyaaa! AHYAAA!" roar the warriors.

"Guides, go reinforce the infantry back there!"

"Yes, Colonel!"

"AHyaaaa AHHYaa!" continues the outnumbered but determined Native American fury.

"Hold up, W.P.!" orders Campbell, while straightening his bicorne. "You stay here with me. Watch my back!

"Simrall! Mount your dragoons and attack the southwest to support Johnson."

"Let's go, boys!" commands Simrall, leading the way.

Because of panic and fear, very few obey Simrall, preferring instead to stand and fire. But even a weak Simrall charge forces an Indian retreat.

"One more attack!" screams Chief Little Thunder.

Very little Indian response is seen by the Americans except for Red Hawk, who comes screaming in, aiming at Campbell with his tomahawk raised. Amazingly, avoiding fired musket balls and slashing swords, his daring charge is met by a surprised and nervous Ohioan swinging a captured Delaware tomahawk. A glancing blow connects with Red Hawk's left skull.

Stunned, Red Hawk stumbles to the feet of sword wielding Colonel Campbell and an astonished Wayne Pastor.

Falling on his boyhood friend to protect him, Wayne Pastor clutches Red Hawks muscular but limp arms and pull them behind his back and ties him as a captive with leather strapping found nearby.

A half hour more of morning daylight allows the U.S. troops to push back the Indian attack, exposing twelve dead militia and infantrymen, dozens of deceased horses and sixty-five troops being treated for wounds by surgeons.

The Indian coalition leaves behind forty-five dead as they hustle away, carrying or assisting their wounded brothers to safety.

At the same time, 112 miles northeast and ten miles from Camp No. 3 on the Maumee River, E.J. and Running Deer are slowed in bringing Captain Johnny Logan to Fort Winchester as they stop to build a sleigh for transporting the seriously injured Shawnee American scout.

"This should move us faster, Johnny. Hang in there, and we will get you help," encourages E.J.

Another hour goes by, and the Captain Johnny Logan group come upon dozens of graves.

A little farther, they pass through an encampment of shanties, redoubts and picket fences protecting and sheltering the sick and starving Americans that would rather be moving toward the Maumee rapids than being stuck in the snow.

"We're not stopping, Colonel Wells," says E.J. "We have a couple Indians who need surgeons right away."

"Keep it going, Carlisle!" uplifts Colonel John Allen overhearing E.J. "Six miles to go till you reach Fort Winchester!"

"Here," says Captain John, tossing the scalp of Winamac at Wells's feet. "Give this to Garrard. Tell him our loyalty should never be questioned!"

With the steeds teamed to pull the sleigh, fatigue from traveling through sometimes knee-deep snow begins to slow the progress until, finally, old Fort Defiance is seen at the point of the Auglaize and Maumee rivers.

After fording the ice-covered rivers, climbing the riverbank and reaching the Fort Winchester infirmary, the injured are laid on tables where surgeons remove musket balls from Johnny Logan and Bright Horn.

Watching the doctors work on the Indians, E.J., Running Deer and Captain John observe Johnny Logan take his last breath.

"That was a gallant effort, fellas," compliments one of the surgeons as he washes off blood from his hands in a wooden bucket of water. "Over twenty miles to get here, did I hear you say? You are good friends.

"Bright Horn, we believe, will be ok. You passed by camp number 3. What's the situation?"

E.J. sits down from fatigue and, sickened by the loss of a great American scout, utters, "Didn't look good."

Running Deer speaks up in his broken English. "The clothing I saw, not warm enough. Need supplies. I'd be prepared for sick people when this weather breaks."

A couple days later, a grave is dug within an outer earthen defensive wall and the picket wall of Fort Defiance overlooking the Maumee River.

Much like Miami war Chief Little Turtle's military funeral service on William Wells' property near Kekionga, a drum and fife-led procession leaves Fort Winchester with the general and troops following behind. Smartly dressed and lined up, the federal troops of Fort Winchester lead the horse-drawn cart containing Spemica Lawba's remains to the grave site.

After placing Captain Johnny into his grave, words by Winchester and E.J. are spoken about his service helping the Americans during the evacuation at Fort Wayne as well as service during the siege and valuable information about the enemy. Bright Horn and Captain John offer some Shawnee spiritual chants and burial rites.

Because of the weather, the service moves quickly, with dozens of infantry and Kentuckians warmly clothed the best they can standing in respect while an eighteen-gun salute, one shot for every state in the union, is fired off.

Meanwhile, in Canada, a Shawnee warrior chief expresses his frustration with Colonel Henry Proctor at Fort Amherstburg.

"While this weather is hard on the Americans, here we sit," preaches Tecumseh. "We should be moving side-by-side up the Maumee, wiping out a new American fort named Winchester and Fort Wayne at Kekionga."

"I completely agree," says Proctor, pacing about nervously, clearly intimidated by Tecumseh, who is again pressing him. "Supplies needed to maintain an army as well as your warriors is the issue."

"What are you saying?" asks Tecumseh. "You have had plenty of time to deliver supplies across the Great Lake to us or through Frenchtown. No excuses!"

"I can only tell you what is happening. Even though we have superior control of Lake Erie, the navy has been sailing at the eastern end near Erie, Pennsylvania. No one has been here recently to take troops or supplies to Maumee Bay since General Hull's surrender and his movement to the prison in Montreal."

"March them across the ice. Ferry them across the river," suggests Tecumseh.

"Now Chief, you know the ice is too thin in places and too dangerous."

"What is dangerous," says Tecumseh, "is the Americans building a great army from the State of Kentucky. They are a different breed of Americans. They fight like warriors! But, perhaps my finely decorated Royal Colonel is too afraid!"

"When the weather breaks, we will be shuttling the British military across the Maumee Bay area. Mark my word."

"Your word is similar to the lies we received when Anthony Wayne pushed us to Lake Erie. All talk. You are making us do the fighting."

"Now Chief, we have gone through all this before. You know we have lost both Canadian and British troops in this conflict. Besides that, the Napoleonic War between France and Great Britain has created delays in supplies and troops."

"Who is more important, an adversary we fought with against you in the French and Indian War or the Native Americans? Your so-called crown needs to make a decision," states Tecumseh.

"The capturing of Americans at sea and forcing them to serve Great Britain in the navy should tell you how committed to helping you we are. Keep in mind, Chief, my empire hasn't even declared war on the United States, yet. Assistance from King George is coming, I promise," concludes Proctor.

Chapter 11

December 1812 — Indiana Territory / Ohio

Wayne Pastor and William Connor have their five guides far ahead of Colonel Campbell's roughly 600-man army, minus eight that were buried at the Mississinewa battle site.

"Glad we were prepared for this weather, Mr. Connor," says W.P. "This is tough."

"As long as we follow the river," says Connor, covering his head and leaning into the rain and wind, "the scouts in advance should pick up the trail to Greeneville."

"The key word is 'should.' Nothing much worse than being lost in the wilderness in the middle of a storm," says Wayne Pastor.

"Don't even talk about that, W.P. You want to jinx us? We are short of food and probably twenty miles to go at this pace," responds Connor.

"Speaking of pace, I'm gonna go back and check with Campbell and see how they are doing."

"Ok, W.P."

After riding back a half mile and finally hearing the drum and fife corps setting the pace, W.P. sees Indian women and children walking in the snow struggling to stay up with the horse-backed soldiers.

"Colonel, you can't stay up with Connor and I. Those Indians need to ride horse back for us to get to Greeneville alive."

"Wayne Pastor, you are right. We need to travel faster. Lieutenant Simrall! Major Davenport!"

The two ride up to the Colonel, "You asked for us, sir?"

"Some of your men are not going to like this, but they need to give up their horses to the Indians. We have to make better time."

"You are right on both accounts," says the irritated Simrall. "Don't you think it's better to lose a few Indians rather than Americans?"

"For your information, Lieutenant, we are all Americans."

With that, the two officers, followed by Wayne Pastor, trot back to deliver the orders. W.P. asks a question.

"Major Davenport, when you have a chance, could I speak to you about the Great Lakes?"

"The Great Lakes?"

"Lake Erie in particular," says W.P.

As frostbite and weather-related illnesses take their toll on the retreating Mississinewa army contingent, captive Indians warn, "You have not seen the last of our warriors! Tecumseh will track you down. He is nearby!"

Wayne Pastor finds Red Hawk and speaks to him in Algonquin for fear of an American reprisal.

"My friend, do you not see the futility of your people. Adjusting to the American way of life is the best decision you can make. Talk to your people."

"I have talked to my people. We have decided on peace. At least most of my people. Why did you protect me, W.P.? I was willing to die for Tecumseh and the coalition."

"Dad burn, Red Hawk, don't you see how the British are using your people?"

"Think of it my way, W.P. My people need them to help us get our land back," says Red Hawk.

"What makes you think the British will not sell the claimed land if they are victorious in this war?" asks W.P.

"Then we will be fighting them again just like the French and Indian War."

"Red Hawk, when does it end? It seems like Native Americans have been fighting over something forever," says W.P. "I don't know your history like you do, but has there ever been peace?"

"Many of our tribes get along very well now. Some down south and across the great river to the west do not like my people. The conflicts go back many centuries."

"See what I mean?" offers Wayne Pastor.

"Carlisle!" yells Colonel Campbell. "Are you still back there? We need you out front!"

"Yes sir!" replies W.P.

"Think about it, Red Hawk. I'll talk to you later."

The next day, while riding next to Major George Davenport, W.P. strikes up a conversation.

"Just between you and me, my real name is George King, but I go by Davenport. Had some business dealings that went wrong, if you know what I mean."

"Don't know about that nor do I want to. Tell me about serving on Lake Erie," inquires Wayne Pastor.

"Oh, it's a terrific body of water, you know. Fresh water compared to the saltiness of the Atlantic. I started sailing when I was seventeen. I've been across the Atlantic a couple times. Seen a lot of the world."

"That's what I heard. I'd like to serve up there," interrupts W.P.

"Well now, the British are controlling Lake Erie, but from what I understand, the United States are inquiring about a sea Captain to turn that around. Are you wanting to apply, Mr. Carlisle?"

"Ha! To be honest, I don't know anything about sailing. I saw Lake Erie once with my father and have this yearning to get back there."

"When we get to Franklinton, let's see what possibilities there are, ok? Rumor was that warships were planning to be built at Erie, Pennsylvania, beginning next month."

"Wayne Pastor! You're not getting paid to jabber back there!" exclaims Colonel Campbell. "Get out front and give Connor a break. Lead the way. We can't afford to get lost!"

"Yes sir, right away sir," says W.P. Departing with his horse plodding through the snow, he turns and flashes a grin and nod at Davenport.

A hundred miles north and east, William Henry Harrison and his 200-man detachment navigate south through the Great Black Swamp by flatboat using the now-thawed rivers to reach a trail that will take them to Franklinton. Pulling Reverend Wallace aside, he makes a strong suggestion.

"I'll tell ya what, Reverend," says Harrison. "With Christmas almost here, you better have a real good sermon to explain why God allows such suffering at those Fort Winchester camps. It reminds me of stories I heard about during the Revolutionary War at Valley Forge."

"I've seen frostbite before," says Wallace. "It's not a pretty site, General."

"I saw diphtheria back at Camp No. 3, Reverend. Ragtag army with no supplies getting to them. Guys in shacks stuck along a river."

"Since we've had a thaw, supplies should be getting through now, don't you think, General?"

"Too late for some of them. What do I say to those who ask why they should believe there is a loving God when they hear of and see this suffering, or the killing of settlers or Indians?"

"Satan brought sin into the world with the first man," explains Wallace. "Suffering reminds us of that. Eventually, all this suffering ends for those who accept Jesus as their Lord and savior. That's why we celebrate Christmas, the birth of our savior. He guarantees eternal life with a new body and no more suffering."

"How does believing reduce our suffering?" asks Harrison.

"Well, knowing Jesus suffered and died on the cross for our sins so believers may live helps. But God does not promise, even for believers, a perfect life here on earth," says the Reverend.

Then the army chaplain pulls out his Bible and quickly turns to Matthew 24:13 and reads aloud, "'But the one who endures to the end will be saved.'"

At Fort Winchester, Brigadier General James Winchester stands up in his office, walks to the door, opens it and looks out to check the weather.

"Merry Christmas, boys," he wishes to his aide-de-camps. "We are moving out in a few days, let's say December 31st.

"Now I know you men saw the order to fall back to Fort Jennings and wait for the gathering of the Virginians and Pennsylvanians. But I'm not going to risk getting bogged down in that Black Swamp and make matters worse.

"The supplies of warm clothing and food are coming in. Heck with Harrison, we are heading for the Maumee rapids and Frenchtown."

"Yes sir."

"Get to Colonels Wells and Allen. Have them transport the sick and invalids back to Fort Winchester and prepare to move forward with those who can."

At Franklinton, in central Ohio, along the west side of the Scioto River in a brick federalist-style building serving as headquarters, Colonel John Campbell reports to General Harrison and explains the action his detachment took at the Mississinewa villages.

"You didn't get to the Wabash River?" asks Harrison. "That was the assignment!"

"The weather got bad. Some of the men weren't dressed for it. And we ran out of food," explains Campbell.

"Colonel Campbell, you had weeks to prepare for this assignment. You're not in Kentucky. It gets cold up here."

"Many of the troops are recovering, if they can, at Fort Greeneville, sir."

"Dad burn, Colonel! Did anything good come out of this?"

"We did bring back forty-two Indian prisoners, mostly women and children. One warrior, named Red Hawk, seemed interested in helping the United States as a scout or spy. A youngster guide and scout for us named Wayne Pastor Carlisle seems to know him from his days at Kekionga."

"Ah yes, Kekionga. The Miami Towns on the Miami of the Lakes, as President Washington called it," says Harrison, removing his bicorne hat and leaning back in his chair. "The source of which all our problems began with a Miami war chief named Little Turtle. At least his family is beginning to help now. I can't tell you, Campbell, how many American settlers were taken to Kekionga as prisoners.

"Bring this Carlisle in. The name sounds familiar."

"Yes sir. He is right outside your quarters waiting to talk to you anyway, sir."

"Show him in."

W.P. strides through the door and half-salutes since he really isn't in the military.

"Wayne Pastor Carlisle?" asks Harrison.

"Yes sir. Thank you for seeing me, sir."

"Who's your father?" asks the future president of the United States.

"He goes by E.J. Carlisle, Elmer James, a veteran of several Indian battles and now this one. He's been stationed at Fort Wayne."

"I kinda remember him. Why is your name Wayne Pastor and not Pastor Wayne?"

"I'm named after Anthony Wayne and, well sir, from what I understand, he was no pastor, sir."

"HA!" Harrison bursts out loud, so loud, in fact, that the guard outside and bodyguard Neil Washburn open the door and stick their heads in.

Harrison waves them back out and responds, "Wayne Pastor, I like you."

"You can call me W.P. sir, if you wish."

"OK, W.P., thank you for your service with Colonel Campbell, and tell me about your Indian friend and your wishes with the United States military in this war."

Back at Mississineway, Morning Bird fears the worse.

"Captured, not killed by the Americans? You are sure of that, Shepocanah," she asks, waiting for Maconaquah to sign to her husband.

"No body of Red Hawk has been found. He must be captured. All of the warriors have been accounted for," says Shepocanah through Maconaquah's signing.

"It is bad enough worrying about my husband, Running Deer. Now I have two involved with this war."

"The warriors put up a terrific resistance to the Americans, preventing them from reaching many villages along the Mississinewa," says Maconaquah.

"You are right, my friend, I should feel grateful," says Morning Bird.

"Red Hawk's companion, White Snake, gave us a warning the night before."

"Wayne Pastor was among the Americans?" asks Morning Bird.

"If that is what his English name is, yes. We must keep that a secret from the Americans," says Maconaquah.

"Yes, that would not be good for White Snake if they find out."

"Now what, Chief Godfroy? What say you, Chief Silver Heels? Little Thunder? Do any of you have an explanation for this attack? It was bad enough they invaded us on the Wildcat Creek," presses Majenica during the review meeting in the longhouse at Mississineway.

"Harrison must have misunderstood what our meaning was back in the fall," says Godfroy.

"Now comes the word from our messengers that Great Britain, our great father, has declared war on the United States," announces Miami war hawk Chief Majenica.

"We should have sent another delegation to Franklinton," says Silver Heels.

"It is too late," says Godfroy, "the victory at Wildcat Creek made us too confident. I suggest you head back to your villages and help those suffering from the damage the Americans did."

"We are not safe anywhere," says Majenica. "We must hope our warriors return soon from the hunting grounds to build our numbers.

Tecumseh cannot be everywhere. He will be asking for more help against the Long Knives!"

Chapter 12

December 1812–January 1813 — Indiana Territory / Ohio

After spending Christmas with his family and praying for Hannah May's return, E.J. Carlisle prepares to leave Fort Wayne for Fort Winchester when a knock is heard on his family's cabin door.

Opening the door, Charlotte views a Native American peering through a beaver-fur hat and robe with black and red war-painted features staring at her. Startled, she reacts and frightens everyone. "Ahhh!"

"It's ok, Charlotte," rises E.J. to comfort her, "it's Running Deer. He's helping the Americans again."

"Oh, thank goodness," says Charlotte. "Come in, Running Deer, and warm yourself up. It's getting cold again. How's Morning Bird?"

Running Deer nods. "Morning Bird is at Mississineway with Red Hawk."

He looks around at Bennie, Teddy and Uncle Isaac. "My, your family is growing. We will find your daughter, Charlotte."

"Thanks for your encouragement, Running Deer," says E.J. as he pulls on his robe and rabbit-fur hat. "We have orders to escort a couple flatboats loaded with supplies to Fort Winchester."

"The river is flowing again with ice in some areas," says Running Deer.

E.J. and Running Deer say their goodbyes and head the short distance down the embankment path to the boat landing on the St. Marys River, just north of the large blockhouse which protects the north side of Fort Wayne.

"Make sure that artillery is chained good," orders Lieutenant Ostrander, "the river is really flowing high and fast. It won't take long to get there if you can prevent yourselves from running into an island or one of those river bends."

"Yeah, yeah, yeah, we've done this before, Lieutenant," says the flatboat skipper grabbing a pole to shove off with his mates.

"Still not the commander yet, huh, Lieutenant Ostrander?" says a grinning E.J. trying to have some fun.

Ostrander turns without answering and steps up the bank toward the fort river gate.

"Alright, we will be following along the Maumee on the south-side trail," informs E.J. "We'll see ya at the bends and straight stretches."

"Yeah, yeah," says the veteran flatboat captain.

With two men helping him, the skipper checks back at the second flatboat, sees they are ready, and pushes off. With their poles orchestrated by the boatmen, they are instantly into the current, picking up speeds of over five miles per hour.

Daydreaming a bit about his own Ohio River flatboat experiences entering the Northwest Territory twenty-two years ago, E.J. snaps out of it.

"Dad burn, let's get going, Running Deer!" yells E.J. "The current looks a little crazy."

E.J. and Running Deer ride to catch up and watch the two flatboats on the St. Marys connect with the St. Joseph River. The two comparatively small streams, then forming the Maumee River, instantly get wider and deeper, helping to avoid underlying rocks and boulders at the fords.

Following the worn tracks northwesterly, some flooding across the trail is sloshed through by their horses, and they are able to advance ahead of the two flatboats.

Waiting at a known sharp-left-turn bend six miles east of the fort, E.J. makes a suggestion. "Let's stay here and see if they can make this curve. Keep an eye out for renegade Indians, Running Deer."

"I have been. You know I am not very popular."

"Ha! Here they come!" says E.J. "Whoa, the second one is ok but the first one is far to the south bank. I think they are going to have to stay between the little island and the bank!"

"They're not gonna make it," says Running Deer, calmly watching the navigators maneuver the sweeper and swing their poles to push off and avoid a collision.

Slamming into the right bank, the jar bounces the initial flatboat around the island and to the left. The impact breaks a chain, and cargo slides to the right, spilling one cannon and a few supplies into the frigid water between the bank and islet.

As the two view the skipper pointing at them and then the spot where the brass cannon went in, E.J. slyly asks Running Deer, "You gonna fish that out?"

"Hmm, pretty deep right there," answers Running Deer, watching the flatboats tandem again and flow away in the centrist current to the left for 300 yards and then a sharp right. "I don't think so. Someone will retrieve it someday."

Back at Franklinton on the training ground, army war veteran Private John Smith is drilling what's left of new recruits for William Henry Harrison's troops, which have left for the Maumee Bay to meet with the disobedient Winchester's left wing.

"Well, who do we have here?" asks Smith observing W.P. and Red Hawk walking up to get reacquainted.

"Private Smith, nice to see you're making yourself useful again," chides W.P. with some of his dad's sense of humor.

"Oh yeah, W.P., and they got real nice water over in the Scioto to take a bath in when I stink! Ha!" answers Smitty, slapping Wayne Pastor on his back. "Been in any good poker games lately?"

"Ha! Not since that last one," answers W.P. "Not sure how that game is supposed to end."

"What is your job?" asks Red Hawk, adapting to perhaps a new role.

"Nice to see you again too, Red Hawk. I'm training federal troops in the morning and the militia from Kentucky and Ohio in the afternoon."

"You know anything about fighting?" asks Red Hawk disrespectfully.

"Well, I trained W.P.'s dad and fought against your dad in the Battle of Kekionga. Served St. Clair—"

"What a massacre! And the Battle of Kekionga was a great Miami victory," interrupts Red Hawk.

"Yeah, well, corrections have been made since then," responds Smith. "Served with Wayne and now with Harrison.

"Perhaps, Red Hawk, you can help teach Americans how to fight the Indians?" asks W.P., testing Red Hawk's loyalty.

After finishing the flatboat assignment, E.J. and Running Deer pass far ahead of Winchester's slow-moving 900 troops that are using sleds to carry equipment. Remorsefully, Winchester leaves behind 300 illness- and weather-related casualties of Camp No. 3.

Some supplies to help the army have gotten through, but the trail is not firm because of thawing and rain, creating hardships. Traversing the gullies and water-filled stream beds puts a strain on Colonel Wells and Allen's command, which is following General Payne and General William Lewis's lead along Anthony Wayne's old north-bank trail.

"We've gotta get off this main trail, Running Deer," suggests E.J.

"Yes, move up into the forest to avoid these villages that may be occupied with enemy," speaks Running Deer in Algonquin, in case his voice carries to unwanted ears.

A few hours later, looking down from atop the bank at the river, E.J. wonders to himself, "Is that General Payne down there?" Knowing Running Deer wouldn't know. "Let's move far ahead of them, Running Deer, and see if any threat awaits. I would guess Captain Ballard and his company will be the next Americans we see."

"Yes, E.J."

Over the next few days, E.J. and Running Deer ride past the rapids on the Maumee as well as Wayne's former battlefield of Fallen Timbers.

A few Indian scouts are encountered and stealthily snuffed out by the pair without them being spotted.

In north central Ohio, with the aid of Red Hawk and other Indian guides, General Harrison has reached the upper Sandusky area with his federal troops and militia from Kentucky. He now turns his attention westerly to the Maumee Bay.

Having found out through messages that Winchester ignored his orders to fall back to Fort Jennings, Harrison is in a forgiving mood when he hears further news that Frenchtown and the Raisin River in Michigan Territory are close at hand for Winchester.

Winchester's requests in the messages for more supplies and troops are met when Harrison sends federal troops, cattle and hogs ahead of his main force.

"So, Major Davenport, this is where I depart the easterners?" asks Wayne Pastor, after guiding Virginia militia General Joel Leftwich from Franklinton.

"Yes sir, W.P., you are heading for a fort called Stephenson on the Sandusky River. That river leads you to Lake Erie, and they will direct you from there."

"That letter from General Harrison and his recommendation for the navy will come in handy," appreciates Wayne Pastor.

"Not exactly the navy, W.P.," says Davenport. "It's kind of a new branch called the marines."

"Whatever. I'll be on the lake?" asks Wayne Pastor.

"Marines can fight on the land and the sea. Wherever you are needed most and probably first," informs the adventurer George Davenport, as he parts westerly from W.P. with Leftwich's Virginians.

E.J. and Running Deer enter Michigan Territory north of the Maumee Bay and close in on scouting the River Raisin when two European-dressed individuals are spotted walking hurriedly on a trail heading south, away from the River Raisin village of Frenchtown.

The American spies leap out from behind a tree pointing muskets and E.J. barks orders. "Hold up there!"

Surprised, the two drop their guns and hold their hands up.

"Ne tirez pas," says one of the individuals.

"Running Deer, take over," says E.J.

"Where are you going?" speaks Running Deer in fluent French learned from his boyhood growing up in Kekionga.

"Our village needs help. The British troops have arrived, and along with unfriendly Delaware warriors, they are ransacking the village and plan to burn down the town," says the spokesperson.

The French Americans continue to rattle on as Running Deer explains to E.J., "Francois Navarre has sent them for help, hoping to reach the Americans unharmed."

"Tell them to follow us, and we will escort them to where they need to go," says E.J.

"Suivez nous," orders Running Deer to the American Frenchmen. "Bring your muskets."

The four ride double and take off in a gallop, hoping to reach Captain Ballard and hand off the Frenchtown residents so that the two spies can get back to scouting the River Raisin.

Two days later, Winchester, who is waiting for Harrison at the rapids, gives permission to Colonel William Lewis and his 550 to move the forty miles north and rescue Frenchtown.

Just a half day after sending Lewis north, while having a few whiskeys and sitting around in his marquee tent, Winchester uncharacteristically grabs Colonel John Allen. "It is urgent, Colonel Allen! We cannnnot afford to wwait on Harrison," he slurs. "Colonel, are yyour men fffit to follow Lewis up as backup?"

"I have 110 able to go and eager for action, General," informs Allen, releasing Winchester's grip, straightening out his coat and bicorne and wondering if the general is just trying to show up Harrison.

"Saddle up then!" orders the tipsy Winchester. "Lewis is pprobably ten miles ahead."

At the River Raisin, hidden by a cluster of trees on the edge of a deep forest next to Frenchtown, E.J. and Running Deer converse. "If the Americans get here soon, this town can be saved. I just worry about more British and Indian allies arriving before and using this as a staging area," says E.J. to Running Deer.

"Ahhh!!! Ahhh!" yells a running Kentucky infantry, with the cavalry and dragoons galloping toward town.

Bam! Bam! B-bam! ignites American musket fire.

The British are seen forming a line to defend their occupied camp.

Bam! Bam! B-bam! return a volley of English Brown Bess muskets, and instantly smoke temporarily obscures the vision of E.J. and Running Deer.

A few British troops are seen falling or bending over from American musket .69-caliber balls that find their mark.

Similarly, Americans fall from British Brown Bess .75-caliber musket balls, producing anguishing cries for help.

Rat-a-tah-tat. Rat-a-tah-tat. British drummers pound an alarm and retreat while they turn toward the frozen River Raisin to cross.

So well-focused and hidden are E.J. and Running Deer, they go unnoticed as 550 men from the 1st Kentucky volunteers regiment led by Colonel William Lewis stream by, attacking the 200 British and Indian coalitionists.

Swords, bayonets, and tomahawks clash.

Rising up from their cover, E.J. and Running Deer are greeted by a familiar voice to E.J.

"Hey, Carlisle," says 5th Kentucky militia officer Colonel John Allen, leading his backup regiment following the storming 1st Kentucky.

"Yes, hello Colonel. Looks like it will be a route!" says the confident E.J., standing with a less confident Running Deer.

As the three watch the militia cross the frozen River Raisin, scalping Indians and British alike, Colonel Allen shouts an order to his troops, "Assure the residents everything's going to be ok. The Americans are here."

"Yes sir," obeys an officer subordinate.

"Come here, Eli,"

"Yes sir."

"As soon as Colonel Lewis returns, we have orders to let General Winchester know what has happened."

"Yes sir," says Private Darnell.

"How many is Winchester bringing up?" asks E.J.

"We should have close to a thousand total," answers Allen.

"Now you'll have to excuse me, E.J. The 5th is going to cover the 1st's retreat back to Frenchtown whenever that takes place."

"Make sure you set up a good defense for a counter attack," offers Running Deer.

"I don't know who this Indian friend of yours is, E.J." says Allen. "But I would advise him to stay close to your side. Some Kentuckians kill first and ask questions later."

E.J. and Running Deer watch Colonel Allen ride across the river and dismount before entering the thick forest with his regiment.

After forcing the enemy across the River Raisin to the north, most of the 1st volunteers chase the British and Indians for two miles, fighting behind fallen logs and upright trees as the Indians counter and then fall back to another defensive position. American casualties increase to thirteen dead Kentuckians and fifty-four wounded as the Indians resist till nightfall and the destination of the Wyandot village of Big Rock is reached.

Back at Frenchtown, "That was a well-executed rescue attack. Well done, Colonel," says town leader Francis Navarre while walking up. "Will this General Winchester be coming soon?"

"Oh, I'm no officer, Monsieur," says E.J., helping a citizen straighten out his house's exterior. "I'm also at no liberty to tell you anything."

"Pardon me. I understand," says Navarre.

Three days later, a confident General James Winchester enters the River Raisin area with most of what remains of his left wing of reserves.

"You've got plenty of time to set up your defenses, General," says Frenchman Jocko LaSalle, a British sympathizer stopping by Frenchtown to deceptively thank Winchester. "The British and Indians are many miles away."

Forty miles farther to the north, shock and seriousness replace the confidence of E.J.

"What do I see through this falling snow crossing the river?" asks Running Deer alongside E.J., both prone and overlooking the Detroit River from a bluff.

Looking up from his map, E.J. clears the fog from his spyglass and peers through the single lens.

"Dad burn, Running Deer! Is that the whole British army?"

"They're crossing the river on the very ice that has their ships locked in!" comments Running Deer.

"We gotta get back and warn the Americans!" says E.J.

At Frenchtown, in the home of Colonel Francis Navarre, a mile from the American camp, General Winchester, his son and aides-de-camp enjoy relaxing in front of a burning fireplace.

"General, my brothers," says Navarre, handing him a glass of wine, "have returned from the north. They say Colonel Proctor and a Wyandot war chief named Roundhead are making their way here from Fort Amherstburg. My brothers would not lie about this, General."

"Ahh," says Winchester in response, "I just got word from a Frenchman today. The British and Indians are many miles away on the other side of the Detroit River. Relax, Francois. Let us enjoy this. We will set up defenses in due time. Besides, Harrison will be here soon with reinforcements."

"You can't trust any old Frenchman, General," says Navarre. "There are spies everywhere helping the British. They pay well for news."

E.J. and Running Deer finally finding where Winchester is headquartered ride in from nearby Frenchtown to inform the General of what they've seen but are stopped at the door by a sentry.

"No visitors," says the guard. "The General has retired for the evening. He is fatigued."

"He needs to know! The enemy is nearby, for crying out loud!" announces E.J. as Running Deer bows his head in disbelief.

"A Captain Nathaniel Hart was here earlier," says the lead sentry nearby, attempting to clarify the situation. "He brought a message from General Harrison that Frenchtown was to be held at any rate. That has been the order dispatched to all officers."

Chapter 13

January–February 1813 — Michigan Territory / Ohio

Leaving General Winchester's Frenchtown headquarters after failing to alarm the general, E.J. and Running Deer head for the town and General Lewis's camp.

Loud music and frolicking from the village on the north side of the river is heard as the townspeople entertain the Kentuckians, offering their cabins inside a picket fenced area to the lucky ones not having to stay in their tent.

"General Lewis," calls E.J. "I hate to interrupt, but Running Deer and I have seen the enemy approaching."

Having had a few drinks and caught up in the merriment, Lewis responds, "Running Deer?" who is that Indian? Never mind. Captain Ballard has not sounded the alarm. We'll be ok. Winchester has assured us from his informants that the British are miles away."

Seeing he is getting nowhere, E.J. and Running Deer ride to find Colonel Allen in his camp.

"Colonel, is Sam Wells around here?"

"E.J.," says Allen, sitting up in his cot, "Wells went back to the rapids and Harrison to explain the success here and to bring his army forward. I would say that Fort Detroit will be back in American control in a few days."

"I hate to put a damper on that thought, but Running Deer and I saw hundreds of British and native Americans crossing Lake Erie heading this way."

"The lake is frozen, again?" asks Allen.

British Colonel Henry Proctor smiles through a burning campfire at coalitionist leader Chief Roundhead five miles north of Frenchtown and strategizes.

"You say your scouts report the Americans have been celebrating and are now sleeping, with very few sentries? That is perfect.

"Chief Roundhead, at daybreak, the Miami, Potawatomi and Ottawa will attack from their position on the right. To our left will be the French Canadians, Shawnee and your Wyandots. At the center, I will initiate the attack with my brigadier-led regulars. The bagpipe and drums alone will force them to run. Ha!" says Proctor assuredly.

Through an interpreter, Roundhead, the top assistant while Tecumseh is in Indiana, contributes, "I suggest attack before daybreak. Catch them sleeping."

"Good idea, Roundhead, and with a hangover. Ha! Let's also put the six cannons to work on your wing. There is an open field for a clear bombardment."

Roundhead reacts with a smile and rises into a war dance, followed by dozens eager to seek revenge on the first-day battle results. "Let's go!" yells Roundhead.

Pounding war drums sound as the warriors chant, dance and keep awake the British bedding down nearby.

AHHHYAYA! AHYAAAHA! BUM! BUM! BUM! BUM!

Since E.J. and Running Deer have done their best to warn the now resting American army, they ride off for Harrison to tell him to hurry. Their absence now only leaves a few sentries existing to issue an alarm.

A few hours later, having moved quietly into position to attack, Proctor is surprised to hear the sound of American bugles ordering the infantry and militia to awaken for the day.

"I don't know for sure, Leroy," says a Kentucky sentry to his paired partner, "but I think I see ... yep! A Redcoat!"

"You sure?" asks Leroy.

"Yep. And I ain't gonna miss."

Raising his musket, the sharpshooter takes aim.

B-BAM! ignites the musket, with blinding powder smoke lingering.

"Jim Bob, I think you got 'im!" informs Leroy.

With that, the entire American camp is alerted as British Canadian infantry start marching forward from 200 yards away.

BOOM! Boom! Boom! Boom! Booom! BOOOM! Canadian militia from the American right fire artillery, overshooting at first, the entire town, but certainly waking everyone up, including the former disbelieving General Winchester.

Readjusting the artillery after daylight brightens the morning a bit, the right flank of the American defense is struck, scattering the militia.

Boom! BOOM!

Kentuckians and American infantry alike make their way to defensive positions; fortunately for the American left and center, that meant behind a protective picket fence and cabins.

Indians on the American right have a clear shot and knock down militia as the Frenchtown defense crumbles there.

Winchester, his son and his aides-de-camp exiting their quarters rush a mile and a quarter to the weakest area of defense, ordering Colonel John Allen and his 1st riflemen to support Sam Wells's leaderless 17th Kentucky volunteers.

Following General Lewis to support the 5th Infantry, Allen and Lewis watch the futility of their troops being overrun by Indians and Canadian militia.

"Retreat!" yells Lewis as he turns toward the 1st, now following him.

Allen, after running up to back the 1st, sees Lewis shot and wounded and urges his detachment to fall back after seeing Lewis captured. Since there is no cover, the Americans are cut down and scalped by the ensuing Indians and Canadians. Escaping the openness and traversing a forested path, Allen is shot in the thigh, causing him to slow, but he urges his men to retreat. Finding a log to sit on, he awaits the results.

"Come on you varmints!" yells Allen, pointing his reloaded musket. "Surrender yourselves! Put your hands up!" he yells at an approaching warrior oblivious to the wounded colonel's order. BAM! Allen fires, knocking the warrior down. He then pulls out his steel sword and pistol to defend himself from hordes of other enemies converging relentlessly. BAM! He hits another Indian.

BAM! comes a return shot from behind, striking Allen dead and making a souvenir of his hair and long knife.

Still thirty miles away, Harrison listens to E.J. and Running Deer explain the Frenchtown situation.

As further news of Winchester's demise is heard, he turns to E.J. and Running Deer. "You know what I'm thinking, don't you boys?" says Harrison. "This regiment I have cannot make a difference in the outcome. In fact, we would probably suffer irreparable damage. With help from the Virginians and Pennsylvanians coming in a few days, I am afraid we will have to retreat to the rapids.

"General Payne, I am sending you forward with 170 men.

Carlisle! I want you and the Indian to lead Payne and help any survivors south to the Maumee rapids."

"Yes sir, General. Hopefully there is someone to bring back."

Lewis and the late-arriving Winchester with his son are captured. The picket fenced, protected Americans at the center and on the left fight on bravely, wreaking havoc on the British frontal attack and forcing an arduous English retreat.

"Give me your jacket, General Winchester," orders Roundhead in Algonquin, ripping it off the captured general. "Now, I am in charge!" says the proud Roundhead. "Colonel Proctor will know who the real leader is! We are now going to wipe out your army, General Winchester, and we will start with you!" says Roundhead, set to have his warriors finish the lives of Winchester and his son.

Proctor, arriving in time, moves in to question Winchester, chuckling at the shivering general and arrogant Roundhead wearing his coat.

"Ha! Write the order of surrender, General, or you will freeze to death as well as get scalped," says Proctor.

"We will not surrender," says the picketed defense leader, Major George Madison, standing under a white flag remembering Harrison's orders to "fight to the end at any rate."

An hour later, the third of three white flags is brought to Madison, bringing him out of the cabin with wounded housed inside.

"The artillery aimed at you will be removed, and safe travel for you and the wounded is assured," reads a further note from Proctor and Winchester that is being read by Major Madison.

Disappointedly, Madison finally relents, seeing no alternative after reading the third and final surrender request from Proctor and resisting the urging of his troops to fight on.

A British and a Wyandot scout arrive breathlessly on horseback, not knowing that Harrison has turned around, with news from the Maumee Bay area. "The Americans led by General Harrison are less than a day from here."

"That does it. We are moving out this afternoon. Collect the weapons and load them on sleds," orders Colonel Proctor, having finally achieved the surrender he sought from Major Madison.

Observing a blanket-covered, humiliated former American leader, Proctor informs Winchester, "General, we will send back doctors and sleds to bring the wounded to Canada as soon as possible.

"If you and your men can walk, you will follow us to Fort Amherstburg. If the men cannot stay up with us, I would have you urge them to stay here," says Proctor, brushing his bright scarlet coat and adjusting his black bicorne hat.

An hour later, Proctor is heard giving the order. "Strike up the drum corps, Captain. Let's march out of here victoriously!"

Rat-ta-tat-tat, Rat-ta-tata-tat-tat, sound the drums led by the Scottish bagpipes playing a lively paced but emotionally sad sound, as tears flow from the surrendered Americans' eyes marching north out of the town following the Detroit Trail.

"Roundhead, your warriors will celebrate at their village tonight!" adds Proctor.

"AHHYAA!" whoops Roundhead after hearing the interpreter's news.

"Ahhhyyyaaa!" chorus dozens of warriors, gleeful of the news as Winchester and his entourage fall in behind Proctor.

Three hours later, a few miles south of Frenchtown, survivors of Winchester's debacle are met by E.J. and Running Deer, who have led Payne's detachment forward.

"Where are your shoes, soldier?" asks E.J.

"We removed them to escape and not be tracked down in the snow," answers the American.

"Smart," says Running Deer. "You surely would have been followed and eliminated."

"How many is that?" asks E.J.

"Thirty-three. If there were more survivors, I think we would have seen them by now," answers Running Deer.

Word of what happened pours out from the defeated troops as Payne's men help them make their way back toward Harrison, who has ordered a retreat to the Maumee rapids to regroup.

"We are going to move toward Frenchtown and see if there is anything left of the village," informs E.J. to General Payne.

"Ok, be careful, Carlisle. We need you and the Indian."

The night after the second Battle of Frenchtown witnesses see injured lying inside residences' cabins in pain from their wounds.

"Who's going to guard us from these savages tomorrow until the sleds get here?" asks a Kentuckian.

"No guards are needed," smiles a British soldier.

Arising early the next morning is Kentucky militiaman Eli Darnell, who helps the wounded the best he can. "Sleds should be here soon," comforts Darnell.

"Don't be so sure," says the British guard as a warrior barges in and starts chattering in the English he knows.

"Your brave Americans who were taken captive yesterday are paying good money for their lives. But their lives have been eliminated anyway! Ha!" laughs the warrior.

No sooner said than more warriors painted black and red walk in and start dragging soldiers outside the cabin into the cold, stripping them naked and tomahawking them.

The ones wounded too badly to move on their own are tomahawked where they lay, stunning Darnell, who is horror-struck as he watches some of his friends scalped and thinking he will be next.

Whiskey is found in a cabin basement and consumed as the upstairs is ransacked. Warriors run from cabin to cabin doing the same to the other of the sixty total wounded.

"It won't be long, and our fate will be delivered," says a Reverend Thomas Dudley to Darnell.

"'Fraid so."

Tired of dragging outside, Kentuckians are stripped, killed and scalped inside and the cabins set on fire.

Algonquin is heard by Dudley and Darnell as Americans surviving the scalping make their way outside to escape the flames but are stopped and tomahawked or grabbed and thrown back inside.

Some Kentuckians, such as Dudley, Darnell and a Dr. John Todd, are taken away as slaves or claimed as personal property by warriors.

"I smell smoke, Running Deer," whispers E.J., sneaking slowly toward Frenchtown for the second time in a week.

"Smells like wood cabins burning," says Running Deer. "I do not think we need to chance our own captivity. The enemy could be all around us."

"You are right," whispers E.J., "our horses are back half a mile. Let's head for the rapids."

As E.J. and Running Deer tread through the underbrush of cover, they reach where they think they left their horses and find themselves surrounded by seventy-five warriors.

"Oh geez," whispers E.J. under his breath.

"Let me handle this," says Running Deer as he holds his hand up and speaks in French, "Can we help you? Est-ce quetu parlez-vous francais?"

"Our chief, here, wants to know what you are doing at this location?" asks a subchief, pointing at a bear-robed and beaver fur-covered leader sitting on his horse nearby.

Recognizing Tecumseh from his visits to Fort Wayne, E.J. takes a deep swallow and nervously pronounces, "Monsieur?" Thinking perhaps a little French he knows will help.

Running Deer nudges E.J. and speaks in French fluently, "We are Canadian French scouts for the crown following the evil Americans."

"We don't know French. Speak Algonquin," orders the Shawnee warrior.

"Je ne connais pas Algonquin," says Running Deer.

"They don't know Algonquin," says Tecumseh in Algonquin. "Send them on. We don't have time for this.

"Send two of our warriors with them to attain information from where they go," continues Tecumseh. "Let's go!" Tecumseh waves his retinue forward, and in a sudden gallop, the seventy-three head up the trail to Frenchtown and Detroit with mud and snow flying behind them.

"Au revois," says E.J. as they leave.

"Don't push it," says Running Deer under his breath to E.J. as two warriors bring the two American scouts their horses.

Chapter 14

February 1813 — Ohio / Indiana Territory

At Fort Stephenson, an infantryman greets Wayne Pastor and the supplies from Franklinton. The major supply depot fort, located on the Sandusky River ten miles from Lake Erie, needs repairs. The blockhouse commander asks, "Before we take the effort to open the gate, what's your business?"

"I bring greetings and necessities from General William Henry Harrison," yells W.P. anxiously from his horse, in front of the federal officer in charge of the supply wagons.

"Yes sir, what he said is correct," says the annoyed officer. "The young scout here has ambitions!"

As the gate is dragged open and the convoy enters, W.P. removes his letter from Harrison and prepares to meet the post commander.

A corporal directs the wagons, and W.P. inquires, "Where's the commander?"

"Out ice fishing," answers the corporal.

"Ice fishing? Dad burn, I like this guy already," responds a smiling W.P. "How do I find him?"

"Go back out the gate and turn left, but take your musket loaded. Most Indians around here are friendly, but not all, as you can tell from our so-called fort. Keep walking to the river, and don't fall through. Ice is starting to thaw."

As W.P. walks to the river, he sees the trail heading north that continues on to Sandusky Bay and a schooner downriver frozen in the ice. Three soldiers walk toward him. The man in the middle proudly holds up five two-and-a-half-foot fish that W.P. identifies as walleye as he draws closer.

"Had some luck!" greets W.P.

"You might say that. Who are you?" asks the middle man, walking briskly past him.

"Here's a letter from General Harrison," says Wayne Pastor.

"Follow us and we'll take a look at it inside. We don't like staying outside too long," says the officer in charge, handing his fish off to one of his escort guards wearing black boots, white pants, a blue coat and a black shako hat.

As the four enter Fort Stephenson and the gates are closed behind, the other officers stop. The commander waves them on and turns to W.P. Extending a hand to the buckskinned, beaver-robed scout, he says, "I'm Major George Croghan. Let's see your letter."

Unfolding and reading, "It says you're Wayne Pastor Carlisle. You related to E.J.?"

"Yes sir, my father."

"What a fine man. Helped out during the siege of Fort Wayne and has been a farmer scout there. I was commander of Fort Wayne for a short spell till they sent me to Fort Defiance. Tried to clean that up, and then they sent me here. This place still has some work needed. Dad burn, Harrison says in this letter you want to serve on the Great Lakes?"

"Yes sir, I do," says W.P. proudly.

"As you probably saw, the USS Caledonia is frozen in, and it might be a few weeks till we get her back out on the river. You know anything about sailing?"

"No sir, I don't, but I can learn."

"You done any fighting?" asks the major.

"Fought some Injuns at Fort Wayne and a few weeks ago on the Mississinewa River."

"Dad burn, we could use some marines. Ever heard of them?" asks Croghan. "They first fought in the Rev War against the British."

"They did? I thought Tripoli against the pirates was their first?" exclaims W.P.

"Hey, you know a little history, Carlisle," declares Croghan.

"Mother tried to teach me as much as she could back at Kekionga."

"I'll tell ya what. That stuck schooner is the best place to start. You can probably shoot. How about shooting from a ship's mast or ropes? Done any rope swinging?" asks Croghan.

"Climbed and swung on ropes while skinny-dipping in the St Joseph River back home."

"Ha!" laughs Croghan.

At Deaf Man's Village on the Mississinewa River, Maconaquah and Morning Bird, along with dozens of women, welcome back the braves who have been in the Kentucky lands hunting. In addition to bringing venison back, captured American settlers from the Ohio River are divvied up.

"You say, Red Hawk fought bravely?" asks Morning Bird.

"From all reports, there wasn't a braver warrior," speaks Maconaquah, watching the wives and mothers greet their husbands and sons.

"If only there had been all these warriors here during the American invasion, perhaps Red Hawk would still be with us," speaks Morning Bird sadly. "Now, I have no children left. Even my husband, Running Deer, could be dead."

"We should keep our expectations alive that the Great Spirit will protect him through his Kitchi Manitou," offers Maconaquah. "Red Hawk is very strong, and his earthly body has not been found, so there is hope he has been captured."

"Maybe so, Maconaquah. Meanwhile, if it is like Kekionga, the American prisoners may be adopted or executed. The young ones most likely will be adopted. The men, if desirable, married off to widows. The desirable women captured, married off to warriors."

"The deceased warriors," says Maconaquah, "will be avenged, especially after the returning warriors hear of the invasion. It will not be pleasant around here for a while. We are glad for the venison, cattle, hogs and horses brought back from Kentucky, but I for one am sick of the torture, violence and war. It just goes on and on."

"Yes, Tecumseh, his brothers and the British seem to think it is the only way to settle disputes," says Morning Bird. "I think taking some children and women with me back to Mississineway and Osage might be best. They don't need to see their husband or father suffer the consequences of war.

"Let's load my canoe with a few of these little ones for the trip downriver to my village."

"Yes, and perhaps my husband, Deaf Man, will allow my two daughters to have a brother or sister."

At the lower Maumee River rapids, General Harrison has the supplies removed and the American blockhouse on the north side of the river is torched so it is not used by the enemy. Leading his 500-man command south and east across the Maumee, deeper ship-worthy water is on his left and the shallower rapids on his right.

The ford is crossed, and the horseback army urges their horses, pack mules, oxen-pulled wagon supplies and artillery pieces up the steep trail that lies vertically next to a forty-foot bluff. The highest point along the entire Maumee catches the eye of Harrison as he looks for Hull's Road at the top of the embankment. He locates the road Hull had built the previous summer on his way to Fort Detroit and the invasion of Canada.

Having cleared the top, Harrison sidles up to Sam Wells. "I feel bad for the 17th you were in charge of, and I would like to head for Frenchtown and avenge the loss," says Harrison, "but even you have to agree that retreating and regrouping at the Portage River blockhouse in the middle of the Black Swamp is the best defensive strategy at this time."

"I agree on all accounts, General, but I just hope Governor Shelby and the people of Kentucky will forgive me—but not forget the defeat at the River Raisin by the British and Indians."

"We won't let them forget, Colonel."

Back ten miles north of Harrison, E.J. and Running Deer have gained the trust of the two coalitionist warriors ordered to follow them and have gradually maneuvered their horses behind the enemy duo to surprise them. "Put your weapons down," orders Running Deer in Algonquin, pointing his musket at them while E.J. slides off his horse to pick up the obeying warriors' weapons.

"Let's take their horses and weapons with us and send them back toward Frenchtown," says E.J. "I'm tired of all this killing."

"Good idea, friend." In clear Algonquin, Running Deer explains to them. "Do not follow us. You are free to join your people. But if you are seen fighting the Americans, the next time, you will regret it. Now go, north!

"E.J., give their knives a heave up the trail for them, and bring their horses and the rest."

"Ok, let's get out of here and see if we can't catch Harrison," says E.J., handing a musket and tomahawk to Running Deer while carrying the rest himself as he awkwardly mounts his horse.

Eighteen miles from the Maumee River at the Portage River two-story blockhouse, a camp is set up with tents encircling the small fortification containing supplies inside.

"I believe, Colonel Wells, if service time doesn't run out and the desertion rate remains reasonable, we could have quite a force here," says Harrison.

"Good thing the road is still ice covered," says Sam Wells.

"That's about the only good thing about this freezing weather. Good thing we don't have to sneak up on anybody. I've never heard so much coughing," comments Harrison.

"Surgeons say its pneumonia, dysentery, typhus—"

"They can call it whatever they want," says Harrison. "It's not good. Do these Indians get sick from this stuff?"

"From what I understand, General, smallpox, measles and other epidemics have been a problem for them over the decades."

A perimeter sentry rides in, dismounts, salutes quickly and addresses Harrison. "Sir, we have the Virginians' scouts reporting that a General Leftwich is leading his troops, supply wagons and artillery in on Hull's Road."

"Well, that's the best news we've had in a while. Go give them a hand, Private, and show them in."

"Yes sir, they're going to need it. That road is more swamp than bridge or causeway."

Another day goes by, and with perfect timing, the Pennsylvanians coming from Pittsburgh and northern Ohio arrive on a northerly road over frozen Black Swamp water and bridges they constructed along the way.

"General Richard Crooks proudly arriving, sir."

"Good, good, General. Your lead scout told me how many you've brought with you. That will swell our numbers to eighteen hundred. We will have an officers meeting tonight at my tent. Correction, General Crooks. We are going to clear out that blockhouse and meet in there."

"Yes sir," says Crooks.

Early evening finds the white-painted interior of the blockhouse dimly lit by lanterns. E.J. and Running Deer, who arrived the day before, are hanging up a crudely drawn map. New acquaintances chat in the background as similar experiences are shared.

"I tell ya, Crooks, we were wading in chest-deep water on what was supposed to be Hull's Road," informs Leftwich about his trip through the Great Black Swamp. "We had to build some flatboats to bring our wagon supplies and eighteen-pounders through, and then ground and then water again."

"Didn't wanna drink that water, did ya?" asks Crooks.

"No, it smells awful," says Leftwich.

"We had to build some bridges and causeways, but we had frozen areas to help and an Indian guide named Red Bird or Red Eye, something like that. A young brave, but he was good. Got us where we needed to get," says General Crooks.

That conversation ends as Harrison walks in, but it perks E.J. up, looking around.

The American scout notices first and then nudges Running Deer as Red Hawk files in ahead of more generals and aides-de-camp.

"Red Hawk, my son!" says Running Deer, walking toward him for a quick hug. "I am happily shocked."

"I can only say I am surprised, my father."

"We will catch up after this meeting," says Running Deer, returning to his seat next to E.J. while restraining a grin and slapping E.J. on his back.

Introductions are made, and Harrison asks E.J. about the Frenchtown humiliation.

After explaining what he saw and heard from witnesses, he reports, "I would estimate five hundred Americans taken to Canada as prisoners. Countless at this time killed and massacred. One witness saw Colonel John Allen shot and scalped."

"Yeah, we know it was bad," responds Harrison. "Step in here, Reverend. Gentlemen, I give you Reverend Wallace of Ohio. We need a prayer and an explanation from your holy perspective before we go on."

After an invocation for guidance and wisdom, Reverend Wallace pulls out his Holy Bible, but before reading, he states, "Killing between men came into the world in the beginning with sin. Combine that with God giving man free will, and we have wars over territories.

"Nations will rise against nations, kingdoms against kingdoms. Even Judea would be attacked and Jerusalem destroyed. Someday when Jesus comes back, it will all make sense, but it will be violent for a while, and then Satan will be defeated, ending all death, disease, sin and destruction. The Bible tells us the outcome in Revelation. Victory is His!

"Dwell some more on this, gentlemen, Isaiah 55:8: 'For my thoughts are not your thoughts, neither are your ways my ways, saith the Lord.'

"I will leave you to your business, gentlemen, with this thought before I go tend to the diseased and dying in our camp. Luke 18:27: 'The things that are impossible with man are possible with God.'

"Pray constantly, my sons, for wisdom and mercy."

Harrison walks back up, "Thank you, Reverend. If you have questions, seek Reverend Wallace out, or better yet, seek the Bible.

"President James Madison, Ole Jimmy himself, has this order for us to follow," continues Harrison, attempting to break the solemnity while unfolding his notes. "We are to take back Fort Detroit and invade Canada. The east coast states are against this war with the exception of Virginia, to which we are greatly appreciative of General Leftwich, here, for bringing his volunteers through horrific conditions. Stand, will you, General?"

Leftwich rises and waves to acknowledge the applause and sits back down.

Harrison continues, "Winchester moved too fast. If he would have waited at the rapids, which were my orders, we probably would be marching past Detroit by now. Word has gotten back to Kentucky about the Frenchtown disaster, and by all reports, Governor Isaac Shelby assures us of hundreds of volunteers from his great state enlisting for service.

"In some cases, they are enlisting for a year's duty. The numbers from Kentucky are many more than was expected. The disaster at the River Raisin is raising the ire to a fever pitch!

"Let me be clear about some individuals in this room. I know the revenge factor is huge, but not all of the Native Americans are fighting with the British. More and more of the indigenous are helping our cause and fighting with us."

Looking at Running Deer busting with pride and then the solemn Red Hawk, Harrison pronounces, "Those that help us against the British, their hostile brothers, should and will be rewarded!"

"HERE! HERE!" shouts E.J. and others in the room ready to bust out of the blockhouse and take on the enemy still many miles away.

"Before I dismiss you tonight, here is my order. The ice on Hull's Road is thawing, and before it thaws completely, we need to head back to the rapids and build a fort! It will be a staging area for the greatest conquest in our young nation's second war for independence. It has to be big and bold to hold many troops, supplies and artillery. I think I know the perfect spot. I saw it on the way here. The spot overlooks the Maumee and the foot of the rapids.

"My apologies to General Crooks, not much rest for you and your men. We leave in the morning!"

"No apologies necessary, General! Let's get out of this swamp, end this war and go home!" says Crooks standing, saluting and then exiting the blockhouse.

Forty miles away at Fort Stephenson, marine training for Wayne Pastor is conducted.

"It doesn't pay as well as the enlisted men, and you have to commit to a full year, W.P.," informs Croghan, the fort commander.

"That's ok, Major. I'm starting to get the hang of climbing ship mast nets and hooking in to fire my musket."

"Keep in mind the ship will be moving and rocking, Carlisle."

"Bring it on, Major. When does this ship sail?" asks W.P.

"We still have ice down the river, and if we sail too soon, the Caledonia could have its hull gashed and sink in the river," advises Croghan.

"I'll tell ya what, Carlisle. How about I provide some provisions and a packhorse, and you head for Erie, Pennsylvania, with that American Indian boy you are friends with? Take three or four of the other boys you've been training with and follow the trail along the lake. You have a horse, and we have horses your buddies can pay for out of their wages."

"How long of a trip?" asks W.P.

"By horseback and if everything goes well, probably four days. They're building some frigates there and probably could use some help. Make a little more money, too. I'll write you a letter of recommendation to give them, and along with Harrison's, you should be in. Getting there may not be easy, though; unfriendly Indians could be along the way. We'll give you an Indian guide to lead the way and interpret to make sure.

"On your way, you will go through a small village called Cleveland. I'll write all this down for you," says Croghan. "There will be a Captain Stanton Shoals there building a supply fort and hospital. Tell him we are making progress at Fort Stephenson. He may think it's Fort Sandusky. Make sure he understands our fort is ten miles upriver from Sandusky Bay, and we are about ready to accept supplies again."

"Wow, that's a lot of information, Major. I just want to be a marine," says Wayne Pastor.

"Do the best you can and give him my letter."

"Better than sitting around here target shooting, I guess," says W.P. "Besides, I'll probably get some good views of the lake I'll be sailing on!" grins W.P.

Chapter 15

Two days after leaving the blockhouse campsite at the Portage River, E.J., Running Deer and Red Hawk sit upon their horses looking across the Maumee River from a forty-foot-high bluff.

Dwarfed by the huge, white oaks in the forest behind them, William Henry Harrison and Army Corps of Engineers Captain Eleazor Darby Wood step off along the bluff for measurements and plan for what will be a huge undertaking. The fort will have to withstand British artillery and both Indian and British infantry attacks, which are sure to come.

"I want the picket wall to follow the contour of the bluff," says Harrison, "making it difficult for an attack from the river. We have seventy-five artillery pieces including mortars, so we need battery nests for them. Blockhouses, my gosh, blockhouses two stories high! A picketed perimeter Captain that we can plan as we continue to step off and talk.

"These white oaks must be vertically embedded three feet with earth ramped up to withstand the twenty-four-pounders the spies say the British have."

"Slow down, General," says the chief engineer, writing as fast as he can. "I've built forts before, and I think we can do this project effectively."

The three mounted scouts listen as the voices trail off.

"This perimeter could be a mile in length," comments Wood. "In fact, I foresee ten acres of interior."

"Tell me, Red Hawk," asks Running Deer, "how is your mother? Is she safe?"

Red Hawk disdainfully looks at his father. "How could you send us away like that?"

"The Mississinewa is as safe as it gets at this time, my son."

"In case you didn't hear, Father, Wayne Pastor and his detachment attacked your so-called safe area."

E.J., attempting to follow along with his weak but efficient Algonquin, hears his son's name. "You saw Wayne Pastor, Red Hawk?"

"To his credit, he tried to warn the villages ahead of time," says Red Hawk, "but there were not enough warriors to prevent many of my brothers and sisters from being killed or captured."

After Red Hawk explains how W.P. saved him from being killed by the Americans, E.J. anxiously asks about Wayne Pastor.

"Where is he, Red Hawk?"

"Where is who? Shall I call you my white uncle?"

"Watch your disrespect, Red Hawk," warns Running Deer.

"Wayne Pastor. Where is Wayne Pastor?" asks E.J.

"When we parted, he was heading for the lake named after the Erie nation. He wants to serve with the Americans at the Great Lake."

"Dad burn, he's no sailor! He couldn't navigate a flatboat if he tried!" states E.J.

Suddenly, Colonel Sam Wells rides along the bluff and joins the three scouts. "Better look out, the axe men are going to start falling timber along this ridge first.

"Your mission, fellows," says Wells, "is to patrol and scout the Maumee Bay area and report any buildup or actions by the enemy."

"Colonel Wells?" says Running Deer.

"Yes, Running Deer is it?"

"Yes. I want to express my sorrow to you about your brother William. He was a brave man. I was with him at Fort Dearborn and saw him die."

"Thank you, Running Deer. His family back at Fort Wayne and I miss him terribly. He had a troubled life after he was kidnapped as a boy in Kentucky."

"By the way, Colonel Wells, I have a daughter that was taken by Potawatomi or Miami warriors during the second Fort Wayne siege."

"I am sorry, Carlisle," says Wells.

"Have you heard of any captives being swapped?"

"No, I have not," says Wells.

"How 'bout you, Red Hawk?" asks E.J.

"No!" answers the unsettled young warrior.

A few weeks go by as Wayne Pastor's scheduled four-day journey to Erie, Pennsylvania, is sidetracked. He and his friends make a little money along the Cuyahoga River helping Captain Stanton Sholes build a Lake Erie supply depot called Fort Huntington.

"That Captain Sholes, Andrew, sure got a kick out of me asking him if he was a sea captain. I think he is still laughing about that," says W.P., mesmerized by the vista of Lake Erie on his left.

"Hey, it was an honest mistake, Wayne Pastor," says W.P.'s new acquaintance with the same ambitions.

"All those guys in uniform look like officers," says W.P.

"Try distinguishing the chiefs apart, especially in the wintertime," says Andrew, the new friend.

"The ice is almost completely off the lake, Andrew, or should I call you Ahinga?" asks W.P.

"That is my Seneca name," says Andrew.

"I once was a Miami and went by White Snake," says W.P. "What does your name mean?"

"It means 'he fights,'" says Andrew. "I guess after I was taken from my family by the Seneca as a young boy, I didn't get along with others very well in my new surroundings."

"Well, I can understand that," says W.P. "My friend Red Hawk and I had some issues along the Wabash River."

"I am still disturbed and sorry about my parents," says Ahinga, "and how their lives were ended when I was young many years ago, but I have gotten used to the Indian way and enjoy it."

"My Great Uncle Isaac had his family wiped out in Pennsylvania and started a new life in the Indiana Territory with my dad," mentions W.P. "By the way, your English is improving."

"It has not been easy, but being around you helps. By the way, W.P., I have been told by my new people that I was taken from Pennsylvania. So we have something more in common."

The trail to Erie, Pennsylvania, skirts the Lake Erie shoreline, and occasionally, small dots on the lake horizon appear and vessels with the british Union Jack flag sail by off the waterfront.

As Wayne Pastor, Ahinga and other friends move on toward Erie, Pennsylvania, William Henry Harrison has to leave the fort on the Maumee that he will name after Ohio Governor Return Meigs and attend family illnesses in Cincinnati.

E.J. and Running Deer, sensing a lull in the war activities, leave the scouting around Fort Meigs to veteran Peter Navarre and Red Hawk and travel to Fort Wayne and Mississineway to check on family.

At the same time in Frankfort, Kentucky, Governor Isaac Shelby organizes volunteers into militia units and turns to Congressman Henry Clay's cousin, Green Clay, to lead 1,200 men to Fort Meigs.

"You served in the Revolutionary War, Green. Do you have it in you to lead these Kentuckians? By the way, dad burn, where did you get a color for a name?"

"Original, isn't it, Governor?" says Clay. "Can't say for sure, but as a businessman and politician, it sure draws attention. I assume my parents were thinking ahead, cause business is good! Ha!"

"I'll say. With forty thousand acres to your name and the number of slaves your family owns, dad burn man, you may own the whole state of Kentucky some day! Ha!" says Shelby.

"Listen, if you can set aside your surveying business for a while, Green, I have a need for your leadership and veteran mind."

"Yes sir."

"William Harrison needs some help up in northwest Ohio on a river called the Maumee. I've got twelve hundred men ready to go. If you accept this duty, and it won't be easy, against those dad-burned

British and Tecumseh folks, I'll give you the instructions. Favors and rewards will be waiting for you when you get back."

"Yes sir. When do the boys and I leave?"

"Thank you, General Clay, if I may be the first to call you that?"

"Of course. Thank you, sir."

"You'll be leaving within days," says Shelby. "Furthermore, and I haven't told anyone this yet, I plan to organize and bring a couple thousand volunteers myself. These old legs of mine ain't done yet."

"Yes sir!"

Three hundred fifty-four miles north, Colonel Proctor walks around tentatively as usual when Tecumseh is in the room.

"These scouts have reported to me that Harrison is building a fort near the rapids of the Maumee."

"Doesn't surprise me. Harrison is not stupid. Let me guess, it is on the south side on the high bluff by the crossing?" says Tecumseh in Algonquin.

"Look, I know you know English, so for the benefit of Captain Barclay here, try to use it so we can dispense with these interpreters," says Proctor.

"I have chiefs with me that do not speak English, so interpretations will continue," says Tecumseh. "My understanding will be better, also."

"No wonder you two never can settle anything," says the one armed British sea Captain Robert Heriot Barclay. "The foolish talk only holds things back. If you take some warriors over there, Tecumseh, and slow them down a bit, I should be able to organize the artillery on the ships that are now free of ice."

"Cattle, supplies, artillery, infantry regulars and Canadian militia can be shipped across the lake and up the Maumee as far as the rapids in a few weeks don't you think Captain Barclay?" asks Proctor.

"I would say that is accurate, Colonel," says Barclay.

"From what I remember," continues Proctor, "the river in front of old Fort Miami, will be deep enough to navigate and unload close to the rapids and diagonal from this American fortress being built."

"Yes, the cannons on these large boats will be invaluable. But don't give me these false promises," says Tecumseh. "General Proctor, is your new rank official now?"

"Yes, I was promoted after the victory at Frenchtown," says Proctor.

"And now you, Captain Barclay," Tecumseh follows up, "We have had enough of the Major Muir-type tactics of rolling big guns into the river and leaving all the fighting to my warriors. That needs to stop, also."

"Hey, we lost some regulars at the River Raisin during that battle and victory!" says Proctor indignantly.

"Yes, I saw the results of the butchery that took place while I was away in Indiana when my warriors and I passed through the River Raisin area," says Tecumseh.

"Your warriors were out of control! In fact, I had Brigadiers that tried to stop the butchery feel the blade of a tomahawk, as well!"

"You will be the next to feel the tomahawk, General!" says Tecumseh as he and Roundhead pull out their weapons and approach Proctor.

"Now boys, boys!" says Barclay, standing up to get between the Indians and the British guards' bayonets.

"Don't you ever call me boy again, Captain, or you will have no arms!" says Tecumseh menacingly, after understanding Barclay's English.

"My apologies, Tecumseh, but this behavior will not get us where we want to be," says Barclay. "And where do we want to be? We want to be invading the Americans in the land they call the United States. And in particular, Ohio and Kentucky. Your homeland, Tecumseh, and a land the Crown of England once claimed."

"Our differences are an issue for another day," says Tecumseh, beginning to calm down and his wisdom surfacing. "My warriors will meet you at the rapids."

"Then, it is a plan?" asks the now standing, sword-drawn Proctor, straightening out his redcoat and black bicorne hat.

"It is a plan. My coalition will be leaving soon," speaks a smiling Tecumseh, looking at the black and red war-painted Wyandot Chief Roundhead.

"Before you leaders get ahead of yourselves," says Barclay, "keep in mind the control of the Great Lakes, and in particular Lake Erie, is key to supplies reaching our efforts. I have five ships and one being built. Only five ships to do that. So don't expect my fleet to be everywhere."

E.J. and Running Deer return to the Fort Meigs area on flatboats with hogs, cattle, artillery bombs, ammunition, and their horses after a short visit to family in Fort Wayne and along the Mississinewa River. The overflowing riverbanks, having been inflated by the thawing snows and rains, make it a fast ride down the Maumee.

Unloading fifteen miles south of the rapids crossing and Fort Meigs construction site, laborious efforts from men, oxen and horses bring the massive, transported goods up the forty-foot-high plateau.

More flatboats from Fort Winchester, Fort Wayne and the Auglaize River depots arrive behind them.

Reaching the top of the bluff, the two friends are noticeably disappointed. "I thought they would have more done," says Running Deer.

"Harrison will not like this," says E.J.

Seeing the commander left in charge, the confrontation begins. "General Leftwich, why is there not more done?" asks E.J. "Why are fort logs being burned?"

"Slow down, and who are you, again?" asks Virginia militia General Joel Leftwich. Not waiting for an answer, Leftwich continues, "The Indians have not been a threat, and the boys have been sick and cold."

"General, the Indians will not stay away forever. We need fortification," says the downhearted E.J. "Where's Captain Woods?"

"Woods got called away to Fort Stephenson to assist the repairs there and put me in charge," says Leftwich. "And who are you?"

"I'm a scout, and knowing General Harrison, he will not be happy when he sees little progress. Where do you want the cattle and hogs?"

Leftwich's subordinates direct the placement of the food on hoof and supplies.

"General Crooks," continues Leftwich, "has been dealing with desertions and expired enlistments. Bonuses to stay on are not convincing many to remain under these conditions."

E.J. and Running Deer ignore their normal duties of patrolling the surroundings, grab double-blade axes and head to the wooded center of a soon-to-be fort and begin chopping on an eighteen-inch-diameter birch tree, hoping the rest of the troops sitting and standing around get the idea.

Two days later, General Harrison arrives back at Fort Meigs from Cincinnati. Having gathered as many infantry regulars as could be spared from the forts throughout the Great Black Swamp, he feels good about the additional 300 troops and supplies brought with him until he reaches the summit.

"Dad burn! What the dad burn you been doing around here, Woods? Where's Woods, Leftwich?!"

"He got called away to Fort Stephenson, sir."

"So what?" yells Harrison. "We have everything marked off. Seven blockhouses, five artillery batteries, picket walls along the perimeter. All marked off with plenty of carpenters available! Why are those few guys doing all the tree cutting. Get off your dad-burned rear ends or those dad-burned Indians and Brits will be doing something to your posterior you don't want!

"Indian signs are all around out there. Saw 'em along the river taking potshots at us. Carlisle, you and your Indian friend put those axes down and get out there!"

"Yes sir, General," answers E.J. as the camp stirs into action.

Chapter 16

April 1813 — Ohio / Erie, Pennsylvania

"There's a bunch of 'em," says E.J. to Sam Wells while halted a mile from the mouth of the Maumee River with the expanse of Lake Erie in the distance.

"Ok, let's make our presence known! Mount up!" orders Wells.

As 300 Americans suddenly appear before the warriors, a quarter mile away their campsite is quickly disassembled, and the braves, a few women and children disappear into the forest to the north.

Wells and company examine the camp and quickly head back to Fort Meigs before an organized Indian ambush of the detachment can take place.

Fort Meigs in a couple months' time has shaped up into a formidable fortress. Ten acres entirely enclosed by picketed walls connecting seven defensive blockhouses still under construction and artillery batteries that contain seventy ordinances are intimidating to enemy spies.

Inside Harrison's marquee tent, the General hosts American citizens from Detroit. "Listen to these folks, will you, Wells and Carlisle?" orders Harrison. "They just arrived with some news."

"The British, Canadian militia and Tecumseh's redskins plan to surround you and bombard you with twenty-four-pounders," says a French-speaking citizen through an interpreter. We saw them boarding their ships with these huge cannons. Gunboats too. Brigs with huge masts that will carry hundreds of regulars and Canadian militia are being prepared and supplied! Tecumseh has hundreds of warriors from the north and west, even the Sioux, Fox, Sac and Menominee, arriving daily at Fort Amherstburg to join him in the attack. Some are already on the Maumee. I don't know how we snuck by them to get to you with this warning!"

"Yes sir, we just saw several hundred of them at the Maumee mouth," asserts Wells.

"Leftwich, do you now understand?" asks Harrison. "General Crooks, are your men ready?"

"The Pittsburgh Blues are always ready, General!"

"I like your enthusiasm, Crooks," says Harrison. "I told Governor Shelby in a message that we need three thousand reinforcements. I don't know how many we will get, but I did receive word that a General Green Clay is on the way with twelve hundred. Will they get here in time is the question. Do you want to add anything, Captain Woods?"

"Twenty-four-pounders can do a lot of damage, sir, when those big iron balls strike or come rolling in here. A lot of men, camp followers, cattle, hogs, you name it are gonna be in trouble. I suggest you start constructing a traverse down the middle of the interior, maybe two of them to slow their effectiveness."

"Just what the heck is a traverse?" asks Harrison, taking his bicorne off and scratching his head.

"We need to pile up dirt or mud twelve feet high with a base twenty feet wide. This needs to be almost the entire interior length of the fort," answers Wood.

"Ok, get that designed, staked out and started," orders Harrison. "Get every man available that's not on guard duty! Even the women! Their lives are at stake, also. Give 'em all a shovel."

"Keep your tents and supplies on the north interior side of the fort," orders Woods. "Until the traverse is completed, the British do not need to see this defense with their spyglasses being constructed."

The next day, Eli Darnell, who had already escaped the Indians at the River Raisin massacre, and a comrade of the 17th Kentucky walk down a switchback trail to the river to check on a friend who went fishing. Sickeningly they see his bloodied, scalped body a few feet from the bank slowly flowing down the river.

"Oh, crap. We can't save him," says Darnell. "Let's get outta here, Georgie, and back up to the fort before the Indians get us!"

"Ayyya! Ayya-yaaaa!" yell Shawnee warriors who spot the two from fifty yards away.

Hustling across the inclined floodplain and then up the zigzagging trail, the Indians chase the Americans with the head start. The forty-foot bluff top draws closer, but so do the whooping warriors carrying tomahawks and muskets. One warrior stops and takes aim.

BAM!

"Zing," hears Georgie as the musket ball flies by his ear just as he makes a left turn.

"Guards! We are coming in," yells Eli almost breathlessly. "Open the gate! Hey! Indians! Indians!"

Bam! bam! explode muskets from the embrasures of the northeast blockhouse No. 3.

"AHYA! Ahya! Yi-yi!" holler the Indians, closing in on the Kentuckians.

"Open that gate, you idiots! Hey! It's Darnell and Georgie comin' up!"

Bam! Bam! explode muskets from the blockhouse again as Darnell is pulled down from behind by a warrior.

BAM!

One more shot is fired, and the first pursuer is dropped. His grip releases, enabling Eli to reach the gate and along with Georgie push it in. He and his lucky friend enter just as another Indian musket ball strikes the right side of the gated framework with a "Zap!"

Two hundred seventeen miles east of Fort Meigs, Wayne Pastor, Ahinga and five of their Indian and American friends follow a Seneca guide into a shantytown that overlooks Presque Isle Bay.

"Sorry, but I'm not very impressed, Andrew," comments W.P.

"I agree, Wayne Pastor. I think I would rather live in my wigwam."

"Ha! We can probably arrange that," says W.P. "This constant rain doesn't help matters, but this is a mess."

The group watch logs being drug in by oxen and draft horses from the forests located nearby through the mud toward sawmills as the rain falling doesn't appear to slow the labor.

The Indian guide leads them to a large marquee tent with an American flag flying above an another older one that is yellow with a rattlesnake and the phrase, "Don't tread on me" stitched on it.

"Now I like that, Andrew!" says W.P. "I think we are at the right place."

A ratty uniformed man with a shako hat stands guard in front of the tent, holding a 1795 Springfield flintlock muzzleloader.

"Hold up, you dad-burned critters," says the guard. "What's your business?"

"We want to be marines," says W.P.

"Never heard of 'em," says the old guard, "and the commodore can't be bothered."

"Did I hear marines?!" shouts a voice from inside. "Show 'em in, Doggie!"

"It might be kinda crowded, sir. There's 'bout seven of 'em. Your Seneca guide wanna go in, too?"

The guide shakes his head no, swings his horse around and departs back the way he came.

"Come on in, boys," hails the voice.

As the American fellows in wool, loose-fitting shirts and cotton pants file in, the Indians loosen their deerskin shirts, and they all take off a variety of beaver or coon-skinned headwear in the warm tent.

"So you want to be marines, do you?" says the twenty-six-year-old commodore from Rhode Island.

"Yes sir," says W.P.

"You all look over five-foot-four-inches tall. Can you all speak English?"

Some heads nod affirmatively.

"Oh it don't matter. Can you shoot straight?" asks the commodore. "Are you all eighteen years of age? Aww, it don't matter again. We need two thousand of you guys. We only have a thousand marines in the whole country, and they are all out in the Atlantic or on the east coast fighting the British."

"Yes sir, we want to be marines and serve on Lake Erie and fight those dad-burned British!" says W.P. confidently. "Don't we, Andrew?"

"Yes sir," says Ahinga in the best English he can muster.

"I like that attitude," says the commodore. "To be honest, the marines don't pay as well as the army, but I'll tell ya what. I have a meeting with Mr. Dobbins, coming in here now. Check back with me each Monday. My name is Oliver Perry, and we'll see what we can work out.

"Meanwhile, I suggest you get a job chopping trees down and build up your muscles and finances. They pay a dollar a day."

"Whoa, yes sir," says W.P. as he leaves with his gang, squeezing by an entering Dan Dobbins, the shipbuilding project manager.

Back at Fort Meigs, the end of April approaches, and British Redcoats are beginning to appear across the river. From the blockhouses facing the Maumee River, the Americans view dozens of English infantry with sympathizers unloading heavy artillery from ships that have floated in.

"See that Injun in that elm tree over there?" asks Major George Todd of the 19th Infantry. "Bet you can't hit him, Eli."

"I'll show you how good the 17th is," says Darnell, grabbing his long rifle and aiming from one of the portals of the No. 2 blockhouse.

BAM! ignites Darnell's rifle as men instantly cover their ears in pain from the noise reverberating in the covered bastion.

"Reloaders!" calls Eli to the men stationed in the center of the blockhouse. "Give me a gun. I'm seeing some redskins moving up on the right."

"AYYY! YII-YII!" call out the natives as Americans take aim out their embrasures.

"Constant hideous yells! That's all we hear from them Injuns," comments Virginian Alfred Lorraine, aiming. "We can't ever let them in!"

BAM! B-bam! Fire the American muskets in response to the warrior Brown Bessies returning fire from behind shrubs and small trees that bounces off the picket and blockhouse walls harmlessly.

"Hey! hey!" shouts Georgie. "You got him, Eli!"

"Got who?"

"That Injun in the elm tree across the river. I just saw him fall!"

Rain also falls constantly as mud and earth is thrown up to build the traverse. Dirt from the outside of the east wall is brought in from the defensive ditches being dug along the wall.

Every man and woman is at some sort of duty as anxiousness from seeing the British frigates arrive on the deeper-watered stretch of the Maumee sets in. Blockhouse observers witness the debarking infantry, artillery bombs, hogs, and cattle for food, and tents and supplies at Fort Miami to the north and west. The very fort that was built to stop American General Anthony Wayne in 1794 makes a nice seaport.

Harrison walks among the Fort Meigs construction and yells ordinances toward a battery commanded by Captain Gratiot.

"Send an eighteen-pounder over there, and see what you get," commands Harrison.

"You heard him. Load 'er up, boys, and let's do it right," orders Gratiot. "First, you will use the wormer and remove any debris from the barrel; second, use the swab ram with sponge and clean the barrel; third, place the powder in with the ladle; fourth, place the ball in the tube, and ram it to the back of the tube; fifth, place the vent pick down the priming hole.

"Hey, if the ball had a cartridge bag, prick that; sixth, pour the fine powder into the priming hole; seventh, use the linstock to light the slow match when I give command."

"It will be over forty-five degrees," says Harrison, "so it is a random shot, but I want you to use the quadrant and plummet for practice.

Aim across the river at that battery almost done, and see if your range is ok."

"Yes sir," says Gratiot. "Ready men? Cover your ears, General! FIRE!"

BOOM!!

The cannon rolls back a little, and an eighteen-pound ball is sent soaring.

The American battery personnel watch as the projectile, in a high arch, crosses the river and in a few seconds achieves a direct hit, sending timber and British cannoneers flying in every direction.

"YEAH! YAY! ATTA BOY, GEN'RAL! HOO-RAA!" cheers every man witnessing the shot from their blockhouse or battery. The cheers heard across the river have a reaction of fist shakes directed at the Americans.

No matter how lucky the strike was, a clear message is sent to the British and Indian coalition that a soon-to-be-outgunned Fort Meigs is something to be reckoned with.

"Has anyone seen Red Hawk lately," asks E.J. "Has he reported in?"

"I haven't seen him in a couple days," says Colonel John Miller of the 19th Infantry inside one of General Harrison's tents that is shielding officers and scouts from the rain while strategic plans are made.

"Neither have I," says scout and messenger Peter Navarre, well acquainted with Red Hawk.

"Do you think he has been captured or worse, Running Deer?" asks E.J.

"If anything like that happened, I would be very surprised," replies Running Deer. "He is too good to let that happen," brags his father. "But I do question his heart."

"Officer, officer?!"

"Yes, what is it," says British 41st Infantry regular Major John Richardson, slowly turning around.

"I can help you enter this American fort and end their aggression," says a Miami warrior, holding a yellow ribbon he has removed from his hair.

"I can't believe you haven't caught on; Indian spies with yellow are helping the Americans.

"Are you here to help us or criticize the British efforts?" asks the annoyed Richardson, walking away.

"My name is Red Hawk. I have been a guide for the Americans but fought at Fort Wayne and most recently on the Mississinewa River with Francis Godfroy, Sakima, and Joseph Richardville."

"How do I know you are telling the truth or can be trusted?" asks Richardson.

"I can tell you about the seventy artillery pieces the Americans have, how many soldiers are inside and their strengths, and a traverse they are building."

"Traverse? You would do this?" asks Richardson.

"I believe in Tecumseh and the attainment of my people's land from the Americans, and that your people and mine share in that same belief," says Red Hawk.

Ninety-seven miles southwest of Fort Meigs, Brigadier General Green Clay of Kentucky arrives at Fort St. Marys via the Little Miami River Trail and splits his 1,200-man militia reinforcements in two to reach Fort Meigs faster.

"Colonel Dudley, I just received word that Harrison has increasing trouble from the British and Tecumseh," says Clay. "You will take half the command and portage to Fort Amanda. Dudley, I want you to flatboat north on the Auglaize through a so-called black swamp to Fort Winchester. And yes, the Auglaize does flow north."

"Yes sir."

"Since the rains have swollen the St. Marys River, my half will flatboat it as fast as we can past Kekionga and Fort Wayne and meet you at Fort Winchester. Leave horses and tents here."

"Yes sir."

"Fort Commander Hosbrook, I need flatboats rigged with sideboard protection," orders Green Clay. "We will be heading into hostile territory our entire trip. The closer we get to this new Fort Meigs, I fear, the worse."

"Yes sir, we'll get the carpenters on that right away, General Clay" responds Captain Hosbrook.

Chapter 17

May 1813 — Pennsylvania / Ohio

"General 'Mad' Anthony Wayne died here in 1796," says Wayne Pastor to his friend Ahinga during a rare day off from cutting mostly white oak and red cedar. After being given a schooner ride across the bay to the thirteen-mile-long but narrow Presque Isle, the boys walk a hundred yards on a beachfront trail.

"There was a fort located here back then called Fort Presque Isle, and on 'Mad' Anthony's way back home to Chester County, Pennsylvania, from the Northwest Territory, he became sick with the gout and passed away," says W.P., laying some early spring wildflowers picked along the way on his grave.

"Why did they call him 'Mad'?" asks Ahinga.

"Oh, the story varies, but I know he did some daring things in the Revolutionary War that amazed some people."

"He must have been a great man," comments Ahinga.

"I think Dad said I was born the day they dedicated Fort Wayne to him," says Wayne Pastor. "I was delivered in the back of a covered wagon."

"That's quite a story, W.P. It seems like the Great Spirit has drawn you here," comments Ahinga.

"The boat captain is waiting on us at the shore," says W.P. "Let's head back across to Erie. Let's go, I'll beat you there!"

"Bet you can't," says Ahinga, sprinting past Wayne Pastor.

"I cannot tell you how important the defense of Fort Meigs is to the defense of the entire nation!" yells William Henry Harrison from the top of the partially completed Grand Traverse.

Standing before him are hundreds of the 1,100-man command that were allowed to leave their posts to listen to the plan and receive encouragement.

"The soul of the United States is at stake," shouts Harrison. "The entire nation from the Atlantic to the Mississippi River and stretching to the Pacific Ocean and our new territories is depending on us!

"As I stand before you, reinforcements are on the way! We must hold on! Every inch of these bastions of hope must be defended to the death! The blockhouse, the picket walls—to the death! So, my fellow Americans, straighten out your gun sights! Sharpen up your bayonets! Remember your family back home! Remember the Raisin! Those dad-burned British and coalition Indians have met their match!!"

"YEAH! YEAH! LET'S GET'EM! YEAH! THEY CAN'T DEFEAT US! YEAH! TO THE DEATH!" cheer the troops and a few women present, waving their hats and raising their swords and guns.

BOOM! BOOM! BOOM! BOOM! BOOM! BOOM! BOOM!

The attack on Fort Meigs has begun, with British artillery attempting to soften up Fort Meigs's defensive works. The Americans fire back.

BOOM! BOOM! BOOM! BOOM!

"The back side only has one, maybe two, blockhouses," says Red Hawk to General Proctor and Tecumseh, "so the main defense faces us. Bust those pickets, and we can run on in."

"I find it hard to believe that you are doing this for us, Red Hawk," says General Proctor. "They could all be wiped out in the next day or two. Don't you know some of them?"

"If it comes down to it, I'd like to spare a couple guys," says Red Hawk.

"Of course. If we can," says Proctor.

Warrior attacks made on the Fort Meigs side of the Maumee are repelled by American mortar blasts from the north and east batteries spraying shrapnel on the Indians and British who are trying to advance their way up to and in Fort Meigs. Rifle and smoothbore muskets fire through the blockhouse portals wreak injuries and death on the aggressors, forcing them to retreat.

After a second day of the same results and casualties, General Proctor calls a halt and conferences with Tecumseh and Roundhead on Captain Barclay's schooner, the HMS Chippawa.

"This boat and the HMS Detroit will continue to fire on the Americans," says Proctor. "The river depth seems sufficient to keep them here."

"You need better aim, Proctor. There is no reason we are not inside that fort!" yells Tecumseh.

"Now Chief, let's give the Americans some credit, the fort has taken some blows, especially the blockhouse on the northwest," says Proctor. "Let's turn this into a siege. We will continue to bombard and weaken them. We have received enough of our own casualties. Let's starve them out and receive a surrender. Give them an alternative: Surrender or be wiped out!"

"I fear you are turning cowardly again, General, just like your Major Muir!" says Delaware war Chief Roundhead through an Algonquin interpreter.

"My infantry is young," says Proctor, "but they will stick it out and stay with it."

"There is no way the Americans can survive what is going to come at them!" says Proctor. "Just have enough warriors on that side of the river to run in there!"

In the marquee headquarters tent, General Harrison holds a meeting.

"We need information, E.J. and Running Deer. Keep an eye on their strengths and any new reinforcements they receive. Report any weaknesses, and more importantly, guide the soon-to-be-arriving General Clay in."

"Yes sir," says E.J.

"I want those batteries directly across from us spiked. Spiked, I tell ya! Rendered useless! Clay's men can do that on their way in. They will have more than enough men to perform that mission.

"Secondly, Wells, you and Captain Miller have the men inside Fort Meigs move their tents to the east side of the Grand Traverse. Keep building it higher, Captain Woods; and as you suggested, build two more traverses running east and west to effectively stop the bombing from our side of the river from the north. I want all that work done tonight and each night so the enemy does not know our strategy!"

"Yes sir!" responds fort engineer Woods

"Captain Oliver!"

"Yes sir."

"I want you to ride for Fort Winchester and wait on General Clay if you have to, tell General Clay to get here now! Tell him it's urgent!

Captain Ballard, escort Oliver partway with fifteen men, and fight your way back into Fort Meigs if you have to. Understand?"

"Yes sir," responds Ballard with a salute and grabbing the reluctant Oliver, pulling him out the tent door with him.

"Quartermaster Christy, nail the American flag up on the northwest battery. Let's let the dad-burned Brits know we are still here!"

"Yes sir."

Assembling and loading food supplies onto eighteen flatboats with sideboards at Fort Winchester are 800 volunteer militia from Kentucky. With almost perfect timing, Colonel William Dudley arrives via the Auglaize and meets Green Clay, who just two days earlier had floated past Kekionga.

Fort Winchester Commandant Major Kain, having heard a couple Kentuckians talking about being anxious for some action, makes his way to Clay and states, "You're heading into trouble, General. We have been hearing the cannons from forty miles away right here at Fort Winchester."

"Is that so?" says Clay. "Maybe they'll run out of bombs before we get there! Ha!"

"Push off! "We'll have to travel the river by moonlight if there is any. Flatboat sweeper! Oar men! Polemen! Be alert, I've been told there are a few bends and islands on this river!"

As Captain William Oliver shows up, he sees that Green Clay has his reinforcements on the way, and he heads back to Fort Meigs.

The next morning at the lower Maumee, bombing resumes. British and Americans use mortars to project bombs with fuses, igniting the bombs overhead and scattering shrapnel onto the enemy below, causing injuries and death from nails, ball bearings, needles and metal objects.

BOOM! BOOM! BOOM! BOOM!

Back and forth, bombs fly across the Maumee. Some bombs explode in the air, others land with a thud, sticking in the mud or rolling from a harder impact area.

"Dig in!" order officers. "Your tents won't protect you much. Shrapnel is passing right through them!"

Troops with shovels gouge caves into the back side of the traverse for protection. Unfortunately, rain continues to pour down, filling the newly formed protection and low areas with water and forcing the digging of drainage ditches instead, endangering the Americans from more shrapnel fragments while they dig.

Propelled twenty-four and eighteen-pound cannonballs fired by the British artillery roll up and sometimes over the traverses, injuring and killing the besieged hidden behind them.

"Open the gates! It's Captain Oliver returning with word of General Clay's reinforcements coming in!" blockhouse lookout's shout.

"Where's General Harrison?!" yells Oliver. "Clay's brigade has arrived!" Oliver says to an aide-de-camp.

"He's in his tent over here in a meeting. Go on in he's expecting you."

"Clay's at the foot of the rapids some eighteen miles south of here, General. Flatboat captains are afraid to move closer without orders."

"Captain Hamilton, ride back upriver with Oliver, and give General Clay these duplicate orders in case one of you doesn't make it," says Harrison, walking them outside.

"Yes sir," says Hamilton, snatching the orders and handing one copy to Oliver.

Watching them ride out the gate, Harrison notices heated twenty-four- and eighteen-pound bombs from the British landing and rolling in hopes of igniting the American ammunition magazine.

"We need to find some better protection, but let's get inside the tent for now, Colonel Wells."

Captains Oliver and Hamilton arrive simultaneously to the eighteen flatboats with orders for Clay to advance downriver as far as he can on the north side.

"With a portion of our force, we are to spike the nearest British artillery and then head across the river to Fort Meigs up on the bluff," reads Green Clay to Colonel William Dudley of the 13th Regiment Kentucky militia.

"Take the first twelve, Colonel. I'll be in the thirteenth, and when you are done, meet me back at the boats. I'll lead you across the river and up to Fort Meigs," says Clay. "Got it?"

"Yes sir," responds Dudley with no questions.

Dudley moves his flatboat to the front as Clay allows eleven more to pass him and get into single file, floating with the current over some rapids in deeper than normal water.

Within a mile of the British shore battery, Dudley hears the artillery of the British exploding and realizes with ever-increasing excitement that they are close.

Unloaded at daybreak, three columns form along the bank with Dudley's men on the right, a Major Shelby leading the left column and another column in the middle led by Major Morrison. Heading northeasterly along the north bank, all movement is as soundless as possible as E.J. and Running Deer wave them on to follow thirty riflemen led by a Captain Combs and nine friendly Indians up ahead.

"This is as good a spot as any, Colonel. Attack before they spot you," whispers E.J.

"Charge!" says an arm-waving Dudley, firing the initial shot at the British battery, chasing the English away and silencing the first battery. Moving swiftly to adjacent one but receiving British and Indian musket balls to prevent them from advancing any farther, Dudley returns to the original plan.

"Spike the cannons!" he orders, but Dudley's left column is thrilled by the chase of Indians up the embankment and follow Major Shelby in that distracted pursuit.

"Spike the cannons, Colonel, and get over here!" yells E.J., trying to prevent further orders from being disobeyed.

"Stop! Return to the boat!" yells Dudley, following the troops up the slight grade past the battery and now Dudley is caught up in the chase himself.

"Stop!" yells Green Clay. "Return to the boats!"

Hearing General Green yelling, E.J. hollers, "I'll get them back, General!" and he and Running Deer scamper up the bank, shouting for the troops to return.

"They don't know what they're getting into," says E.J. to his partner.

"Neither do we," says Running Deer, as they observe warriors closing in behind Dudley and his men and tomahawking taking place.

"No! No!" Harrison screams from behind a picketed wall as he views his plan that initially went well beginning to go awry. Waving his arms helplessly, he bellows, "Come across the river! The Indians are getting behind you!"

The warning goes unheard as Harrison and others watch the beginning of an ungodly scene unfold before them.

Clay, not being able to wait any longer, orders his boat across the Maumee before being enveloped, himself. With over a hundred of his remaining troops on the southeast bank awaiting him, they are forced to fire on natives just to scale the south embankment to Fort Meigs.

E.J. and Running Deer fortunately find themselves having their arms pulled behind them by British infantry and tied as prisoners as they watch the American Dudley force being tomahawked.

Dudley is seen being shot in the leg and torso, knocked down, scalped, stripped, and unbelievably dismembered.

Between vomits, E.J. turns to the Englishman next to him and asks, "How can you allow this to happen?"

Running Deer, being escorted next to E.J., observes more of the same and mumbles, "Just don't watch, E.J. I am not proud of my people at this time."

Along with survivors of Dudley's regiment, the two are led to the encampment around old Fort Miami. Some militias are pulled out of the single file and are either tomahawked and killed or kept as personal property and therefore protected.

Tecumseh comes galloping in with several of his entourage and begins shouting in Algonquin, "Stop this inexcusable behavior! Stop this massacre! This is not who we want to be! Treat them as prisoners!

"No more of this abuse! You do not know what you will be causing!" pleads Tecumseh in near tears as he dismounts and pulls some of the Americans away from the aggressive warriors.

"Lead them as prisoners to our camp," orders the disheartened war chief.

Just as suddenly, General Proctor rides in, takes a gander at what has taken place and, from his horse, admonishes kneeling Tecumseh. "Have your warriors gone mad? Have you lost control? Have you no decency?"

Tecumseh stands back up with venom in his eyes and retorts in English, "Go put your petticoats on, General."

Running Deer observes warriors on either side of him and E.J., giving them long, hard looks as if they have been recognized. Running Deer, understanding the Algonquin and French languages bantering about concerning E.J. and himself and fears the worse. He hears talk about their bravery and beating hearts and takes a deep swallow.

After reaching the Indian and British camp of old Fort Miami, braves push the British soldiers aside, and the two are now kept captive by warriors despite their British guards putting up resistance.

Indignant looks are given to the Brits by northern Michigan Indians as the American scouts are untied but directed to a single file line of mostly Kentuckians.

"What's next, Running Deer?" asks E.J., weakened by the experience so far.

"They are preparing a gauntlet," says Running Deer, sighting two Indian lines forming approximately five feet apart and twenty-five yards long, with women up front holding willow switches followed by warriors, some dressed in confiscated American militia clothing and federal uniforms, grasping clubs and tomahawks.

Chapter 18

May 1813 — Ohio / Indiana Territory / Pennsylvania

Sickened by the failed mission and what he is seeing across the river, Harrison turns to Reverend Wallace for some counseling and strolls toward the gate he expects General Green Clay to arrive through soon.

"What can I say to these men and their families when this is all over, Reverend?"

"Jesus spoke two thousand years ago about future wars," begins Wallace, "about nations rising against nation and kingdom against kingdom. That wars and rumors of war would be heard of, that even Judaea would be devastated, Jerusalem besieged and taken by Gentiles, and the temple defiled and destroyed."

"Yes Reverend, but that was a long time ago," says Harrison.

"And this is now, General," says Reverend Wallace. "God's word is for all time."

Across the river, E.J. and Running Deer await their fate while standing in a long column. Guarded on both sides by warriors, the single file leads to an old Indian tradition of running the enemy through a gauntlet.

While watching fifty or so Americans and some American friendly Indians attempting to pass through unhurt toward the river and fort but failing, Running Deer has a plan as they keep stepping forward, watching unconscious or dead comrades pulled out, stripped and mutilated.

"Follow me, E.J., the far end warriors are not getting any action. I think the front will let us get through toward them. We will take a hard turn left before we reach the anxious ones, bust through the line, and head for the river."

"Ok," says E.J., shuffling forward anticipating his death, praying for forgiveness of his sins and accepting Jesus as his Lord and savior.

"Here we go, E.J., follow me," encourages Running Deer. With a burst of accelerating speed that he still has from his younger days, he jumps over fallen, piled-up Americans, sprinting so fast that tomahawks and clubs have a hard time connecting. Meanwhile, E.J., despite having a difficult time staying up, makes it through as the recoil of the heavy weapons allow just enough time for the white man to pass unscathed and make a left turn between surprised warriors, then following Running Deer right turn toward the Maumee River. Passing a Miami brave and British officer leaning against the northern wall of old Fort Miami, they can hear several irate warriors following.

"AHYI! AHYI! YAYAYA HYAAAA!"

"Who was that?" asks British Major Richardson.

"With very little clothes on, it is hard to tell," answers Red Hawk, turning to watch the two plunge into the cold Maumee and swim desperately to the center, "but they looked kinda familiar."

Five warriors with muskets and tomahawks hustle after them and stop at the riverbank. To the left of the HMS Chippawa anchored offshore, the scouts free styling it connect with a swift current as the warriors raise their Brown Bessies.

BAM! BAM! BAM! discharge the muskets.

Zing! Zing! Splat! musket balls pass by and strike the water near and far.

"Ohh, ohh! I've been hit!" says E.J.

"Shhh," says Running Deer, "sound carries out here. How bad is it? You alright, buddy?" whispers Running Deer.

"Yeah, maybe," replies E.J., treading and flowing with the river. Feeling around his body for the wound he answers, "Sorry, I swam into a stick."

"Sheesh," responds Running Deer, withholding laughter. "Let's climb on this island here and get our bearings," suggests the friendly Miami.

Red Hawk and Major Richardson walk away from the wall of Fort Miami together through the Indian encampment that minutes earlier hosted a gauntlet. They observe hands, feet and fingers laying around.

String tied to meat hanging over a boiling kettle is held by braves wearing American pants and shirts.

"You want a bite?" offers one in English who knows Richardson.

"Um, no thanks," says the British major.

Nightfall at Erie, Pennsylvania, catches Wayne Pastor and company counting their money after a few weeks of hard labor cutting trees that will be used to build American warships on Lake Erie.

Walleye and bass, caught late in the day by a couple of their Erie Indian friends, lay in a pan over an open fire outside their makeshift wigwam and tent.

"What do we have for supper, boy?" says a muscular backwoods lumberjack walking toward the fire.

"Looks like a good meal," says his just-as-muscular friend while grabbing the cast-iron frying pan.

"Hey, put that down," says W.P.

"Or what? You lily pad!" says the first lumberjack.

"This is what!" answers Wayne Pastor as he reaches back to deliver a haymaker punch.

Halfway to making contact with the lumberjack's jaw, the buffed bully reaches up with his huge right hand and catches W.P.'s fist. Beginning to squeeze his knuckles together the vice grip of the lumberjack takes W.P. to his knees.

"Stop, Stop!" cries W.P. "You can have it! You can have it! Let 'em have it, fellas!"

"Darn right, we can have it," says the lumberjack.

"And put that musket down, Indian boy, if that's what you is!" threatens the first bully while pointing a small flintlock pistol at Andrew. "You don't want to get your blood all over our fish, do yas?" he asks, walking away.

A couple moments go by as the bullies promenade through the shantytown chowing down the confiscated fish.

"Maybe I'm just not cut out for this part of the world," says a dejected Wayne Pastor, massaging his hands together to relieve the pain. "Maybe I'm not good enough for the marines. I've had some army training back at Franklinton in Ohio, and Croghan taught me a little rope climbing at Fort Stephenson, but I wasn't prepared to handle the situation tonight, Ahinga."

"You have been trained for war, W.P. It will be different next time. Marines, from what I understand, need to be able to fight in any manner."

"Perry hasn't explained that, and there are no marines around here," says W.P.

"Let my fellow Seneca and I show you some combative moves," says Andrew. "To be clear the Seneca prefer negotiating first, so we are all still learning. That weapon I pulled was not wise.

"If you pull a weapon, you must be prepared to use it. You are athletic, W.P., and will catch on quickly to the other part. Those two will be around again, and we will show them how marines fight. Let's begin tonight, W.P. Step out here and let me show you some warrior tactics."

"Ok."

"Each night, we will build on the previous," says Andrew.

"Don't forget, we check in with Commodore Perry tomorrow," says Wayne Pastor.

"Forget about that for now, W.P. Start beginning to understand who you are and be in tune with your body and surroundings."

Back at Fort Meigs the next day, bombing across the river takes place again.

BOOM! BOOM! BOOM! BOOM!

Bombs burst overhead with fragments falling everywhere, but the prepared Americans crawl into their caves dug into the traverse away from the enemy fire.

A messenger arrives at Harrison's command post. "Blockhouse No. 4 reports the British and Indians crossed the river last night with artillery and are setting up to fire on us from this side of the river, sir."

"Thank you, Private," responds Harrison, sitting next to General Green Clay.

"Sergeant?"

"Yes sir."

"Bring me Colonel Miller and Captain Sebree."

"Yes sir."

"We'll use them to take care of that nuisance on the north side of our fort.

"Now tell me, General Clay. How many do you estimate survived Dudley's massacre?"

"Hard telling," says Clay. "Those that escaped are still coming in."

"I'm sending a courier to Governor Shelby," informs Harrison. "We need three thousand Kentucky draftees as soon as possible and I'm sending a courier to Franklinton and Governor Meigs asking him to send Simon Kenton forward with his Ohio militia. We need better training and discipline. Men that will follow orders without question. I like our bravery, though, and fighting spirit. With three thousand more troops, I think we can invade Canada."

"Man, that's ambitious," says Clay. "We gotta get outta here first, sir."

"You haven't been around me much, have you, Green?"

"Look out, blockhouse No. 3! Here comes one at you!" calls out a militiaman standing on top of the Grand Traverse. "Here comes one toward you now, blockhouse No. 1!"

WHUMP! is heard as the top floor of blockhouse No. 3 is hit by a British twenty-four-pounder, sending wood and soldiers flying in all directions.

"Dad burn, the Redcoats got lucky," says Harrison.

"Somebody else got lucky," says Clay from a north portal on the east side of the No. 6 blockhouse of Fort Meigs.

E.J. and Running Deer reach a fort entrance barely clothed near the commander's protective bulwark, with scout/messenger Peter Navarre next to them.

Staring at the Grand Traverse, a fatigued Harrison mumbles, "Somebody needs to get that man off that hill before he gets killed."

Just then, an explosion from a rocketing ball that hit without a warning, burst, and the traverse soldier is no more.

"Bravery or a fool?" mumbles Harrison, climbing down the interior ladder of the blockhouse. "Show Peter and these guys in, guard."

The door is opened, and Navarre walks in ahead of the pair. "Geez, go get these guys some clothes, Sergeant."

"Yes sir."

"Found them climbing up the bank downriver, General," says Navarre. "Say they escaped an attack that Colonel Clay or somebody made across the river while I was gone along the lake scouting."

"Yeah, that's about it, Peter," says Harrison. "They weren't the only ones. General Clay is right here with Captain Combs and Lieutenant Underwood. Combs and Underwood escaped captivity."

"So did we, General," speaks up E.J., "but first we had to escape the gauntlet."

"Can't be, General," says Underwood. "No one escaped that gauntlet; it was completely surrounded with Indians and British."

"Wait a second, not only that," says Captain Combs, "I saw the Indian here. What's his name?

"Running Deer," says Harrison.

"Yes sir, that's it. Running Deer's son, Red Hawk, who is supposed to be scouting for us, walking around with a British officer. I heard him giving information and the British officer calling him by name."

"Red Hawk would not help the British!" says Running Deer.

"Sorry Indian, I saw your son!" says Combs.

"Yes sir, and let me add," says Underwood, "I saw these two taken captive by two British grenadiers and led to the Fort Miami encampment. Meanwhile, it sickens me to tell you this, but butchery took place in front and behind them."

"Two officer witnesses that saw this, and Red Hawk has not reported for several days," says Harrison.

"They ought to be hung, General," says Combs.

"Yep, string 'em up," says Underwood. "Can't have the traitors around."

"General Clay and I will have to consult with each other over this matter. Until then, Sergeant, keep the two in the containment blockhouse but away from the Indian captives."

"Yes sir," says the sergeant.

The next day, Harrison makes his rounds and notices ammunition is getting low in the artillery batteries.

"Offer a gill of whiskey," says Harrison, "for every British cannonball eighteen pounds or less that has landed in Fort Meigs."

As word gets out to the troops, scurrying that is taking place on the parade grounds is smiled upon until British bombardment recommences.

"Dad burn, I didn't think our boys would run out there during the bombardment."

"Those boys are thirsty, sir," says Colonel Wells, chuckling.

"Yeah, but some of them bombs may explode if they have a lit fuse on them," says Harrison.

"General!" says an infantryman in blockhouse No. 2. "There's a British messenger approaching with a white flag."

With the bombing stopped again, a message from the Brit is handed through a small gate and then delivered to a pompous Harrison, pleased to hear from Proctor and Tecumseh.

"They want us to surrender, Sam," says Harrison.

"Oh yeah?" responds Wells.

Harrison immediately writes a response and reads aloud for Wells to hear, "Tell General Proctor that if he shall take the fort, it will be under circumstances that will do him more honor than a thousand surrenders."

"What are you going to do, General?" asks Green Clay, walking up to the gate area and white flag outside.

"What the heck do you think we're going to do? We are staying put, General. We are actually in good shape. I think the Indians will get impatient and leave."

"You know them better than I do, General," says Clay.

The next day before bombing resumes, percussion instruments are heard in the fort.

Prum! Prum! Prum! Rata-tat-tat, Rata-tat-tat, Rata-tat-tat, Rata-tat-tat, Rata-tat-tat!

E.J. and Running Deer, dressed in new deerskins, boots and moccasins, are escorted and drummed out of the fort.

Directed toward the east main gate, comments from Wells are heard. "But General, they have always been loyal. At least I know Carlisle has," say Wells.

"I know, that is why I am giving them new rifles with ammunition and horses," says Harrison.

Troops are lined to the gate, as is customary, but no tar and feather antics, cheering or mockery is heard.

"Listen Wells, at this point, with eyewitness testimony and both Red Hawk and Running Deer fighting with the Indians before, he is seen as a traitor. Clay and I have concluded that we can't trust them and can't take a chance," say Harrison solemnly.

The gate opens, and E.J. allows Running Deer to go first, pulling the reins of his new government-issued mount. E.J. follows but hands the reins of his military horse back to a guard. He then exits and hugs his old reliable horse, Thunder, who somehow knew to come to Fort Meigs's east gate.

Climbing aboard their rides, Running Deer asks, "Now what, E.J.?"

"Let's go home, Running Deer, I've had enough of this army."

Chapter 19

June–August 1813 — Pennsylvania/Indiana Territory/Ohio

"What are we going to say to Commodore Perry, W.P.?" asks Andrew. "We've been cutting down twelve trees per day, so now we can be marines?"

"He told us to report every Monday, and that's what we are going to do until he tells us different," says Wayne Pastor.

"Hello, Doggie. Is Commodore Perry here today?" asks W.P.

"Who wants to know?" asks old timer Doggie, the marquee tent guard for Perry.

"Dad burn, Doggie, you blind? You ought to know us by now. It's Carlisle and Ahinga the Seneca."

"Oh yeah," says the guard, withdrawing his musket bayonet. "Commodore Perry? Carlisle is here again."

"Yes, send them in, Doggie," says Perry.

W.P. and Andrew walk in and salute with their left hands.

"Whoa, you guys are getting big!" compliments Perry, returning a salute. "That forest work is putting some muscle on you.

"I have a thousand militia from Pennsylvania in town protecting the shipbuilding, so perhaps one of them can show you some military etiquette on saluting and marching."

"Yes sir," says W.P. "Sounds like the Marine Corps dream of ours is moving forward?"

"I have to be honest with you men. We are hurting for more sailors, marines, carpenters, cannoneers, you name it. The British have been committing impressment; that is, they are capturing our ships and forcing our sailors to sail for them.

"Like I said before, being a marine doesn't pay much and there are no land grants for your service after the war, but I got word from Secretary of War John Armstrong, who gave the marine Commandant Franklin Wharton permission. In other words, you and your crew are in."

"Yes sir," says a grinning W.P.

"I want you to report to the sloop, the USS Trippe, and acting Master George Senat at the docks tomorrow morning. You will notice some large two-masted brigs at the dock. Yours will be a smaller, single mast. Bring your friends along and any recruits you have been talking to."

"But we've never sailed before or even fired a cannon," explains Wayne Pastor.

"You want to be a marine, don't you?" asks Perry.

"Yes sir."

"How 'bout you, Indian or whatever you are? You want to be a marine?"

"Yes sir," says Ahinga.

"Then report at 8 a.m. You will be taught everything you need to know, and if we have any uniforms, you'll get that," says Oliver Perry. "Good luck!"

The boys salute awkwardly and leave the marquee tent. Walking back toward their shanty wigwam excited about their opportunity, the lumberjack bullies come calling again.

"If it isn't our fishing buddies," says the first lumberjack, reaching out to shove Ahinga.

With that movement, Ahinga grabs the lumberjack's hand and pulls the bully toward him, leveraging him into Ahinga's hip and flipping the big man over his back and to the ground. Ahinga lands a right elbow to the bully's chest.

"Why, you no-good redskin!" yells his friend, yanking his flintlock pistol out of his belt. That draw is quickly met by a swift kick to the gun hand by Wayne Pastor's foot, knocking the weapon into the air, causing a harmless discharge.

BAM!

Seamlessly, the second bully's arm is brought behind his back by W.P. and he is forced to his knees.

"Stop, stop, you'll break my arm!!" yells the second lumberjack.

"That's the end of this nonsense, ok, gentlemen?" commands W.P.

"In fact, you want to join the navy, don't you?" adds Ahinga, negotiating the Seneca way.

"All the fish you can eat tonight!" adds W.P. with a smile at Ahinga.

"Sounds like a deal, doesn't it, Max?" says the first defeated paper tiger.

"Yeah, we've been thinking about it anyway, honest. Let us up, fellas," says Max.

"OK, but just so you know, your life will end the Seneca way if you double-cross us. Get it?" says Ahinga.

"Yes sir, Ahinga is it?"

"Yes, Ahinga."

"And one more thing," says Wayne Pastor, twisting a little harder, "the British are the real enemy, not us. Stop by for supper tonight, and we will fill you in on the marine and navy situation."

"Ok, ok!."

Riding into Fort Wayne on the south trail of the Maumee River are former Harrison scouts E.J. Carlisle and Running Deer. As they pass Fort Wayne's south main gate and head for E.J.'s residence on the west side of the blockhouse, Lieutenant Ostrander gives a wave, and E.J. disinterestedly nods back.

"Dad's back! Dad's back, Ma! Yells E.J.'s oldest son, nine-year-old Bennie.

Uncle Isaac halts the farm horse, drops the plow and high-steps it through the furrowed field to greet his nephew and Running Deer.

Charlotte and little seven-year-old Teddy come out of the two-story log cabin with E.J.'s wife drying her hands on her apron and the youngest son reaching for his dad.

Dismounting their horses, they both are surrounded and hugged. With the news of the horrific siege at Fort Meigs reaching Fort Wayne, it is a great relief to see them ok, physically.

Upon entering the cabin, sitting down for some hot stew and beginning to relax, E.J. and Running Deer reveal the story of their time with Harrison on the lower Maumee.

"Only by the grace of God did we survive the gauntlet. We will probably never get over what we saw, and hopefully never see what we saw again," says E.J.

"I hope you don't either," says Uncle Ike, "but don't count on it. We have Indians lurking around here, and the war is not over yet."

"Yeah, you're right, Uncle Isaac."

"I better go check in with Captain Moore and see if he wants me or us around here," says E.J.

"Thanks for the food," says Running Deer. "I need to head on down the Wabash to check in on Morning Bird. I don't know when I will see you again, friends, but I'll keep an eye out for Hannah May."

"Thank you, Running Deer," says Charlotte, standing up in her layered cotton dress to give the Miami warrior a hug.

"Stay in touch, Running Deer, and stop in again when in the area. If we are still here," says E.J.

"I have a feeling you will be, E.J."

Hugs from the Carlisle boys and a handshake from Uncle Isaac and E.J. put Running Deer on his way.

"I haven't received any word from Harrison or the government, so as far as I'm concerned, you are still employed around here," says Commander Captain Moore of Fort Wayne. "Indians have been seen on the outskirts of the forest, so be careful when you're out there."

"Thank you, sir, I will be."

"And E.J., I believe you and Running Deer's story."

"Thank you, sir, that means a lot."

Days later, Tecumseh, Roundhead, General Proctor, Captain Barclay and guest Miami spy Red Hawk conference at Amherstburg, Canada.

"Taking ships across the lake sure beats horseback riding the long way around," says Red Hawk, naively eager to contribute.

"So we failed at Fort Meigs," says Roundhead through an interpreter, "but we bludgeoned them pretty good."

"But did we inspire the Americans?" questions Proctor.

"What do you mean, General?" asks Roundhead.

"The butchering and out-of-control behavior may act as a motivation for the Americans for revenge," answers Proctor.

"Here we go again, my British General friend. Anything for an excuse for failure!" says Tecumseh, standing in disagreement.

"If this is not going to be a productive meeting," says Captain Barclay, "I need to prepare to bring supplies in from the east. My ships and I will be leaving soon."

"After the Prophet and I venture into the Indiana Territory to stir up support, we will come back and plan another attack on Fort Meigs," says Tecumseh, sitting back down.

"I would say that makes sense, Tecumseh," says Barclay. "Fort Meigs will be a major supply depot, along with a Fort Stephenson on the Sandusky River, for an eventual attack on Canada. Another problem is a place called Erie, Pennsylvania. Warship building by the Americans is taking place there. Regrettably, the port is hard for our warships to get to and disrupt the activities."

"From growing up at Kekionga, you may want to consider an attack on Fort Wayne again," says Red Hawk, not believing he is actually contributing. "The St. Marys River from Fort Barbee is sending supplies through there regularly to Fort Meigs."

"Yes, there are many forts in the Black Swamp that are assisting in the flow of food and supplies," says General Proctor. "Once we destroy Fort Meigs, the rest of the forts will fall like dominoes."

"Now you are talking, Proctor!" says Tecumseh gleefully.

Along the Wabash River downstream from the Mississinewa, an elderly Indian couple have three American pioneer children helping them with chores and adapting to a new way of life.

"The older white boy is a big help to us," says the woman in Algonquin to her husband. "The older girl is ok, but the little blond girl cries and refuses to learn our language."

"Perhaps she needs held and loved more, my wife," says the husband. "Our way of life is still new to her."

"I agree," says the wife. "Oh! I miss our warrior son. Nothing can replace a blood relative, but we need help as we age, my husband."

"I am too old and impatient to teach," says the elderly brave. "Let's find the little girl a younger couple to take her. Perhaps a trade for an older boy to help us hunt and work around here."

A couple weeks later, back at Fort Wayne, a mile up the St. Marys River from the fort at a sharp right bend, Red Hawk leads a group of Miami and Potawatomi warriors in ambush.

Hiding in the trees and brush on the north side, they watch flatboat after flatboat pass by in the fast-moving current heading for a stop at the American post. As the boats at the bend swing closer and closer to the north embankment, the Indians wait their chance.

Three men struggle with poles and a sweeper to steer the last supply boat carrying bacon, flour, and other necessities around the bend to the right.

The Indians, seeing their chance, the command from Red Hawk is given. "Fire!"

BAM! Bam!

Eight Brown Bess muskets discharge at the white occupants, striking the supplies and an American. The flatboat is forced out of control and rams the north bank, spilling some provisions into the water and onto the river's edge.

"Take what you can!" calls Red Hawk, "including their scalps. Hurry! The fort surely heard the shots and will be coming soon."

Two of the Americans are eliminated and a third is winged trying to swim to the south bank and drowns as the flatboat, now unstuck, proceeds easterly toward the Maumee and St. Joseph rivers.

Major Joseph Jenkinson, in charge of the flatboat fleet, follows along the bank on horseback but is too late to make a difference. He stops and watches the Indians scamper away, then spurs his horse and heads to his commander, Colonel Richard M. Johnson, who had just reported in with his 700 horse-backed American dragoon unit.

Having heard the shots, the unit remounts and take off, attempting to track the ambushers.

After a several-mile tracking mission of the marauders, Johnson and his brother, Lieutenant Colonel James Johnson, return upset about the immediate follow-up but pack up supplies for an incursion toward Five Medals Village the next day.

"Captain Moore!" yells Johnson at the Fort Wayne commander. "You are to secure the surroundings when supply boats come in. Dad burn, Captain, three killed within a mile of the fort? Total neglect, sir, neglect!"

On Lake Erie, after a few weeks aboard the USS Trippe, Wayne Pastor, Ahinga and fellows that they recruited begin to become familiar with terms and orders issued by Lieutenant Thomas Stevens as they sail the Presque Isle Bay and Lake Erie shoreline near Erie, Pennsylvania.

Men of all walks of life are learning the marine and navy way on the fly. "Climb that ship mast net, Carlisle, and get to the rigging! Faster! What are you going to do when the real fighting begins? Follow him, Ahinga, and be ready to hand Carlisle a loaded musket!

"Hang on up there, boys, don't be falling on us. The waves make things a little more difficult," yells Stevens, observing winds kicking up five-foot to eight-foot swells.

"Now you Indians arrange yourselves to pass up the loaded musket! At the same time, pass down the spent rifle. Faster! You two have to load faster! You act like you never seen a musket!

"Blimy! You're in the navy, not on a flat war path! You ain't in some cozy blockhouse either, mates! You're gonna be getting fired upon by some of the greatest marksmen in the world!

"You, below! Dad-burned lumberjacks! You haven't fired off one round of the eighteen-pounder yet! Come on now, Max! You too,

Buford! The British will be blasting you to kingdom come if you can't load faster. Why, I ought to send you all back to the forests!"

BOOM!

"Well, congratulations!" continues Stevens. "Next time, aim it out the porthole! You blundering rookies! Good thing we have carpenters back at port to fix that! Ha!! Reload, but don't blow yourselves or the ship up, you dad-burned fools!"

"Mr. Stevens!" calls down Wayne Pastor near the top of the single mast above the sail.

"Lieutenant Stevens!" calls W.P. again.

"Yes, mate! What you got up there?"

"There's a ship with Union Jack sailing toward us. I think it's British!"

"You don't say.

"Helmsman! Turn the Trippe about and head us back to Presque Isle Bay and Erie!" says Lieutenant Stevens.

"Our 'squids' and marines are not ready for this, and it looks like the British are coming back to this end of the lake," comments Stevens to the first mate.

"Come on down here, Carlisle, before you fall! You're having too much fun up there! You too, Indian, or whatever you are!"

Back at Fort Wayne, Charlotte walks in through the front door of her cabin and finds an exhausted E.J. rocking Teddy on his lap.

"E.J.!"

"What's that, Charlotte? Everybody ok?"

"I just got news from one of the officer's wives that we have a new fort commander in Major Jenkinson, and that shooting we heard the other morning was Lieutenant Ostrander firing his musket at some geese flying overhead from inside the fort against orders."

"He should know better than that," says E.J. "Geez, you're just full of news today."

"The worst of it is that Fort Meigs is under attack again. Where did you say Wayne Pastor is?"

"Red Hawk told his dad and I that Wayne Pastor was going to Lake Erie," explains E.J., rubbing his eyes, "and in particular Fort Stephenson to become a marine. I just wish Red Hawk or Running Deer knew where Hannah May is."

"Oh, I long for my little baby girl, too, honey," agrees Charlotte, tearing up for a good cry but snapping out of it. "What in the world is a marine?" asks Charlotte. "Never mind, it doesn't matter. I want you and Running Deer to get up there and bring our boy back!"

"I'm way ahead of you, Charlotte. I sent an Indian friend to the Mississinewa villages a few days ago asking for Running Deer to return to Fort Wayne. If he is not here tomorrow, I'm leaving by myself."

"You get Red Hawk back here, too! Morning Bird's gotta be worried sick."

Chapter 20

July–August 1813 — Ohio / Pennsylvania / Lake Erie

"You want me to do what, Governor Shelby?" asks Private John Smith at Franklinton, Ohio.

"Watch a pig," says the sixty-two-year-old Kentucky governor.

"Now, you know I like you and would vote for you if I still lived in Kentucky, but I gotta draw the line somewhere!"

"Private Smith, you've always been loyal to the U.S. government according to General Charles Scott, who met you messaging for Anthony Wayne at Fort Greeneville."

"Yeah, I remember General Scott, but babysitting a pig, sir?"

"He's our lucky charm, Private," says Shelby. "Ever since the little porker has been following us, I have been receiving good news about the war.

"That little pig fought another pig in his pen back at Frankfort, crawled under the pen fence to follow us and, dad burn, man, even swam across the Ohio River right next to my boat."

"You ain't putting me on, are you, Governor?" asks Smith.

"No, Private, it's all true. You can't make something like this up," says Shelby.

"What exactly are my duties with this pig?" asks Smith.

"All ya gotta do is keep him safe. Don't let any yahoo turn him into bacon. See that he follows us. Feed him and do whatever a pig needs done."

"Come on, Governor, I'm more important than this," begs Smith.

"If anything in this war starts going wrong, we'll have pork chops, but if the momentum continues this way, I'll see that you are rewarded generously when the campaign is over," coaxes Governor Shelby.

In northern Ohio, the hunt for Wayne Pastor is on.

"Getting around that Black Swamp was not easy, Running Deer. I'm glad you caught up with me," says E.J.

"I was more nervous about passing General Harrison's headquarters at Fort Seneca ten miles back since Fort Meigs is being attacked again and we already got drummed out of there."

"Now I kinda understand what you are going through being a man without a nation," sympathizes E.J.

"If the United States loses this war, do the British want us on this land?" ponders Running Deer. "What if the Miami do not want me back? Am I still Miami? Am I going to have to fight Red Hawk, my own son? It is all so confusing."

"God knows who we are, and that's all that matters. The answers will unfold soon. Here's the Sandusky River. Let's follow this to Fort Stephenson. I understand it is located on the west side, so let's stay on this path," reasons E.J.

"This beautiful river stream sure winds around," comments Running Deer.

Breaking free of the river forest trail, E.J. whispers, "There's the gate, Running Deer. Let's hope they let us in."

"Scouts Carlisle and Running Deer making an inquiry!" shouts E.J. up to the blockhouse.

"What's your inquiry?" responds the guard to E.J.

"We are looking for the whereabouts of a Wayne Pastor Carlisle!"

Voices are faintly heard on the other side of the double-door picketed gate.

"Of course, get in here, Carlisle and Running Deer, you say?" asks Captain George Croghan. "Not familiar with him, but if he is a friend of yours, E.J., heck yeah, come on in."

"Keeping things buttoned up, I see, Captain," says E.J.

"Injuns and British spies are out there, you know. Dad burn, you are a sight for sore eyes, as they say," says Croghan. "Good to see you again, my friend. I will always appreciate the help you gave me in my first assignment at Fort Wayne.

"If you're looking for Wayne Pastor, he left for Erie, Pennsylvania, back in the spring before the first Fort Meigs battle. He took several individuals with him. Says he wants to be a marine and contribute to the war. He's still up at Erie, I assume."

"I can think of safer ways to contribute to the war, but that sounds like my son," comments E.J. "Mind if we spend the night, Captain?"

"Stay as long as you want, but I must warn you, we are expecting trouble any day. After the second siege at Fort Meigs by the redskins and British failed, we got word the English were sailing here to destroy the supplies we have stored and get an easy victory to build their confidence."

"Ohhh great," says Running Deer sarcastically.

"You think we should leave, Running Deer?" asks E.J.

"It would be the wisest thing to do, but we aren't always the wisest, Ha!"

"Don't let me whitewash our chances. We can use all the help we can get, fellas," says Croghan. "We have 160 men and one six-pounder. So, I don't blame you if you want to go."

"The fort looks solid, Captain," says E.J.

"It ought to. Captain Eleazor Wood came over before the Fort Meigs siege and designed the repairs. It was in pretty bad shape. Then I went back with him and fought in the first siege there."

"We were there, too. Can't believe we didn't see you."

"It is a huge fort, and I was located at a northeast-side gun battery."

"E.J., we don't have a choice. We are needed here," states Running Deer. "Besides, I didn't tell you this at the time, but the forests around here are crawling with warriors."

"Yes sir, Running Deer," says Croghan. "We've been seeing them, too. I'm just glad we took those supply boats downstream this morning and sunk them."

"Sunk them?" questions E.J.

"Yes sir, hopefully they will prevent the British warships from coming up to our fort and blasting us to kingdom come," informs Croghan.

After E.J. and Running Deer get settled in, a messenger from General Harrison arrives for Croghan from Fort Seneca.

"You take this message and tell General Harrison, Sergeant—that is, if you can get back to Fort Seneca—we are surrounded by hostile Indians. We fear being massacred if we give up the fort and try to march to Fort Seneca," says the twenty-one-year-old nephew of William Clark.

"Probably a good decision, Captain," says E.J., overhearing his response. "What else can we do around here to prepare for an onslaught?"

"We have plenty of bayonets in the supplies," says Croghan. "Take the 24th Infantry and have them tie those bayonets to the top of the pickets to prevent the enemy from scaling."

"Yes sir."

"Running Deer, we have plenty of shovels, I want a ditch dug along the wall to the left of the north center blockhouse that is ten feet wide and seven feet deep. Take two companies of the 17th to start that effort."

"Ok," says Running Deer, looking for an officer to find the shovels and lead that assignment.

"I think if we get attacked, they may use that ditch in front of the blockhouse for protection, and we will have a surprise for them," advises the strategizing Captain Croghan.

"Sandbags! We need sandbags, Sergeant! Take the rest of the 17th and place sandbags around the outside of the pickets to brace for bombardment!"

"Yes sir!"

"Do you see it, Quartermaster?" asks British Commodore Barclay. "Point of sail should be the mouth of the Sandusky River. Snap to it,

Mr. Thomas! Ask the men aloft if they can verify the river mouth and inform us of sandbars."

Yelling of orders and questions are called out to the barrel men in the crow's nest and boatswains supervising the main deck as the approach is made.

"Signal the gunboats to move ahead of us to enter the river first. The wind is astern, Quartermaster. We need hazard information, Lieutenant," orders Barclay. "Come on, men! Work together now. Have the oars ready, mates. We do not want to run aground! Find the channel!"

"Our troops are anxious for a victory, Captain Barclay," says General Proctor, in command of his 500 grenadiers and regulars on board. "Get us as close to this Fort Stephenson as you can. Your long guns and carronades will come in proudly if we get within range."

"You've got a winding river up ahead!" yells a barrel man aloft.

"We've been down this river before, and it has good depth only so far, perhaps ten miles," advises Barclay.

In Fort Stephenson, more orders are given in preparation for the anticipated invasion. "Move the French and Ottawa colonists inside the fort for protection," orders Croghan.

"Since you are right there, Mr. Carlisle, open the gates and let them in, sir. They have been in this community for a number of years and have been friendly and helpful!"

"There's the British, Captain!" yells the northeast blockhouse observer closest to the river. They are unloading downriver. The sunken boats worked! They cannot navigate closer!"

Captain Croghan climbs to the second story of the center north blockhouse and pulls out his single lens spyglass.

"They are a mile away, but the smaller gunboats floated over and are moving closer. The British infantry is unloading," describes Croghan to everyone within earshot.

E.J. and Running Deer join the fort commander and gaze out the portal, and with the naked eye, they spot the artillery pieces being rolled down the gangplanks.

"I see old General Proctor," says E.J. "I'd recognize that proud peacock anywhere."

An hour goes by, and the Indian leadership of Shawnee Tecumseh, Canadian militia Major Robert Dickson and Wyandot Chief Roundhead meet with Proctor on the edge of the forest on the north side of Fort Stephenson. The enemy summit is seen breaking up as the coalition brain trust join their commands.

"I see a Canadian militia advisor with the Indians. I'd say they are done with Proctor. New British leadership could be a problem for us," remarks Running Deer.

"I would imagine Tecumseh is frustrated but still needs the British," says E.J.

"Here comes a Brit with a white flag, Captain!" says a guard, peering out the center blockhouse.

"I'll be right up and communicate from the portal."

The British-accented voice of a Colonel Elliott is heard calling up to Croghan.

"The General Proctor wishes you greetings and an offer to surrender the fort, Commander, in order to prevent any unnecessary bloodshed! We cannot prevent a complete massacre of all inside by the two thousand Indians waiting in the forest if the battle commences."

Indian drums and howling can be heard in the background as the warriors prepare mentally for the assault.

"I have the terms written on this document explaining the concessions expected from General Proctor! Read and sign, and I shall return it promptly to the honorable General Henry Patrick Proctor representing the Crown of England!"

Croghan looks around for a moment.

"Lieutenant Shipp, step out there and tell 'em, 'No surrender.'"

The lieutenant exits the fort gate and strolls to Colonel Elliott.

"Our commander wishes to inform General Proctor there will be no surrender from the Americans and no one to massacre when the fort is taken, for everyone inside will not give up while able to resist."

"'Shipp, come back in here,' orders Croghan. "We're going to blow them to you-know-where!'"

Within five minutes of the white flag meeting, British bombardment from the gunboats on the Sandusky River, three six-pound cannons and two howitzer batteries on the north side of Fort Stephenson open up.

BOOM! BOOM! BOOM! BOOM! BOOM!

"Here we go again," comments E.J., Running Deer and Croghan almost simultaneously, remembering Fort Meigs.

For twenty-four hours, the 150-by-300-foot rectangular fortress protecting 160 Americans and villagers takes an estimated 500 six-pound cannonballs with little effect.

During the night, the five artillery pieces are moved within 200 yards of Fort Stephenson and project more terror at the inhabitants, but the white oak, sixteen-foot-high pickets ward off the bombs.

"If and when they attack," orders Croghan, "hold your musket fire till they reach the fifty-yard marker. Do you see 'em out there?"

"Yeah, but dad burn, Captain, that's kinda close, don't you think?!" exclaims E.J.

"We don't want to miss," answers the commander. "Bombardiers, load up Old Betsy with grape and cannister shot. In fact, double-load it!'"

"'Old Betsy,' who is she?" asks Running Deer, nervously watching the British artillery barrage through a porthole.

As the English and Native Americans double-step forward, the Americans hold their fire.

Sharpshooters move up to the portholes of the three blockhouses and picket ramparts ready to fire, as reloaders behind or below the Kentucky infantry riflemen are ready to hand or reload the firearms.

"FIRE!" yells Croghan. The order releases a horrendous explosion of muskets, projecting a wave of musket balls onto the invaders from riflemen inside of the fort.

Bam! Bam! B-bam! Bam! B-bam! B-bam!

"Fire 'Old Betsy'!" commands Croghan.

BOOM!

Nuts and bolts, musket balls, rocks and other objects that make a good grapeshot induce contact with British and Indians alike on the north side, forcing a withdrawal all around the fort by the invading force. Injured and dead are seen being carried off the field to English surgeons in the forest behind them.

"Well, Round 1 seems to be over," comments E.J.

"Did you men see any ladders or axes?" asks Croghan. "I think they thought their cannons would be sufficient."

"Load up Old Betsy and fire a few more rounds with cannonballs this time. Use different portholes. Make them think we have more than one six-pounder," orders Captain Croghan.

BOOM!

"We are done with this," says Tecumseh to Chief Roundhead and Major Dickson, watching in the thick woods on the south side of the fort. "I will not allow my warriors to be sacrificed by this incompetent Proctor."

BOOM!

Old Betsy propels another American cannonball out of a different porthole, causing confusion about the strength of the Americans.

"Commodore Barclay, I think I detect a weakness in the northwest corner of their fortress," surmises the frustrated Proctor.

"Ok, I'll direct the gunboats to concentrate there," says Barclay. "Messenger, take this order to the gunboats to commence firing on the northwest corner."

"Yes sir."

Later in the afternoon, the British assault force of 300 regulars double-time under the cover of cannon fire and resultant smoke.

Two hundred tall grenadiers averaging six feet two or taller march around in parade fashion to the south side of the fort in order to intimidate the Americans. In their crimson coats and black pants and holding shimmering, bayoneted Brown Bess muskets, they prepare to attack in coordination with the 41st foot regiment on the north side.

"Well, ain't they fancy," comments a Kentucky sharpshooter while spit tobacco drools down his chin.

"Here they come, Captain," informs E.J., "but they don't even have ladders to scale the wall or axes to break in."

Climbing back up the interior ladder of the center blockhouse, Croghan directs, "Make sure that Betsy is loaded with grapeshot shrapnel. Point the barrel toward the west porthole."

"Yes sir, it's loaded, Captain."

"Keep the porthole shut till I give command," orders the captain.

Heavy rounds of musket balls from the Kentucky militia double down again on the British infantry. A British officer is seen pointing to the ditch dug along the picket wall to the north of the blockhouse.

The British, thinking they have found cover from the American musket sites, jump into the trench but are surprised when the porthole opens and they hear the command, "Fire!"

BOOM!

Projectiles of all shapes and sizes fly in all directions toward the infantrymen in the ditch, killing and maiming dozens.

"AH! Ah! Eeeyi!" sound the Brits in pain.

Americans follow the cannon shot with musket fire from the blockhouse, inflicting more casualties.

"They're retreating on both sides of the fort, sir!" calls one of Croghan's officers.

Behind the British lines, a conference takes place.

"I am concerned about Harrison showing up to aid the Americans," says General Proctor to Major Dickson and Commodore Barclay.

"Major Dickson," says Proctor, "this evening after dark, have the warriors creep in and bring our dead and wounded off the battlefield."

"Yes sir."

"Commodore, we can't let Harrison come in here and finish us off or take us captive," says Proctor. "Tecumseh will not be happy, but we are going to sail out of here tonight, regroup with our flotilla and head for Canada."

Chapter 21

As Commodore Perry's eyes sweep over the sleek new USS Lawrence propped up by braces in a creek called Lee's Run, he turns to the sailing master and asks, "Captain Dobbins, in your opinion are we seaworthy?"

"I will defer to Ebenezer Crosby," says Dobbins.

Ebenezer Crosby, the master shipwright, looks the brig over and flatly states, "It's the best I can do in the time we are allotted. One ship to build is tough enough, but Secretary of Navy William Jones wanted four!"

"Until we get these four vessels fitted and out there," says Perry, "we are outnumbered by the British."

"Slide them in," says Henry Eckford, architect and designer. "I'll vouch for them. Heck, the Lawrence and Niagara are twins, so if one goes down, the other pro'bly will, too! Ha!"

"If you don't mind Mr. Dobbins, I'll launch the Lawrence," says Perry. "Jesse Elliot can take the Niagara, and we will sail around the bay a bit and then head for the sandbar. With the size and weight of these sisters, the challenge is to get them over the shallows with only six feet of water underneath."

"Get your crews ready, Commodore. Time's a wastin'!" orders Dobbins.

With nearly a thousand viewers gathered to witness the launching spectacle, Perry nails a list of men he has approved and desires to a pine tree. The captain points to Wayne Pastor standing up front and gives a thumbs-up to be a part of his sailors and marines.

Long cannons, carronades and ammunition brought 130 miles from the manufacturers in Pittsburgh are loaded on sloops and schooners first. Transferring to the larger brigs will take place after the sandbar issue is resolved.

The smaller schooners and sloops already fitted float over easily, then with some coaxing, the Lawrence does as well, but the Niagara gets stuck.

Just as luck would have it, the billowing white sails of the heavily armed British HMS Detroit captained by Commodore Robert Barclay scuds forth and is spotted by Perry's top crew occupying the crow's nest. Perry's experienced flagmen signal two American schooners nearby, the USS Ariel and USS Scorpion, to confront the British warship that is still two miles away.

The Detroit has noticed the USS Niagara stuck on the bar and is pressing toward it.

BOOM! BOOM! Long guns from the American ships blast away, convincing Barclay to turn around without further excitement.

"Well, that was a good sign," says Perry, observing Detroit's actions from the quarterdeck with his helmsman. "Now, let's get the Niagara off the bar and out to sea!"

After extensive hard labor to raise and float over the barrier and to bring aboard the artillery and ammunition from the schooners and sloops, Captain Perry lines up his half-uniformed sailor and marine crew for inspection and expectations.

"I am glad to see the white trousers have come in and you are fitted. The blue or gray shirts and jackets will be issued as soon as we see them delivered.

"I know only perhaps ten of you have much experience at sailing or fighting at sea, so all of you can expect continuous drilling over the next month or less to prepare for a sea battle. Perhaps the biggest battle of your life! As I look around at all of you, I don't care if you are white, black, Indian or even a lumberjack! You are all Americans to me, and your country is counting on you!

"The British must be defeated on the Great Lakes, and it starts right here on Lake Erie! General William Henry Harrison and Green Clay of Kentucky have held at Fort Meigs on the Maumee!

"And in an unbelievable God-fearing miracle, a victory at Fort Stephenson has shifted the British and Indian forces to Amherstburg, Canada!

"The President of the United States, James Madison, has laid on us the unenviable task of stopping one of the most renowned navies on earth. Since perhaps the greatest army on the planet has been defeated twice by the United States of America in two separate wars, the expectations of our victory is substantial!

"Now men, report to your stations, the ship's corporal will be training you extensively! You are dismissed!"

"Captain Perry," says Wayne Pastor, nervously walking up to the commodore after his speech. "I, I just want to thank you for this opportunity you've given my crew friends and I to serve with you."

"Let me know how you feel after we are done on this mission," says the now twenty-seven-year-old Perry. "I have served in the West Indies and the Mediterranean Sea against pirates and a little patrolling off of Africa. This is my first go-around at this level, so let's look sharp, and good luck, W.P.!"

"Yes sir!"

Three hundred sixty-five miles to the southwest along the Mississinewa River, a young five-year-old white girl finds herself living in a Miami Indian village with Chief Silver Heels's family.

"Does she know Algonquin?" asks Maconaquah visiting from Deaf Man's Village.

"Some progress with Spotted Fawn is being made," says Silver Heels, using the girl's new Indian name. "I cannot go play with her and interact like young people, but watch this."

Silver Heels points to the sun, and the little girl dressed in Indian leggings and a deerskin dress reacts, knowing the drill. "Kizis," she says in Algonquin.

Without prompting this time, Spotted Fawn says, "Nibi."

"She is thirsty, Silver Heels," says Maconaquah.

Silver Heels points to a bucket of water and waves her permission to drink.

"You're going to have to talk to her instead of pointing, Chief. She is not a dog. How do you expect her to learn?" instructs Maconaquah.

"Yes, I know, I know," says Silver Heels. "I don't have the patience like I should. The village is slowly returning to normal after the American invasion last winter, and Spotted Fawn has been very helpful since many of the women were taken as prisoners.

"Perhaps you take Spotted Fawn to Deaf Man's Village with you. Your husband needs help, and your daughters, Cut Finger and Yellow Leaf, can help her with transitioning," says Silver Heels in Algonquin.

"Nij animosh," says Spotted Fawn in Algonquin as she spots two dogs running by together.

"Yes, nij animosh," repeats Maconaquah, confirming Spotted Fawn's attempt at the Algonquin language.

"Silver Heels, I think my daughters would enjoy having another sister around. If Deaf Man does not approve, I will sadly bring her back," says the former white captive girl herself, Francis Slocum.

At Fort Amherstburg, General Proctor, Tecumseh and Chief Roundhead consult with Captain Barclay about the next move.

"We appreciate you shipping many of my people and I to this side of the lake into Canada, but we are running low on food," says Tecumseh. "Did we fight so hard for you against the Americans to cross this vast lake and starve to death?"

"Yes, Barclay, my army has gone to half rations. You must get supplies to us," adds Proctor.

"The Americans have ten ships and control the lake," responds Captain Barclay, satisfied to this point with staying up the Detroit River near Amherstburg for protection.

"My informants have been telling me it is a ragtag, motley crew of Americans manning these ten ships. What are you afraid of?" pressures Proctor.

"My navy is afraid of nothing. We will blow them out of the water when the opportunity exists. We just need favorable weather conditions on the lake."

On the south side of Lake Erie, William Henry Harrison follows his marching band past the victorious Fort Stephenson. Hundreds of American military personnel, equipment and camp followers from Franklinton and Urbana flow through Fort Seneca to Fort Stephenson and head for the departure port at the mouth of the Portage River.

"He's not serious," says Colonel Sam Wells to Captain George Croghan.

"It sure sounds like he court-martialed me," says Croghan. "Has he gone mad? Has the pressure of the war gotten to him?"

"To the contrary, Croghan, after the circumstances were explained to him and he heard your quick explanation, I am happy to announce to you that you have been promoted to major. Congratulations, George!" says Wells.

"No disrespect to you, Colonel, but you'd think he could have done that himself."

"The war is moving on, Major, and Harrison is meeting Naval Captain Oliver Perry at the Portage River," says Wells. "The British in this part of the country are on the run. If luck has it, we can finish them off soon. Your victory here is monumental, Major Croghan."

Suddenly distracted, Colonel Wells notices familiar faces, "Dad burn if I don't see E.J. and Running Deer," says Wells, "After you got run out of Fort Meigs, I thought I'd never see you guys again."

"We are looking for our sons, Colonel," says E.J. "Hello, sir, it is nice to see someone who had faith in us and stood up for us at Fort Meigs."

"You don't have to sir me. It is good to see you two again."

"There is no more evidence needed as proof of their loyalty to the United States, Colonel," remarks Croghan. "They were a big reason why we held off the British. They didn't have to stay. There was time for them to leave before the British got here."

"You don't have to convince me, Major Croghan."

"By the way, Colonel Wells, why didn't Harrison send a relief corps to help us out?" asks E.J.

"Other than the fact the general thought he would be outnumbered by the British and Indians, I cannot comment."

E.J. and Running Deer watch as hogs, cattle, packhorses and squeaky oxen-drawn wagons carrying supplies and pulling artillery pass by Fort Stephenson.

"Look at this with Governor Shelby, Running Deer," says E.J., talking over another drum and fife band that is setting the pace.

"You sure that is Kentucky Governor Shelby?" asks Running Deer.

"Heck yeah, no one has as nice a horse as Shelby's thoroughbred," comments E.J. "Actually, on second thought, I think my faithful, animal-companion, appaloosa Thunder, is better," he says loud enough to be heard by passersby.

"Speaking of a faithful companion, looks like that little pig has found one! Ha!" says E.J.

"Ha!" laughs Running Deer for the first time in months.

"What are you doing, Private Smith?" asks Running Deer. "Did the army finally find a job you can handle?"

"I'll have you two yahoos know I am escorting the good luck charm of the governor of the Commonwealth of Kentucky. Porky and I are becoming very good friends, and no one has attempted to turn him into pork chops yet," says Smith, maneuvering the pig with a six-foot show cane and patting his jacket, "at least not as long as I have my flintlock pistol ready! Ha!"

Governor Shelby's 3,000 Kentuckians and camp followers ride and walk by, and then E.J. and Running Deer hear another familiar voice.

"Get on your horses and lead the way, Scouts!" yells the six-foot-three-inch General Simon Kenton ahead of the Ohio militia, advancing to the Portage River, also.

"That's the man, Running Deer," says E.J., "that loaned me his long rifle to save you from a sure roasting along the Maumee."

"Your friend there took the shot, Running Deer, and what a shot it was!" gushes Kenton pulling up.

"You boys need to join us and get out front," says the living legend.

"Not sure Harrison wants us with him," says E.J.

"Ah, Harrison. All he wants are some dead British and to be president someday! Ha!" says Kenton. "Mount up; if William Henry says anything, he'll have to deal with me!"

Hundreds of white wedge and marquee tents making up the camp of Simon Kenton's Ohio militia are set up near Governor Shelby's Kentucky volunteers when a lone rider approaches the now-relaxing Simon Kenton with a message from Shelby.

"Carlisle! What the heck did you get yourself into now?" asks Kenton after receiving and reading the note.

"What's that, Mr. Kenton?"

"Shelby wants you and your horse at his tent pronto. He says be ready to race."

"Race? Dad burn. What did that John Smith say to him?" wonders E.J. aloud.

"It better be good, 'cause Shelby doesn't mess around," says Kenton.

E.J. and, out of curiosity, Running Deer ride into the Kentucky camp containing more wedge tents and camp followers fixing meals, to find Smith, a small pig sitting on Shelby's lap and the governor's bay-colored thoroughbred horse, wearing a sleek, new, lightweight saddle and bridle.

"Private Smith says you said your horse could beat mine!" announces Governor Shelby not so quietly.

"Now I didn't exactly say—"

"Let's put a little wager on this, Carlisle. You did say it was Carlisle, didn't you, Private?"

"Yes sir, I did, Governor, the one and only E.J. Carlisle," grins Smith.

"Smitty, you dad-burned liar. I didn't say my horse could beat the governor's."

"Sounds like you might be chicken, Mr. Carlisle!" says the governor out loud so that many of the Kentuckians camped around could hear him.

"My horse against E.J. Carlisle's Appaloosa, straight up. See my aide-de-camp if you want in, boys!"

"Yeah! Yeah, count me in, Governor!" yell several Kentuckians, gathering around and waving bills.

"You against me on our horses, Governor?" asks E.J. over the betting voices. "How far we gonna race?"

"Half mile, and I ain't gonna ride. I'm too old. Private Smith is my jockey."

"What, Governor? Me?" asks Smith, removing his shako hat and not grinning anymore.

Bettors look over at the gangly Smith and start yelling again.

"I wanna change my bet!"

"I'm changing mine also, and I want odds!"

E.J. leans over to Running Deer and says, "You're riding for me."

"What? Don't pull me into this, E.J.," whispers Running Deer in return.

"You'll do great, and we can make a killing on this. That Smitty boy doesn't know anything about riding and look how big he is."

"I don't know, E.J."

"I'm changing riders, also," says E.J. to Governor Shelby. "The Indian, here, is riding for me!"

"I'm changing my bet!" calls out another Kentuckian.

"Me too. I based my first bet on the Hoosier riding!" says another.

"He ain't no Hoosier," yells Smith. "He's from Pennsylvania!"

"Settle down now, boys. The bets are final except for Carlisle and I," says the governor. "What you say, E.J.?"

"My horse for yours," says E.J.

"What?" says Running Deer. "You can't lose Thunder!"

"I know it. That's why you're gonna win," says E.J.

"All right," says the governor. "I don't own many Appaloosas."

Governor Shelby sends out two officers to stand next to two trees a hundred yards apart and several hundred yards in the distance.

"Alright you riders, we've got a nice meadow here. You will head for the tree on the right, go around on the right, turn left and head for the other tree, then turn left after you round it and head back, crossing a line between Carlisle and me that I'm drawing with my sword! Get away back there. They's gonna be ridin' in hot!"

"Good luck, Running Deer," says E.J.

"I'll tell ya what, Carlisle, since your horse is somewhat smaller, I'll spot ya fifty yards."

"No, no Governor!" yell bettors. "I want my money back!"

With no argument from E.J., the horses and riders take their mark as Shelby raises his model 1805 flintlock pistol for the start.

"I hope you know what you're doing," says Private Smith to Shelby, sitting awkwardly in the saddle.

"Ready!"

BAM!!

The horses take off, and the white-coated, black-spotted Appaloosa bolts far ahead with his noted short-distance sprint ability. Smitty, swatting the thoroughbred lightly with his riding crop, is beginning to gain as they make the first turn.

Thunder cuts quickly around the tree and heads for the second. Running Deer's long hair blazes behind him, contrasting with Thunder's shorter mane.

After the second turn and heading to the finish, the governor's horse noses even with the tiring Thunder. With 200 yards to go, it's the thoroughbred with the lead, then Thunder with a heel kick from Running Deer, then Smith's swat takes him into the lead. With twenty yards to go, they are even when Running Deer gives another heel kick, and at the finish, Thunder is declared the winner by a nose.

Dozens of Kentuckians yell and whoop and roll on the ground in laughter or anger, depending on their wager.

"Wooo-ha!" yells an exhausted but relieved E.J., as Running Deer returns with Thunder.

"Don't you ever do that to me again, E.J.," says a smiling Running Deer.

"Here you go, Carlisle. I'm a man of my word," says Shelby, handing him the reins from Smith.

"Sorry, Governor," says Smitty.

"Aw, that's ok. It was a great race. Shoulda never given him a head start," winks the governor at E.J., helping Smith down off his mount.

Chapter 22

September 1813 — Ohio/Lake Erie/Indiana Territory

Captain Perry and General Harrison exit the latter's marquee tent. They stop to take a long look at the South Bass Island barely visible that day in Lake Erie. Parting from each other, the feuding continues with a parting shot. "Get it done, Captain!" says Harrison.

Perry's success at stopping the British supply route from the east to the western half of Lake Erie and making the British Army and Royal Navy relocate near Amherstburg along the Detroit River is still not satisfactory to Harrison.

Ticked off, Perry turns and follows Harrison a few steps, "I have a third of my crew down with dysentery and do not deem them ready to attack, General, unless given permission from my surgeons," says Perry.

"I hate to think you are afraid, Commodore, but we need to strike when the opportunity is nigh," responds Harrison.

"I will check on my crew and then the weather conditions in the morning," says Perry. "Meanwhile, the USS Ohio will be sent to Erie for more supplies."

"That still gives you nine ships with which to enter the Detroit River and attack the British, Captain!" says Harrison.

"My fleet and I will prepare but bide our time until dawn, General."

That evening, Perry returns to his flagship, the USS Lawrence, after another meeting, this time with his eight ship captains in a marquee tent on the South Bass Island.

Climbing up the rope net and swinging his leg over the railing he looks around and begins, "Look sharp, boys! Prepare for battle tomorrow!" he yells. Unfurling a dark blue flag with white lettering that says, "Don't Give Up the Ship," Perry explains the significance of the statement while having the symbolic flag raised under the eighteen-star American flag.

"The name of the ship you are sailing, the USS Lawrence, is in memory of a heroic friend of mine, Captain James Lawrence! He lost his life earlier this summer in a sea battle with the British thirty miles out from Boston! Mortally wounded and with his final, dying breath, Lawrence gave his last order, 'Don't give up the ship!'

"Now boys, think of our purpose, our assignments, our country, and rest well tonight! Be ready to go in the morning!"

W.P. gathers his marines together for a last word with them. "I've never been in a naval battle before, but Perry makes it sound like it's gonna happen tomorrow. You Indians," asks Wayne Pastor as Ahinga translates for him, "are you ready to load and hand those muskets and rifles up to Ahinga and me on the ship mast nets?"

Five Seneca, Erie and Wyandot braves now turned American allies shake their head affirmatively.

"Good. Make Chiefs Cornstalk, Tarhe and the Great Manitou proud of you."

"How 'bout you lumberjacks? You'll be manning a carronade when we get in close to the British warships. Your side of the ship, remember, is the starboard side. The right side, Max and Buford. You got it? You'll be below deck. The boatswain mates are not allowed to let you up once we are on our way. You know your tasks. Keep firing away and listen for commands."

The two shake their heads nervously, contemplating the next day.

The next morning is September 10th, and if the crew of the flagship Lawrence isn't already awake, it will be now as the barrelman in the crow's nest yells, "There they are, Captain, the British to our northwest coming out of the Detroit River! Looks like six warships heading this way."

"Look alive, boys. Follow the tacking Ariel and Scorpion, coxswain!" yells Perry. "The British have the weather in their favor,

Lieutenant," comments Perry looking up at the American and battle flags.

The Lawrence is followed by the USS Caledonia, Niagara, Somers, Porcupine, Tigress and Trippe. Each boat captain follows the preplanned order and awaits flag signals for anything different.

The British schooner HMS Chippawa leads the fleet of six warships bearing down with favorable winds toward the USS Lawrence. Next in line for the British are the Detroit and it's seventeen long guns and two carronades, the Hunter with eight long guns and two carronades, followed by the Queen Charlotte armed with three long and two carronades, and the Lady Provost with three long and ten powerful carronades. The Little Belt containing two long guns brings up the rear.

Perry signals his fleet to match up according to size estimated by their naval training and experience. Tacking and maneuvering by the U.S. force into the breeze and the three-foot green waves of Lake Erie proves a challenge.

W.P. and Andrew are already holding their muskets and preparing to climb the ship mast nets to fire down on the British decks.

Almost two hours after first sighting each other, the HMS Detroit, under the command of Barclay, discharges first with a long gun, but the cannonball falls short, creating a large splash and stern warning to the Americans that a battle is looming.

Suddenly and amazingly, the wind shifts from southwest to southeast, now favoring Perry's fleet and slowing the British to almost a standstill.

"We've got the weather, gentlemen!" yells Perry excitedly. "Signal the fleet, boatswain, we are heading for the Detroit. Lieutenant, have the others match up! The Niagara should be following us!

"Coxswain, take us to the Detroit! Boatswain, set the sails and rigging! To your battle stations! Sand the deck, Corporal!"

Blazing away with long guns as the Lawrence approaches the Detroit, Perry holds his eighteen carronades for close fire.

BOOM! BOOM! BOOM! BOOM!

The Lawrence is joined by the Scorpion and Ariel, taking on the Chippawa as well as the Detroit. The Caledonia and Somers take on the HMS Hunter and Queen Charlotte as the Tigress and Trippe try to get organized with the Porcupine and head for wherever they are needed. Unexplainably, the American ship Niagara holds back a third of a mile away.

Wayne Pastor and Ahinga climb up the ship mast nets carrying their loaded muskets strapped over their right shoulders. The Indian marines follow the sharpshooters, spacing themselves partway up to hand loaded guns and pass down spent ones.

Across from W.P.'s boys are another team of U.S. Marines climbing up with the same purpose.

Attempting to get inside the long gun range of the British to take advantage of his carronades, Perry directs the Lawrence while taking hits and casualties.

"Where's the Niagara?" questions W.P. above the thundering cannons.

"I don't know!" yells Andrew from just below him.

"The Niagara should be here to take on one of these Brit ships!"

Both the Detroit and the Queen Charlotte slam away at the mid-deck water level area of the Lawrence, with shells, shrapnel and resultant splinters of wood flying everywhere.

"We lost our Indian help!" says Andrew. "We gotta go down, W.P.!"

"I've got one more shot, Andrew," says W.P. as he watches a fellow marine sharpshooter fall from his netting to the deck below.

"Dad burn! I see who got him," says the hatless blue-jacketed Wayne Pastor, aiming at a Brit at the top of the Queen Charlotte.

Bam! cracks Carlisle's rifle, and he watches the enemy sharpshooter fall to the wood deck fifty feet below.

"All right, get down, Ahinga. I'm following you!"

The Lawrence's deck is covered with dead and dying Americans as British carronades blast ball-and-chain-like shrapnel from the HMS

Detroit, ripping into the masts above W.P. Rigging topples over, just missing him and Andrew, crashing down on the decking below.

"I need help!" pleads Max, the bloody former lumberjack as he climbs up through an unguarded hatch from below deck.

"We'll get you a surgeon, Max!" says W.P., the now descended American sharpshooter trying to gain his balance on the blood-soaked, sandy deck.

The ship sways, and Max, unable to sustain his balance, is thrown against a side railing and overboard, splashing into Lake Erie too injured to swim.

"Lieutenant Yarnell, take over the ship!" says Perry, ironically lowering his "Don't Give Up the Ship" flag.

"Yes sir!" answers the injured first lieutenant.

Grabbing Wayne Pastor and Ahinga, Perry says, "Come on, boys! We are heading for the Niagara. Help Cyrus and I lower this longboat!"

"Yes sir," says Wayne Pastor, as all four miraculously are missed by shrapnel and musket balls flying about.

"Row hard, boys!" says Perry, proudly standing and pointing toward the Niagara as cannonballs and musket fire from the English splash harmlessly around them during their one-third-mile sculling.

On the British warship HMS Detroit, the one-armed Commander Barclay, who is injured in his good, right arm, jubilantly yells from the quarterdeck, "They are retreating! The commander of the Lawrence is boating away, and the Lawrence's flag is being lowered! Dad burn if we didn't beat 'em!"

"Commander!" states a boatswain, viewing flag signals. "The Queen Charlotte informs us that their Captain Finnis has died from wounds, and a junior officer is taking over."

"Tell 'em to stay away from us, boatswain."

"Flagman, you heard the commander!"

"More bad news, Mr. Barclay," chimes back the boatswain. "Captain James Garden, because of injuries, has turned his command over to a junior officer."

"Commander!" yells a voice from the crow's nest. "The Americans in the Niagara have set sail for us!"

"No, it can't be!" replies Barclay.

Struggling to hold his spyglass still, Barclay eyes the USS Niagara, now with Perry taking command from Elliot, bearing down with long gun cannons hurling twenty-four-pound balls.

BOOM! BOOM! BOOM!

Direct hits on the Queen Charlotte's quarterdeck forces it out of control, and it slams into Barclay's Detroit.

"Get us away from the Charlotte, Quartermaster!" yells Barclay. "Return fire, Lieutenant!"

BOOM! BOOM!

Sliding between the two largest British warships, the Niagara's helmsman maneuvers with port and starboard carronades spraying shrapnel and eighteen-pound cannonballs into the British sides and across the deck of both ships, wreaking havoc above and below.

Having climbed the mast nets of the Niagara, W.P. takes aim with a fresh group of marines. "I have a good shot at the Detroit quartermaster, Ahinga," says W.P. "Watch the guy in the black bicorne on their quarterdeck steering the ship."

Wayne Pastor, wasting too much time, receives a musket ball from a British sharpshooter topsman. It nicks and whizzes past his right ear.

"Dad burn, I've felt that before," remarks W.P., remembering his siege of Fort Wayne close call. Repositioning himself while blood from his ear trickles down on his right shoulder, W.P. aims his 1795 Springfield at the quartermaster and fires.

BAM!

Then W.P. grabs a loaded Harpers Ferry 1803 rifle from Andrew and fires at the British topsman.

BAM!

Watching the Brit tumble sixty feet to the deck below, W.P. hears Ahinga exclaim, "You got their helmsman below in the leg, W.P., and the British are lowering their flags!"

"Cease fire, men!" orders a shouting master-at-arms, obeying Perry's command.

All six Union Jacks of the British ships are lowered.

Some cheers are heard, but thoughts are with over 250 combined British and American casualties either lying on ship decks, below deck or floating in Lake Erie.

"Master-at-arms, I'm going to give you a message that I want delivered to General Harrison at Fort Seneca as soon as possible. It reads," Perry says as he scrawls the words, "'Sir, we have met the enemy and they are ours, two ships, two brigs, one schooner and one sloop, O.H. Perry.'"

210 miles to the southwest in the Indiana Territory, a young American girl plays happily with Indian friends, thirteen-year-old Cut Finger and four-year-old Yellow Leaf, the daughters of Maconaquah.

"Since we have lost two sons at an early age, my husband," says Maconaquah through sign language, "I thought having and raising another child would be helpful to you and our daughters. I love the laughter the young bring us."

"I still mourn the loss of our two sons at an extremely young age," says Shepocanah. "I fear I am too old to give you another child, Maconaquah, so I cannot turn away this gift from the Great Manitou."

"Her language is still a barrier," says Maconaquah, "but our two daughters are helpful in that regard," concludes the signing wife and mother.

"Look who we have here?" says an Algonquin-speaking, tin-capped white man pulling along a haggard old mare with saddlebags.

"Wolf!" says the traveler calling back his other animal companion. "You 're ok, he's just curious. He won't harm you folks."

"Johnny Chapman! Welcome back, says Maconaquah smiling. "It has been a while since we have seen you."

"Where have you been for so long?" signs Deaf Man, grinning.

"Not too sure about my signing, Maconaquah."

"He wants to know where you have been," speaks Maconaquah in her language.

"Well, my fine Indian couple, I've been visiting relatives in southern Ohio, watching armed troops marching by to the north and staying out of harm's way."

"War has come to our river valley, Johnny," says Maconaquah.

"That's what I heard and saw as I passed through Silver Heels's village back upstream. Do you think it is over?"

"Don't know," signs Deaf Man, allowing Maconaquah to interpret. "News does not travel fast to our village, and that's the way our traders, trappers, and people like it. No one is excluded along our river unless they come for trouble."

"No trouble here," says Chapman. "In fact, I bring some corn and apple seed with me for you. Figured the Americans left a food problem with your people."

"Thank you, yes they did," signs and says Maconaquah.

"Looks like you have a new addition to your family. Ha!" says Chapman. "They sure grow fast around here. Last time I was here, you had two daughters. Unless that's a neighbor girl I haven't seen, looks as if you sprouted one."

"Spotted Fawn! Spotted Fawn!" calls Maconaquah in Algonquin twice. "Come and meet our friend, Johnny Appleseed!"

Spotted Fawn's eyes light up, and a smile forms as she, without hesitation, approaches and hugs the wolf, glances at the horse and walks up to Chapman wearing her Indian leggings and dress.

"She acts like she knows you, Johnny," says Maconaquah. "That's the least shy she has been since I have known her."

"All kids seem to," begins Chapman in English, then switches to Algonquin. "All kids seem to take to me and my stories."

"Mr. Chapman, I'm Hannah May. Hannah May Carlisle," says the white girl in English.

Chapter 23

September–October 1813   Ohio/Lake Erie/Canada/Detroit

On a brisk sunny day, a small American schooner bobs in western Lake Erie. Sailing south toward the Ohio shoreline a few days after the Americans' great victory in the Battle of Lake Erie, Oliver Perry and General Harrison discuss what's next.

"Well, we have seen Detroit and Canada from this ship but I want you to see something else, General Harrison," says Perry. "See that little island to the left?" asks Perry as he points.

"Yes, Commander," answers Harrison while checking with his spyglass. "What about it?"

"It's only about eight acres in size, but that island will have to be a last jumping-off point before we land our forces in Canada. It's called Little Sister Island. It is about twelve miles from South Bass Island."

"Yes, and South Bass Island is how far from the Portage River port?"

"Fifteen miles or so," says Perry.

"We have accumulated what, about sixteen British and American ships and schooners but still not enough room on those vessels for five thousand men and their horses?" asks Harrison.

"I figure we can't take the horses with us."

"Well, I don't like that, and it won't make the men happy," says Harrison.

"No choice," says Perry. "Besides that, some of our militia volunteers will have to travel by longboat and row across. That's why the island hopping," explains Perry.

"Dad burn, man! Is that safe?" asks Harrison. "This isn't the Ohio or Maumee River! That's open water! Are we sure the British navy on Lake Erie has been subdued?"

"The weather this time of year is conducible, not that a rare storm couldn't occur. Let's put the non-swimmers on the larger crafts just in case."

"You're assuming I'm gonna approve of this venture," says Harrison.

"The British, according to that American spy we pulled on board back there, are planning a retreat to the east as we speak, General. This is the fastest way to Canada. Furthermore, spies near the Niagara River say there is no current British threat heading this way and we have the Detroit River blockaded."

"I'm convinced," says Harrison. "As soon as we get back to the Portage River, I need to get a message off to Colonel Johnson and his brother James to take the land route from Fort Meigs past Frenchtown to Detroit. His 500 cavalrymen can bring extra horses with them, and we'll ferry the whole lot of them across the Detroit River to Canada."

"I thought Johnson was in Fort Wayne?" asks Perry.

"Naw. He delivered supplies from there to Fort Winchester and Fort Meigs and, last I heard, is sitting around anxious for orders. Oh, that Kentucky Colonel Richard Johnson destroyed some hostile Indian villages up in Michigan but will be happy to finally get into some serious action," says Harrison.

"Won't the British at Detroit have something to say about Johnson just waltzing in and ferrying across?" asks Perry.

"Commander Perry, with Richard M. Johnson and his boys passing Frenchtown and the remains of the massacre that took place there, the battle cry, 'Remember the Raisin,' will be ringing in their ears, and the British at Detroit will feel the wrath of the whole state of Kentucky bearing down on them!"

At Fort Amherstburg, Canada, General Henry Proctor faces the scrutiny of Tecumseh and Wyandot Chief Roundhead once again.

"If we had more British artillery and troops at Fort Stephenson, that supply line would have been shut off," says Tecumseh.

"Yes, I know. But with that little fort and your couple thousand warriors with us, the victory should have taken place anyway," retorts Proctor.

"Besides what Tecumseh says," adds Roundhead through interpreters, "a foothold attained in northern Ohio would have carried us to victory over the state of Ohio and the entire Northwest Territory!"

"Where were your warriors when my grenadiers attacked both sides of the fort and suffered death and injuries?" counters Proctor.

"Where were the ladders and axes to scale and chop our way into the fort?" asks the frustrated Tecumseh, countering back.

"Another poorly planned battle strategy, and then add the defeat of Commander Barclay and his mighty British fleet, and we have a problem," states Tecumseh, realizing a portion of his Indian coalition dislikes the developing circumstances and are going home.

"Don't tell me the coalition you formed has taken most of the casualties. Walk around, Chief. The Crown and it's young countrymen have sacrificed and suffered also."

"We have many warriors scattered in the forests around Fort Lernoult at Detroit and around Amherstburg. The Americans will suffer greatly if they invade us."

"I have a little over six hundred troops. At one time, you had as many as five thousand warriors at this location. My spies tell me they have that many Americans ready to move this way," informs Proctor.

"You are not telling me—"

"Yes, Chiefs," says Proctor, interrupting and pointing to a map, "our only option is to burn the forts, gather as much food as we can, and make our way to British reinforcements by land back east to Queenston Heights at Lake Ontario."

Two hundred thirty-six miles to the southwest along the Mississinewa River, John Chapman escorts a little American girl, Spotted Fawn, with his horse loaded with bagged apple seeds. The ever-alert, constant wolf companion leads them to the Mississineway Indian village on the Wabash River.

"You have been talking nonstop, Hannah May, about your where-a-bouts and the adventure you have been on. You make it sound like you are not sure you want to return to your family," says Chapman.

"Oh, Mr. Appleseed, I do miss my mother and father and brothers, but living among the Indians and learning their way is so peaceful. I never saw the war the Indians talked about when I could understand their language. But I saw the sorrow the American army brought when that happened," says Hannah May.

"The sorrow that war brings, sadly, has been felt on both sides," says Chapman. "By jiminy, we are almost there. Maconaquah and her family are waiting for us. To finish, Hannah May, God wants us all to live in peace and love on the earth that he created."

"Thank you, Johnny Chapman, for bringing Spotted Fawn here as you promised," speaks Maconaquah. "The canoe ride was swift, and we have been visiting with Morning Bird."

Kekionga friend Morning Bird advances from behind the family and gets a glimpse of Hannah May for the first time in over a year, knowing instantly despite the girl's Indian clothing that she belongs to Charlotte and E.J. Carlisle of Fort Wayne.

The six-year-old thinks Morning Bird looks and sounds familiar, and it jars her memory as she hugs her family's friend, Morning Bird, in return.

"It is good to see you are well and have been taken care of by my people," says Morning Bird in broken English that she hasn't used in some time.

"Well, Chief Deaf Man," says Chapman, "I know your customs well. I assume her return to her American family is not automatic."

"You are right, Mr. Chapman," signs Chief Deaf Man. "This girl has been given to Maconaquah and I and belongs to the Miami. Without a trade or equal compensation, she stays here for now. The tribal council will meet and decide the outcome."

Back at the Portage River mouth at Lake Erie, sixteen schooners and over seventy longboats are aligned to take over 5,000 Americans and American allied Indians island-hopping across Lake Erie to Detroit and Amherstburg, Ontario, to pursue General Proctor and the Tecumseh warriors.

"You can't take that pig on the ship, Smitty!" exclaims E.J., waiting with Running Deer, Kenton and hundreds of others to board.

"Hey, you tell Governor Shelby that."

"If horses can't go, neither can a pig. Besides, he will probably end up bein' barbecued on a spit," jokes E.J.

"The pig, according to Shelby, will probably try swimming across the lake to stay up with us, E.J. Your horse may have won that race, but you're not winning this argument. Porky is going with us by boat!"

"There are always speeches, E.J.," says Running Deer.

"Yeah, but you may like this one," says E.J., watching the seventy-two-year-old, six-foot-four-inch-tall Wyandot Chief Tarhe step forward in front of slouched, coon-skinned and shako-hatted Americans holding their muskets and rifles of choice by their sides. "It's one of yours."

In broken English, the old war chief begins. "I want to thank your General Harrison for inviting my two hundred warriors to join you in the defeat of our former father from across the great sea!"

"Let the victory be swift and ours!"

"AHAYAYA! HAYAA!" yells Tarhe in his chilling war cry that is mimicked by his war party, also pounding drums. The cry echoes across the small bay and is heard by ship members, including Wayne Pastor and Ahinga on the USS Niagara.

With a wave of Tarhe's arm, the warriors quiet. The appreciative Kentuckians and Ohioans, cheering the fact they are being helped by the war cry instead of fighting it, finally quiet.

A young Reverend Isaac McCoy steps up to speak in front of Harrison and begins to speak authoritatively.

"Oh! You cheer them now about fighting with you, but how many of you offer your whiskey and rum to these poor, first-nation aborigines? Take advantage of them in your pursuits of land and greed? God sees your sins and assures us that if you don't repent, eternal hell awaits you!"

"Thank you, Reverend, for your message," says Harrison, annoyingly stepping in to move things forward.

"Men!" begins William Henry Harrison. "Before we depart for a foreign nation that lies across the Great Lake that spans before us, I just want to thank the volunteers from Kentucky, Indiana and Ohio as well as the federal troops assembled. I urge you to remember, we are the sires of the Revolutionary War, and to fight as our forefathers did for freedom! Finally, I will leave you with this before we depart, 'Remember the Raisin!'"

YEAH! YEAH! BUM! BUM! BUM! BUM!

Thunderous cheers, pounding of Indian drums and the blaring of brass horns from the army musicians are heard all the way to the occupants of their first destination, South Bass Island.

One minute goes by until Harrison steps forward to wave his arm. Music and drums stop as the task at hand becomes a reality.

"Before we load up, check with your officers on where your horse will be located when you return! Now a prayer from Reverend Matthew Wallace of Cincinnati!"

"Yeah! You tell us, Reverend!" yells a southern Ohio citizen.

"Remove your hats, please! Father in heaven, we gather here in your presence, understanding that some of the gentlemen before you going into battle will not be coming back," Wallace pauses as the crowd hushes. "That their life on earth may end in combat or by accident. Father, remind the folks before me that life on earth does not have to be the end! That eternal life with You can be simply achieved! All they have to do is confess their sins to You! Ask for forgiveness from You! And sincerely in their heart accept Jesus as their Lord and savior!

"Let me read to you Ephesians 2:8: 'For by grace you have been saved through faith. And this is not your own doing; it is the gift of God!' Amen!"

AMEN! repeat the men and women saying goodbye.

A few days later the American ships are spotted. "There they are!" nods and points Colonel Richard Mentor Johnson, a future vice president of the United States, to his brother James.

"What? Those ships out there?" asks James as he and his brother lead 500 cavalrymen past Frenchtown for Detroit.

"We'll kind of shadow them along the Detroit River," says Richard, who briefly a few miles back stopped and paid homage to the fallen at the River Raisin. "I'd say from what the spies told us, Fort Lernoult is about thirty miles away."

Close to a hundred longboats and a couple schooners with artillery land on the southern shore of Canada with no resistance. The Americans are fortunate to have crossed the forty-five miles of Lake Erie and reached the shore with no incidences.

"All right, let's form up," orders Simon Kenton to his Ohio volunteers.

"E.J. and Running Deer, this old map shows the king's town of Amherstburg straight north five kilometers from here. That's three miles. Sorry we don't have horses for you, but take whomever you want and scout what we may see."

"Yes sir, General. By the way, that boat ride reminds me. Didn't I see you along the Ohio River about twenty years ago at a place called Maysville, Kentucky?" asks E.J.

"Dad burn, I knew I'd seen you before. You were with some pretty gal waiting for a flatboat or something."

"Ha! That pretty gal became my wife, and we settled in a place called Fort Wayne."

"Yeah, I've been there. A place by the portage and Indian village named Kekionga. Oh, that was a rough place at one time," says Kenton.

"Yep, that's it," says E.J. with a slight wave, walking the trail north with Running Deer heading for the enemy compound.

Farther up the Detroit River, Harrison and Perry dock their ships at Detroit and are greeted by mostly friendly citizens explaining in a hard-to-understand French language that the British had vacated Fort Lernoult, ferried the river and were last seen heading north toward the Thames River mouth by horseback and bateaux.

"We put the fires out and were able to save most of the fort, sir," says Colonel Richard Johnson to the just sailed in General Harrison, at the river docks of Detroit.

"We will leave General McArthur with a brigade of his troops at Fort Lernoult, give it to Lewis Cass to command. Then ferry your cavalry on horseback and artillery across the river and follow those scoundrels," orders Harrison. "By the way, Governor Shelby, we need to change the name of that fort from Lernoult to Shelby."

"Whoa, that'd be an honor."

"Tecumseh, I have a feeling the Americans will not follow us past Sandwich," says General Proctor. "Let's rest and follow the Thames River easterly tomorrow."

"As usual, I don't trust your instincts," responds Tecumseh. "The Harrison I know smells blood and will be following us. You better be ready to deliver the American blood, Proctor."

"I say fight them here," says Roundhead.

"I smell smoke," says E.J. "Cooking fire?"

"No, logs of a fort," analyzes Running Deer instinctively.

Breaking through an opening of a forest surrounding Fort Amherstburg, the scouts witness the king's soldiers finishing off setting the British fortress ablaze and riding off.

Before E.J. can say anything about putting the fire out, warriors of Chief Tarhe, anxious for action, take off running toward the escaping English. The British, having seen the Wyandots' fast approach, give a spur to the side of their horses and ride northerly through the forest trails.

"We can save it, Running Deer," says E.J. "Let's form a bucket brigade and put it out."

Arriving an hour later at Fort Amherstburg, Simon Kenton assigns troops to stay and protect the smoldering fort and artillery that will be left behind by Americans to fortify a repaired and future Fort Malden.

"Let's go, boys," orders Kenton. "We are heading to the town port. I was told a couple American schooners will be there. The schooner captains will take us and a portion of our force up the river to Perry and Harrison."

"Not much daylight left, Mr. Kenton, and I don't want to be left out here with British sympathizers around. Could be trouble," suggests E.J.

"I agree. Let's find the boats and get up to Detroit at least," says the frontiersman general striding westerly toward the Detroit River.

The next day, British spies report to Proctor that Tecumseh was right. The Americans are closing in from south to north toward the town of Sandwich at the Thames River.

"Break camp! Let's get out of here, Tecumseh! The Americans are approaching," says an anxious Proctor. "The bateaux can get us far up the Thames, where the Americans' large ships cannot sail or be oared."

"What are you, General Proctor, an animal with your cowering tail between your legs? Fight here and have some respect for yourself and our cause. You have some artillery and guns but very little food," says Tecumseh.

"How far do you think we will get, General?" asks Roundhead. "We are already on half rations."

"Roundhead is right, Proctor. Starve or fight, choose your poison," options Tecumseh.

"Just a ways up the Thames. There is a chance we can live to fight another day. The Americans have five thousand soldiers and warriors with them. Another day, we will have the advantage," urges Proctor.

"Our combined twelve hundred do not have a chance without favorable ground."

"Well, at least we can find that and make a stand!" agrees Tecumseh.

Just arriving at Fort Lernoult at Detroit in Michigan Territory, Running Deer's son, Red Hawk, expects to see British soldiers standing guard, but instead, a thousand Americans under Generals Duncan McArthur and Lewis Cass have taken over.

Watching Americans repairing the damage the British did before abandoning it, Red Hawk disappointedly speaks to Ottawa and Miami warriors resigned to the same conclusion.

"The British are no more?" asks Red Hawk in Algonquin.

"They left after setting the fort on fire," answers a Miami warrior from the Indiana Territory.

"Tecumseh?"

"He is with the British leading a small force that is loyal to him," informs the Ottawa warrior.

"I am loyal," says Red Hawk.

"Go ahead, follow him. He and the coward Proctor have traveled north to the Thames River, which they will follow northeasterly. Go give your life for him," says the Miami warrior.

"Why were you late getting here to join the coalition?" asks the Ottawan.

"I missed the British boat from Fort Stephenson. I was in Ohio and Indiana interrupting supply lines of the Americans."

"Too bad. Many of the warriors here will have nothing to do with the unreliable, arrogant, selfish British. We see no other option. Chief Tarhe thinks joining Americans is best."

Red Hawk nods, turns around and leads his horse back the way he came, disillusioned.

Chapter 24

October 1813 — Ontario, Canada/Kekionga

Following the British and Indians up the Thames River in Canada the Americans have a problem. "The schooners need to be unloaded. We can't go any farther without running aground," informs Commodore Perry. "I also request permission, General Harrison, to follow along with you. We can place guards here to stay with the ships."

"Of course, Commodore, but you may have to walk. The horse shortage is catching up with us," says Harrison.

Governor Isaac Shelby follows the two down the gang plank.

"Governor Shelby, if you don't mind, sir, we have a pony available for you to ride."

"That's ok, Harrison. I'm not too proud to ride a pony. Better than walking, at my age. Ha!" says Shelby.

"Oink, oink, oink," squeals the governor's pig as Private John Smith prevents him from jumping over the schooner's railing.

"Porky wants to join ya, Governor!" yells Smith.

"Let him down the gang plank, Private. He can follow us. That pig won't have it any other way!" exclaims Shelby.

"Dad burn, Governor," says Harrison. "I thought you were saving him for breakfast and lunch! Ha!"

"You know, Governor, that pig's not eligible to vote. Ha!" adds Perry.

"He's our good luck charm, gentlemen," says Shelby, settling in on his pony. "He'll follow us and maybe even lead the way. He's pretty smart. Ha!"

"Strap a gun on him, Governor!" shouts a good-natured aide-de-camp. "He may capture Tecumseh himself! Ha!"

Perry and Harrison just shake their heads at the sight and dismiss the fact that Simon Kenton, E.J., Running Deer and the bayonet-gunned Ohio volunteers are swiftly passing by in the Proctor pursuit.

"Get the artillery unloaded and hook 'em up to the workhorses! Move them forward. We can't let the scoundrels get away!" grovels Harrison.

A couple of hours later, Colonel Richard Johnson rides in with seven captured British and Indian coalitionists for the commanders to interrogate.

"Caught 'em red-handed destroying bridges so we can't cross the Thames, General."

"No questions necessary. Hang 'em!" shouts Harrison.

"You heard 'im, men!" says Johnson, grabbing rope off the artillery wagon. "We can pro'bly do three at a time at that large tree branch over there. Loan us your horses, you three cavalrymen."

"Now you know we can't do that, General," says Perry.

"Why? Wayne would!"

"We're not Anthony Wayne. And after what we told the Indians about massacring the enemy—"

"Hold up, Colonel Johnson," says Harrison. "Keep 'em tied, but bring them over here."

"I know, I know. I'm just trying to scare 'em so they talk more, Commodore," says Harrison.

"The prisoners told me earlier the British and Indians are now on the north side of the Thames and moving toward a place called Moraviantown," says Johnson. "Figure we can cross to the other side if we put the foot soldiers on the back of my cavalrymen and ride double."

"Sounds like an excellent idea, Colonel Johnson. Where can we cross that is shallow enough?" asks Harrison.

"Place called Arnold's Mill just up ahead. The men are backed up, sir, waiting for permission to cross."

"Heck yeah, get 'em across, dad burnit!" barks Harrison.

Two miles west of Moraviantown, British rear guard spies trailing Proctor and Tecumseh report the Americans closing in.

"We have to set a trap, an ambush," says Proctor. "Tecumseh, it looks like you and Roundhead are going to get your wish. This swampy area on our left appears like a good defensive position."

"Let's do it, Proctor. Enough of this turkey flight! Choose the ground that is best for your regulars, and my warriors will adjust to defeat the Americans."

"Ok, see that smaller swamp in the middle of the partially forested ground? My troops will man both sides so it splits up the American attack from this road. The Americans have the river on their right and will have to confront us in the boggy area."

"Yes, the marsh to the left that is forested should provide the best protection for Roundhead and my warriors," says Tecumseh, with the Wyandot chief nodding affirmatively.

"Bring them on!" says Roundhead in Algonquin.

On the Americans come, but with scouts E.J., Running Deer and Simon Kenton using information gathered from rare sympathetic villagers, they lead the way forward.

With horses tied to tree branches a half mile back, the three scouts stay in the forest as they parallel the road that travels to and from Detroit.

"Come on," says Kenton, "stay up with me. Stay low through this marsh up ahead. We'll get as close as we can to spy their strength."

"Lead the way, Mr. Kenton. Never thought I'd see a General doin' the scouting also." whispers E.J.

"Crap, those militia boys have enough officers leading the way, they won't miss me for awhile."

"Running Deer, steer to the left," says E.J. "I hear warriors over there. See what you can see."

High-growing marsh grass makes it hard for anything to be seen, but a low voice is heard, "I see a skunk in my way," whispers Running Deer, "and he won't move."

"Oh, geez," says E.J.

"Oh, he got me," says Kenton instead of Running Deer.

"Skunk?" asks E.J.

"I wish," says Kenton softly, "Timber rattler. Here, have a look," he says as he tosses the headless snake he whacked toward E.J.

"That's a northern water snake. That ain't no rattler."

"Never mind," jokes Kenton.

"Geez, Mr. Kenton, let's head back."

"Just a little farther, boys. I think I have a gage on an ambush," says Simon.

Twenty minutes later, Colonel Richard Johnson and his brother James ride up to where the three scouts left their horses. Recognizing the rides of the trio searching ahead, they dismount and follow, encountering the returning scouts ten minutes later. While Kenton holds his rag-covered painful snake-bitten wrist, E.J. and Running Deer explain the Indian and British situation ahead while walking back to the horses.

Commanders Harrison, Perry and Shelby show up and listen to Johnson's plan of sending in twenty volunteers on horseback to draw fire, and then as the enemy is reloading, the several hundred volunteers and infantry that have creeped in close will attack full force.

"It's an old trick that's been used successfully many times," says Harrison. "Those brave boys going in first to draw the fire will deserve a medal."

"We can arrange that," says Shelby as a squirmy Porky wants in on the action. "Keep the pig back, dad burnit, Smitty."

On the British front line, the weary and hungry British soldiers listen for commands.

"Here they come!" yells Proctor to his British regulars while observing twenty Kentuckians galloping toward the British and Indians on both sides of the swamp.

"Don't fire!" yells Tecumseh. "It's a trick!"

BAM! BAM! Bam! B-bam-BAM!

Ignoring Tecumseh's warning, or thinking he said to fire, the British and some Indians discharge their guns, bringing down fourteen Americans that signals an immense charge from Kentuckians and Ohioans, screaming, "Remember the Raisin! Remember the Raisin!"

BOOM! BOOM! explode American artillery, with more fear than death causing the early surrender of the British regulars.

"For God's sake, men, stand and fight!" orders a brigadier to his brigade, disgusted with the embarrassing effort and weapons being thrown down and arms being raised.

Richard Johnson, seeing that his brother James has the British left under control, signals for the 300 cavalrymen, who he had assigned to himself to ride through the swamp toward Tecumseh's and Roundhead's positions on the American left, to join the U.S. militia.

Initial shots from the Indians do not allow them time to reload, and hand-to-hand tussles ensue, with hard-charging Americans meeting head-on with Indians in the swamp forest.

Bam! ignites Tecumseh's reserve pistol, striking and knocking Colonel Johnson off his horse. His warrior instincts kicking in, Tecumseh sprints in to finish Johnson off with a scalping knife.

BAM! Bam! Bam! BAM! Bam! Bam! fire several guns from Americans, attacking in numbers too much for the Indian coalition to stop.

Several Indians carry off their dead, wounded and dying. E.J. stops and catches his breath while watching the scalping and mutilation of Indians take place.

"We're not going to do that, Running Deer," says E.J.

"Good decision," says Kenton, standing nearby and leaning on his long rifle.

"Which one's Tecumseh?" asks a militiaman.

"He's not here," says the knowing Kenton, waving his white cloth-wrapped hand at the Kentuckian. He's over by Roundhead."

"You need to find Proctor, that's who you need to find!" urges E.J. to the Kentuckian.

"He took off in a carriage," offers a member of Lieutenant Colonel James Johnson's right flank, arriving too late to help against the Indians that are still alive and scattering away.

"That's enough of this, E.J.," says Running Deer. "Let's go home."

"Geez buddy," says E.J., lightly slapping Running Deer on the back while winking at Kenton, "you stink. Couldn't you avoid that skunk?"

"No friend, I couldn't."

Ten days after the Battle of the Thames, E.J. and Running Deer ride slowly from the northeast on the Maumee Trail, leading a packhorse with supplies and the losing Shelby thoroughbred. French trappers and their Indian wives across the river in Kekionga wave at the two.

E.J. waves back as they approach a cemetery near the fort. "Guess we know what happened to Lieutenant Ostrander," says E.J., stopping his horse and viewing the lieutenant's tombstone, along with three others near the path to his log cabin. "I always kinda liked him," says Running Deer, "in a strange kinda way."

"Well, I'll give him this. He was the commander of Fort Wayne for a little while," mentions E.J., bracing himself for Charlotte, Uncle Isaac, Teddy and Bennie, who are sprinting toward him and Running Deer.

Dismounting Thunder and handing the reins of his new thoroughbred to Running Deer, he is nearly pulled down to the ground by the hugs and squeezes. Running Deer alights and gets his share of pats and affection, as well.

"Whoa, you boys are getting bigger and stronger. I won't say that to you, Charlotte. You are still as gorgeous as ever."

"Well now, isn't your vocabulary improving," smiles Charlotte, smothering E.J. with kisses.

"Where's Wayne Pastor, E.J.?" asks Charlotte between kisses.

"Now Charlotte, I knew you were going to ask me that, but W.P. told me he would be visiting Fort Wayne real soon. He and a friend he made are marines and are sailing Lake Erie with a Commodore Perry."

"He's still on that lake?" asks Charlotte.

"Yep. We saw him on the USS Niagara, and I think his friend introduced him to a pretty Seneca girl."

"My son's got a girlfriend?"

"Not only that, but look who has a wife and daughter coming back?" says Uncle Isaac, pushing the crowd to see Morning Bird, Johnny Appleseed, Maconaquah and a two-inch-taller Hannah May.

"Oh, my God!" says Charlotte, falling to her knees in thanks. "Thank you, Lord!

"John Chapman! I knew if anyone could get my daughter back, it would be you!" bursts Charlotte. "Come here, Hannah May, my precious one!"

"Thanks, Johnny," says E.J., shaking his hand vigorously.

"Oh, it wasn't me so much as it was Maconaquah and her husband," says Chapman.

"I don't know you, ma'am," says E.J. to Francis Slocum, "but my son Wayne Pastor has told me about you."

"Gotta speak Algonquin, E.J.," says Chapman.

"Oh yeah," says E.J., and then repeats for Maconaquah's understanding.

An hour later, Running Deer and E.J. finish telling part of their adventure while rocking in their chairs on the porch, sipping cider.

"And Harrison didn't even recognize you and Running Deer at the Thames?" asks Charlotte.

"Either that or he was too busy trying to hang prisoners. Ha! Look who's here, Running Deer?" says E.J., nudging him.

Red Hawk rides in, causing some consternation from the southeast blockhouse.

E.J. waves to the guards, signaling it's ok.

"Our son," says Running Deer and Morning Bird together, standing up and walking toward him.

"Mother, Father, I am back to negotiate for our people, if the white man allows it."

"Well, we are off to a good start here," says Running Deer. "We still have to convince the hostile ones to put down their tomahawks and the whites to eliminate their prejudices toward the Native Americans. You'll make a fine Indian representative, Red Hawk."

"Running Deer, what's that smell on you?" asks Morning Bird.

"Yeah, Dad, why do you smell?" asks Red Hawk.

"Never mind," says Running Deer.

"Dad burn, look who's also arriving. If it isn't Private John Smith on a nice Kentucky thoroughbred."

"Watch your language, E.J." says Charlotte.

"Yes ma'am. Come in, Smitty, and have some of Mr. Chapman's cider. Never mind his wolf."

"Well, he looks pretty fierce to me, but I don't mind if I do," says Smith.

"You get that pig back to Kentucky?" asks E.J.

"Went as far as Urbana, and the governor took over from there."

"Pig? What pig?" inquires Charlotte, brushing Hannah's hair.

"Oh, that's a story for another day," says E.J.

"Here comes a flatboat delivery," says Smith. "I'm expecting a delivery from Governor Shelby."

"Let's all go down and see," says E.J., stumbling out of his rocker. "We could all use some exercise this late afternoon."

The flatboat sweeper docking his large raft yells out, "Is there a Private Smith among you folks?"

"Yeah, right here, Mr. Sweeper," calls Smitty.

"I have this envelope for you first, Private."

John Smith opens it and reads aloud, "It's from Governor Shelby and says, 'Thank you for the pig help. Job well done. I'm a man of my word. Enjoy the deed that allows you some government land, and the contents in the wood-framed box is yours, also.'"

"What's that in there?" asks E.J.

"You're gonna need some help lifting it," says the flatboat sweeper.

"Let's see what's in it, first," says Smith.

Prying off the wood casing protecting the contents with a loaned crowbar, Smith exposes a large copper tub."

"Dad burn, if it isn't a bathing-type barrel of some sort! No more cleaning up in the river, boys and girls! And just in time! Running Deer, you stink! You can take the first bath! Ha!" says Smitty, howling with everyone else.

Chapter 25

October 1920 — Aboite Township, Allen County, Indiana

"We think you're all set with your new phone line, ma'am," says Nyle. "Stan and I are a little late getting back to the shop and will have to be taking off shortly."

"Bye, ma'am," says Stan. "You have an interesting house and property."

"Bye, boys. It's been nice spending some time with you," says the lady with the new phone line.

The boys load their tools into the phone truck and position themselves to leave, but the vehicle won't start.

"Here comes a guy," says Nyle hopping out, raising the hood and looking at the Ford Model T engine.

"What's the problem?" asks the stranger with long hair tied back by a bandana and attired in overalls and moccasins.

"Engine won't turn over," says Nyle.

"Ok, you boys crawl back in and try to start it again," says the stranger, fumbling around the motor.

BRRRUM! The new 1920 truck starts up.

"Good deal," says Stan, getting out to thank the stranger and to close the hood. "Thank you, mis—"

But before Stan can finish, the stranger walks away, heading for the house, then turns and says, "Now, don't come back here."

With Stan gathered back in, Nyle reverses out the driveway onto Redding Drive and heads east toward Fort Wayne.

"You're awfully quiet," says Nyle. "What'd that guy say?"

"He said, 'Don't come back.' Walked away and just disappeared."

"Just disappeared?" asks Nyle.

"He was there, and then when he got about halfway to the house, he disappeared. At least, I think he did," explains Stan.

"Geez, what do we have, another Ostrander?" asks Nyle. "Let's go back and make sure he's ok."

"I don't think so, brother. We're a little late as it is."

Snapping out of his funk, Stan makes a suggestion. "Let's go in on Jefferson and turn left on Clay."

"Left on Clay and go by the rock?" asks Nyle.

"Yep, and cross over the Columbia Street bridge and turn right onto Edgewater Avenue," says Stan.

"Ok. What you got on your mind?" asks Nyle.

"Today's the 130th anniversary of the Battle of Kekionga," says Stan.

"Oh, you and Bob Gavin and your history again! Nobody cares about that."

"Some of us do, and that battle started along this street down a ways. There's a marker there now."

As the boys drive along the river, Stan wonders aloud, "We couldn't have been the only ones finding things buried in this neighborhood. What, with sewer lines and water mains being installed ..." says Stan, trailing off.

Turning right to cross the Tecumseh Street bridge to the shop, they make their way to the phone company building and yard.

"Hey, there's Josh and Jake," says Nyle, pulling up alongside of their Model T.

"What's going on, undertakers? Ha! Picking up some old bones again?" asks Nyle.

"We hope not. Actually, we are waiting on Aunt Martha. We're taking her home."

"Yeah, she's usually locked the doors by now," says Stan.

"We went in to get her, but she says she wanted to talk to you guys about what she saw," says Jake. "In fact, she was acting like that Mrs. Harrington on Begue Street a few years back."

Stan and Nyle walk in the building and up the stairs to Aunt Martha's office, where she stands at her large picture window overlooking the Maumee River and the Lakeside neighborhood.

"Oh, iiit's yyyou bboys. Good," says Aunt Martha, nervously waving them over to the window.

"What's going on, Martha?" asks Nyle. "You're acting a little jittery."

"Fellas, I was standing here looking across the river into the Lakeside neighborhood waiting on my nephews to pick me up from work, and I had a vision. Maybe you can explain it."

"What did you see, Martha?" asks Stan.

"I saw … oh, you guys will think I'm crazy."

"No, go ahead Martha, what'd you see?" asks Nyle.

"Well, I saw men in old uniforms, some on horses, crossing the shallow river. The neighborhood had no houses but a lot of gardens and burned cornstalks, and Indian people were running everywhere. Men on horseback were riding around, and then it ended."

"What ended, Martha?" asks Stan.

"The vision. The vision ended."

"The Battle of Kekionga," whispers Stan immediately, staring across the bridge into Lakeside.

"Time-warp travel?" suggests Nyle. The three stare in silence for a few moments.

"WHAT are you guys staring at?" asks Jake from behind, smiling.

Startled, the three jump and turn around.

"Don't you ever do that again, young man!" says Aunt Martha smiling and catching her breath. "You trying to give us a heart attack?!"

Epilogue

The War of 1812 continued on after The Battle of the Thames River and ended combat wise on February 18, 1815, with the Battle of New Orleans.

The War of 1812 actually lasted thirty-two months and sadly was officially over two weeks before the Battle of New Orleans that took place on January 8, 1815.

Tecumseh's movement ended with his death at The Thames River near Moraviantown, Ontario. Also dying were thirty-three Indians including Roundhead, eighteen British, and twenty-seven Americans. 579 Indians and British combatants were captured. 246 British soldiers escaped to Lake Ontario with General Henry Proctor.

Ryegate, Michigan was renamed Tecumseh in 1912.

Whitley County, Indiana and Whitley County, Kentucky are named for Colonel William Whitley of Kentucky, who died in the initial charge at the Battle of the Thames. Spearheading the attack, he was one of the twenty volunteers to draw the fire of the British and Indians that brought down fifteen Americans including Whitley.

Arguably one of the most significant results of the war was the burning of the White House on August 24, 1814. Reportedly, the British feasted in the White House prior to torching it. A portrait of George Washington was saved before the British had arrived by first lady Dolly Madison. A portrait of Chief Little Turtle was unable to be removed before the burning took place.

Casualties in the Battle of Lake Erie were forty British killed and ninety-six wounded, the Americans lost twenty-seven killed and ninety-four wounded. Six British ships and 306 British sailors were captured including Commander Robert Heriot Barclay.

At the Battle of Fort Stephenson, the British lost twenty-six killed and forty-one wounded while the Americans had just one fourteen-year-old boy dying and seven wounded. It was significant that a combined force of 3,300 British and Indian forces could not overcome an American defense of one-hundred-sixty infantrymen.

During the Siege of Fort Meigs there were fourteen British killed, forty-seven wounded and forty-one captured. The Indians lost nineteen killed and one hundred-twenty-one wounded. The Americans lost 160 killed, 190 wounded and 530 captured.

Dudley's defeat produced 220 American deaths and 350 captured. Over 600 Kentuckians were killed, captured, or wounded.

To be clear, after the two-day second siege of Fort Meigs in July of 1813, the British and Indian coalition moved on to Fort Stephenson at modern day Fremont, Ohio, and that siege was turned away by the Americans.

In the Michigan Territory, the Frenchtown Battle of the River Raisin, January 18 - 23, 1813, brought over 350 Americans killed, 560 or more captured or wounded. The British and Indians lost over twenty killed and 150 wounded.

The Counties of Allen in Indiana, Ohio and Kentucky are named after Colonel John Allen who died in the second battle of Frenchtown while leading the first Regiment of Kentucky Riflemen.

At the Battle of the Mississinewa, the results cost twelve Americans their lives, forty-eight wounded. The Miami lost thirty-eight warriors while the Delaware lost ten braves. Many of the Americans returning to Fort Greeneville, Ohio after the expedition were malnourished and frostbitten resulting in three-hundred American casualties from those effects.

The November of 1812 Battle of Wildcat Creek, also known as the second Battle of Tippecanoe and nicknamed 'Spurs Defeat,' brought seventeen American deaths and three wounded out of the sixty-man detachment. No Indians were reported killed in this encounter.

Over 300 of General Winchester's Kentucky troops died and were buried at Camp Number three located six miles downriver from Defiance, Ohio. Nicknamed 'Fort Starvation' these graves were uncovered by Wabash and Erie Canal workers during the 1840s and a marker exists at Independence Dam State Park today.

No casualties from either side were reported from Chief Five Medals' second siege of Fort Wayne.

Approximately 15,000 Americans died during combat or from disease in the War of 1812. 8,600 British and Canadian soldiers died from disease and battle in the war. It is reportedly unknown how many total Native Americans lost their lives.

Lyrics to the Star Spangled Banner in the form of a poem were written during the War of 1812 by Francis Scott Key at Baltimore, Maryland during the bombardment of Fort McHenry.

The largest War of 1812 living history reenactment in the United States is the Mississinewa 1812 event located near Marion, Indiana every October.

Casualties listed previously are not to glorify war but to acknowledge the sacrifice made for freedom from tyranny that the US enjoys today.

The body of Tecumseh reportedly was never found after the Battle of the Thames. Some individuals claimed they knew which body was Tecumseh but pointed those wishing to collect body part souvenirs into different directions.

Furthermore, it was rumored the body was carried off the field of battle by warriors and buried in an unknown location. Colonel Richard Mentor Johnson claimed that during the battle he killed Tecumseh and with that fame it propelled him to the Vice-Presidency of the United States in 1837.

Accreditation and Further Reading

"Battle of Frenchtown, The," _http://riverraisinbattlefield.org_. n.d.

"Battle of Fort Stephenson, The"
http://birchard.lib.oh.us>battleoffortstephenson.n.d.

"Battle of Lake Erie, The," _http://battlefields.org. n.d._

"Battle of the Thames River, The," _http://battlefields.org/learn/war-1812/battles/battle-thames. n.d._

"Battle of Wildcat Creek, The," _http://military-history.fandom.com._ n.d.

"Colonel John Allen and the River Raisin Debacle,"
http://warfarehistorynetwork.com>articles.

"Dudley's Defeat," Siege of Fort Meigs,
http//:ohiohistorycentral.org>dudley'sdefeat. n.d.

"Fort Meigs," The War of 1812, _http://fortmeigs.org. n.d._

"Fort Meigs," http://ohiohistorycentral.org>fortmeigs. n.d.

"Franklinton, Ohio," _http://ohiohistorycentral.org. n.d._

"George Croghan," _The Project Gutenberg ebook of George Croghan_,
Prepared by the Public Library of Fort Wayne and Allen County, 1953.
Release July 28, 2021. [ebook #65941]

Griswold, Bert.J., _The Pictorial History of Fort Wayne, Indiana._ Chicago,
IL: Robert O. Law Company, 1917.

Hahn, Dennis J., "Samuel Wells, 1754-1830,"
http"//kykinfolk.org>kymilitary. n.d.

"Henry Proctor," http://battlefields.org>henryproctor. n.d.

Holy Bible, The

Knoll, Denys W., USN (Ret.), "The Battle of Lake Erie, Building the Fleet in the Wilderness," Naval Historical Foundation, *http://navyhistory.org*. n.d.

Lossing, Benson J., *The Pictorial Field Book of the War of 1812*. New York, NY: Harper and Brothers, 1868.

"Matthew Elliott," Dictionary of Canadian Biography Volume V (1801-1820) Matthew Elliott, *http://biographi.ca>bio>elliott-matthew se*. n.d.

Naveau, Ralph, "Roundhead, Biography of Wyandot Chief Roundhead," Friends of the River Raisin Battlefield, http://riverraisinbattlefield.org. n.d.

Pickard, Bill, "It's the Bomb!," *http://ohiohistory.org*. n.d.

Raynor, Keith, The Battle of the Mississinewa, *http://thewarof1812.ca/mississinewa*. n.d.

Sandi, "Kentucky's first Governor and a Pig," *http://groups.io>topic>>kentucky'sfirstgovernorandapig*. n.d.

Slocum, Charles Elihu, *History of the Maumee River Basin*, Indianapolis, IN: Bowen and Slocum, 1905.

"Tecumseh," Tecumseh A Biography of the Shawnee Chief, 1768-1813, *http://warof1812.ca>tecumseh*. n.d.

"William Connor," Connor Prairie Blog, William Connor and and the War of 1812, *http://connorprairie.org*, April 12, 2021.

Front and Back Cover Artwork
"Battle of Lake Erie", Sept. 10, 1813 - Rufus Fairchild Zogbaum - 1910
Howard M. Metzenbaum U.S. Courthouse - Cleveland, Ohio
Fine Arts Collection - U.S. General Services Administration

The Taming of Kekionga: 1812-1813

Characters in the Approximate Order of Appearance

(F) Fictional Character

(NF) Non-Fictional Character

Nyle (F) – Telephone worker.

Stan (F) – Telephone worker

Bob Gavin (NF) – Local historian

Tecumseh (NF) – Shawnee war chief

General Henry Proctor (NF) – British General

Tenskhatwa (NF) – The Prophet, brother of Tecumseh

Major General Isaac Brock (NF) – British colonial administrator

General William Hull (NF) – American General, War of 1812

Major Adam Muir (NF) – British army officer

Matthew Elliott (NF) – British Indian agent

E.J. Carlisle (F) – Elmer James, American farmer, scout and spy

Wayne Pastor (F) – W.P., son of E.J. and Charlotte Carlisle

Lieutenant Philip Ostrander (NF) – Officer at Fort Wayne and for a few days Commander of Fort Wayne

General William Henry Harrison (NF) - United States General and future President of US.

Running Deer (F) - Miami Indian warrior and scout

William Wells (NF) – Deceased brother of Colonel Sam Wells

Private John Smith (NF) - 'Smitty,' Messenger and special assignments

Charlotte (F) – Wife of E.J., mother of Hannah May, Bennie and Ted

George Croghan (NF) – At one time or another Commander at Forts Wayne, Fort Defiance and Fort Stephenson

Red Hawk (F) – Son of Running Deer and Morning Bird, Miami warrior

Benjamin Stickney (NF) – Indian agent at Fort Wayne

Lieutenant Dan Curtis (NF) – Officer at Fort Wayne

General John Payne (NF) - Commander of Kentucky light dragoons

Lieutenant Colonel William Lewis (NF) - Kentucky volunteer officer

Captain William Garrard (NF) – Kentucky light dragoons officer

Colonel Sam Wells (NF) – Led Kentucky 17th Regulars

Ensign James Liggett (NF) – 17th Regiment Kentucky scout

John Chapman (NF) – Johnny Appleseed, land opportunist and gospel spreader

Major George Davenport (NF) – Sailor, fur trader, merchant, adventurer

Chief Five Medals (NF) – Potawatomi Chief

Colonel James Simrall (NF) – Kentucky first Regiment Light Dragoons leader

Chief Coesse (NF) – Grandson of Chief Little Turtle

Captain James Rhea (NF) - Commander at Fort Wayne during 1812 siege

Uncle Isaac Carlisle (F) - Uncle of E.J. and Charlotte, merchant at Fort Wayne

Black Loon (NF) - Miami warrior

Chief Winamac (NF) - Potawatomi war chief

Cornelius Washburn (NF) – 'Neil,' Scout, Indian fighter, body guard of Harrison

Peter Navarre (NF) – American scout, messenger

General James Winchester (NF) - Tennessee Revolution war veteran officer

Morning Bird (F) - Wife of Running Deer, mother of Red Hawk

Antoine Bondi (NF) – French trader and trapper at Kekionga

Captain Johnny Logan (NF) – 'Spemica Lawba,' Shawnee scout for Americans

Bright Horn (NF) – Shawnee American spy

Colonel John Allen (NF) – Kentucky militia leader, noted for having three US counties named for him

Henry Clay (NF) – War hawk politician of Kentucky

Lewis Wetzel (NF) – Deceased Indian fighter and pioneer

Maconaquah (NF) – 'Francis Slocum,' Indian wife of Shepoconah, Chief Deaf Man

Roundhead (NF) – Wyandot chief allied with British

Reverend Matthew Wallace (NF) – Army chaplain for Harrison

James Madison (NF) – 4TH President of the United States

Lieutenant Harrison Munday (NF) – 17th Kentucky Infantryman

Chief Charley (NF) – Miami chief near Mississineway

Majenica (NF) - Miami Indian chief

White Loon (NF) – Miami Indian chief

Silver Heels (NF) – Potawatomi chief

Captain Squirrel (NF) – 'Annikoosa,' Miami Indian chief

Simon Kenton (NF) – Legendary frontiersman, General of the Ohio militia

Captain Hugh Moore (NF) – Commander at Fort Wayne from 1812-1813

William Atherton (NF) – Kentucky fort engineer and frontiersman

Bennie Carlisle (F) – Son of E.J. and Charlotte

Hannah May Carlisle (F) – Daughter of E.J. and Charlotte

Kumskauka (NF) – Younger brother of Tecumseh

General Samuel Hopkins (NF) – Kentucky militia leader

Colonel Russell (NF) – Kentucky militiaman

White Cloud (F) – Shawnee warrior

Colonel Miller (NF) – Kentucky militiaman

Colonel Wilcox (NF) – Kentucky militiaman

Private Wade (NF) – Kentucky militiaman

Captain Beckes (NF) – Kentucky militiaman

Elias Darnell (NF) – Kentucky militiaman

Colonel Allen Trimble (NF) Ohio militiaman

Teddy Carlisle (F) – Son of E.J. and Charlotte Carlisle

William Connor (NF) – Guide and frontiersman

Mathew Elliott, Jr. (NF) – Son of Indian British Indian Agent Matthew Elliott

Colonel John B. Campbell (NF) - Led Americans at the Battle of Mississinewa

Francis Godfroy (NF) – Miami chief

Joseph Richardville (NF) – French Canadian trader

Pecanne (NF) – Miami chief

Metocinyah (NF) – Miami chief

Captain John (NF) – Shawnee spy for Americans

Nathaniel Vernon (NF) - Federal infantry Pennsylvania Pittsburg Blues

Ivan Davis (NF) – Kentucky militia

Captain Bennoni Pierce (NF) – Officer at the Battle of Mississinewa

Major Bell (NF) – Officer with the Pittsburg Blues

William Northcutt (NF) – Kentucky militiaman

Chief Little Thunder (NF) – Miami warrior

General William Hull (NF) – American General

King George III (NF) – King of England during the War of 1812

General Joel Leftwich (NF) – Virginia militia General

Francois Navarre (NF) – Frenchtown, Michigan resident

Colonel William Lewis (NF) – American federal officer at River Raisin

Captain Nathaniel Hart (NF) - Kentucky militia officer

Leroy (F) – American militiaman

Jim Bob (F) – American militiaman

Major George Madison (NF) – Officer of the 1st Kentucky Rifle Regiment

Reverend Thomas Dudley (NF) – Private in the 1st Kentucky Rifle Regiment

Dr. John Todd (NF) – Surgeon, 5th Kentucky Volunteer Regiment

General Richard Crooks (NF) – General of the Pennsylvania volunteers

Governor Isaac Shelby (NF) – First and fifth Kentucky Governor

Captain Eleazor Darby Wood (NF) – US Corps of Engineers

Captain Stanton Shoals (NF) - Commander at Fort Huntington, Cleveland,OH

Ahinga (F) – 'Andrew,' Marine with Wayne Pastor

General Clay Green (NF) – Kentucky General of volunteers

Peter Navarre (NF) – American scout

Captain Robert Heriot Barclay (NF) British Naval Commander on Lake Erie

Georgie (F) – Kentucky volunteer

Commodore Oliver Hazard Perry (NF) – Commander of US Naval fleet on Lake Erie

Alfred Lorraine (NF) - Virginia volunteer

Captain Charles Gratiot (NF) - Fort engineer at Fort Meigs

Sakima (NF) –Potawatomi Indian warrior

Captain Daniel Hosbrook (NF) – Ohio militia officer

Dan Dobbins (NF) – US Navy sailing Master

Colonel John Miller (NF) – US Infantry 19TH Regiment Commander at Fort Meigs

Major John Richardson (NF) – British 41st infantryman

Colonel William Dudley (NF) - Leader of the 13th Kentucky militia Regiment

Major John Kain (NF) - Ohio militia Commander at Fort Winchester

Captain William Oliver (NF) – Special messenger for Harrison

Captain Hamilton (NF) – Messenger for Americans

Captain William Sebree (NF) - Kentucky militiaman

Captain Leslie Combs (NF) – Kentucky militiaman

Lieutenant Joseph Underwood (NF) - Kentucky militiaman

Doggie (F) – Pennsylvania militia guard for Commodore Perry

Major Joseph Shelby (NF) – 1st regiment Ohio Militiaman

Major John Morrison (NF) –Officer with the Kentucky 9th regiment volunteers

Max (F) – Lumberjack at Erie , PA

Buford (F) – Lumberjack at Erie, PA

Lieutenant Thomas Stevens (NF) – US Naval ship Commander on Lake Erie

Lieutenant Jesse Elliott (NF) - US Naval ship Commander on Lake Erie

Henry Eckford (NF) – Ship builder

Lieutenant Shipp (NF) – Messenger for George Croghan at Fort Stephenson

Major Robert Dickson (NF) - British Indian Department officer

Ebenezer Crosby (NF) – Master Shipwright at Erie, PA

Lieutenant John Yarnell (NF) – USS Lawrence Commander after Perry left

Captain James Garden (NF) – British ship Commander at Lake Erie battle

Colonel Richard Mentor Johnson (NF) – Kentucky military officer

Major Joseph Jenkinson (NF) - Commander of Fort Wayne from 1813-1814

Lieutenant James Johnson (NF) – Brother of Richard Mentor Johnson

General Duncan McArthur (NF) – Ohio State militia General

General Lewis Cass (NF) – Michigan militia leader

Chief Tarhe (NF) –Wyandot chief friendly to United States

Josh (F) – Undertaker and nephew of Aunt Martha

Aunt Martha (F) – Telephone Company employee

Jake (F) – Undertaker and nephew of Aunt Martha